The Stone in My Pocket

The Stone in My Pocket

Published by The Conrad Press in the United Kingdom 2021

Tel: +44(0)1227 472 874
www.theconradpress.com
info@theconradpress.com

ISBN 978-1-913567-61-3

Typesetting and Cover Design by: Charlotte Mouncey, www.bookstyle.co.uk

The Conrad Press logo was designed by Maria Priestley.

Printed and bound in Great Britain by Clays Ltd, Elcograf S.p.A.

The Stone in My Pocket

Matthew Keeley

For Mum and Dad
You are not Helen and Colin

1

August 1999

At first I thought it was the cat. Sometimes Freya would be out there in the garden at night yowling to come in or chattering at birds she couldn't catch. Or if it wasn't her, maybe a fox. I'd heard them howling like babies in the dark a few times. Then it wailed again. No, not a wail, duller than that – a moan. That's when sickness lurched in my stomach. The same kind of plummet when you realise you've been caught lying again or your parents ask you a question you don't want to answer. I knew the noise wasn't Freya or a fox or any animal.

It was coming from a person. A voice.

I wouldn't have heard it if my bedroom window hadn't been open. I only did that in summer. The TV that I wasn't supposed to be watching this late was already turned down low, but I clicked the mute button, amplifying the groaning voice seeping into the room. Then I turned the lamp off to get rid of my gormless reflection in the window and let me see out there. But the blue-white light from the TV still danced against the walls and glowed on the glass.

The voice snuffled to a stop. They, whoever *they* were, must have spotted the lamp turning off. Must've seen me. The bushy edge of a moonlit conifer shuffled in a sudden breeze and I pictured a man out there; someone drunk or homeless hiding in the dark trying to break in and rob us. I've no idea why I thought of that. Weird what fear conjures. Drichton wasn't exactly crawling with Sunday night binge-drinkers and I don't think I even saw a homeless person until I was about eleven and in Edinburgh for the day on a primary school trip. A dark-skinned woman with a patterned shawl around her head had held out a paper cup to me. I thought she was doing a magic trick until the teacher shoved me along by my shoulders.

I crouched by the open window. The voice was there again, gulping in juddered breaths like something wounded. It didn't sound like a kid or someone my age, but I couldn't tell if it was a man or a woman or even how near they were. I pulled the window open a little more and squinted out. Clouds drifted and the moon bathed the garden in grey-blue sheen. But it was empty. No cat roaming under the bushes. No fox rummaging in the wheelie bin. No woman with a cup. The old, rusted swing chains weren't even squeaking in the wind. And beyond the back fence the black river gurgled past, higher than usual. No one could escape out there when it was this dark without falling in. But I still felt eyes prodding at me from some secret place. I'd learned the sensation years ago. Shivering, I swallowed and poked my head out into air that now felt too cold for August. I peered down to see if someone was standing right beneath me, pressed against the wall, but there was nothing except blank concrete slabs. And the moaning had stopped. I ducked back in and yanked the window closed like I'd just flung a spider from a glass.

Most other people might've shouted for their parents or rushed to their room to tell them. But there was no point in telling my mum and dad. They wouldn't believe me; stopped listening to my 'nonsense' years ago. 'Back to bed, Nathan,' it'd be. They'd tell me the noise was only Freya or maybe something a little more clichéd about it being the wind or that old houses just creaked at night. That's usually a stupid explanation for things like this in books and films.

I turned to the muted TV to see Mulder and Scully scarper with torches around a dark building chasing some black creature. Not helping. Nick would ask me at school if I'd watched it, but I'd been taping it so I could catch up another night. Maybe when I hadn't just heard a disembodied voice in my garden. My mum had caught me in the middle of an episode one night last year and banned it: 'it'll cause more nightmares, Nathan'. What other seventeen-year-old still had their parents telling them what they weren't allowed to watch? Nick's parents had been letting him watch horror films since before high school. That's what he'd told me, anyway.

I switched the TV off and clambered onto the bed feeling like poison was swilling in my guts. At least it's what I imagined poison would feel like. Every few seconds I'd turn to the window, thinking I could hear it again. But the voice was just an echo in my head by then. I never can sleep early on a Sunday night – especially not before the start of a new school term – but now the idea of tucking myself into bed and drifting off was a joke. I pulled my knees towards my chin and checked my watch. Almost midnight. I flicked the switch on my lamp and lifted the book from the bedside table, pulling my makeshift bookmark – a Love Videos loyalty card I'd lifted from a pile in Dad's shop – out from the middle of *Mysteries Unsolved: Beasts and Aliens*. Everyone at school just tucked over the corner of whatever page they'd read to in a book but

I'd always hated that. I think my mum had told me not to do it once when I was little and the tick had wedged itself in the pages of my brain.

I'd had most of the *Mysteries Unsolved* series for years but I only used to look at the pictures and read the captions under the weirdest ones. My mum hadn't even wanted me to keep them when we'd moved house but Dad had slid them in a cardboard box for me. I found them in my wardrobe a few weeks ago and started reading them again after discovering the late-night *X-Files* repeats.

I glanced down at a page with a printed photograph of a blurry, dark human shape between tree trunks. Was that what was out there? Calling for me to listen? I looked to the window then closed the book again, shoving it back to the table. My mum had probably been right about the nightmares. It had been months since she had shaken me awake in darkness. I didn't want that to start again.

My final plan was to scuttle to the chair at my desk and turn on the little spotlight lamp above my model: the Empire State Building. Finishing the silver paint on the needle helped me forget what I'd heard. For a while at least. The last time I remembered seeing on the clock was 2:58.

I woke myself up, my feet squirming like thrashing fish outside the rumpled covers. I didn't remember climbing into bed or turning the lights out and I'd fallen asleep on my back, which I never did. When I pushed myself up onto my forearms, I saw it. Her. Him. The shadowed figure standing in my doorway.

I swallowed a scream, my tongue numb and my body a useless plastic mannequin. Hurling my limp arm across to the lamp, I smacked it onto the floor then half-lunged out of the bed to grab it, fumbling with the switch, panting. Light flicked back into the room and I tumbled out from the covers, my hip thudding onto the floor. When I spun around it was gone. The door was open and nothing was there. Just flowery hallway wallpaper filling the space and the quick pumping of my heartbeat punching my ears.

☆

In my dreams, hours later, I was tiny, living inside the Empire State Building model. It filled up with silvery water and I couldn't get out. A familiar man's giant face stared at me through the window and I heard the sound again: the muffled, keening voice. But it wasn't coming from the man outside. It was *my* voice, drowning.

2

My mum was already in her blue uniform with hair and makeup sort-of done by the time I crept into the kitchen with my tie in hand, collar up. I hadn't even wanted to step into the hallway from my room that morning, wondering what might be lurking around the corner, watching me. Of course, there was nothing. But in *here* I was being watched. She raised an eyebrow as soon as I entered and I knew she must have been fighting the urge to either eye the clock conspicuously or motion to her watch with a pointed finger like every other Monday morning. But she didn't. Instead, she flicked to the next page in her auction guide, eating dry toast. Maybe my last year of school would be different from the previous five.

Dad was milling about, still in a vest and ancient pyjama bottoms that made him look about fifty years older than he was. He slurped his cereal every few seconds, fixated on the news. I don't think he'd even noticed me coming in. Telling them about a voice in the garden and a ghost standing at my door in the middle of the night was probably not what they'd have wanted to hear about just then. Neither of them had come to check on me after I'd fallen out of bed. Although that didn't mean they hadn't heard me. I could imagine them grumbling out of sleep, one of them prising their eyes open and waiting to make sure it wasn't a burglar before flopping back down, telling the other one not to bother. Just Nathan again.

Years ago, in Spain – when we used to go on holidays like

that with Granddad – I'd woken up at night in our apartment and could see little red lights blinking in the distance across the fields and convinced myself it was a UFO; a few weeks earlier Dad had let me watch *Close Encounters of the Third Kind*. I ran into my parents' room crying and screaming about the aliens watching me. They let me sleep at the bottom of their bed and shook their heads at me in the morning. I didn't tell Granddad about it.

There were other things I thought I saw when I was younger too, but my parents told me they weren't real. Now it was happening again, but with sound effects.

I peered past Dad and out of the kitchen window, trying to spot some clue in the garden – a glove or scarf left behind, a miniature crop circle – but nothing. There hadn't been any footprints or occult symbols etched on the walls in the hallway upstairs either. Maybe I'd had so much practice making up stories for other people that I was starting to do it to myself.

With bleary eyes I navigated around Dad to make my breakfast before slumping into a chair opposite my mum.

'Nathan, you've put far too much sugar on that.'

She wasn't even looking at my cereal. Or me. I didn't answer and she wasn't looking for one. Besides, engaging in a discussion about food would inevitably lead to my favourite 'you aren't getting enough vitamins and minerals' lecture.

'Damnit, Freya's meant to be going to the vet this afternoon. Annual check-up.' Dad had taken a break during a weather report to thumb through scraps of paper and postcards bursting beneath old holiday magnets on the fridge. 'I can't leave the shop early again, Helen.'

My mum sighed and took her time dislodging something

from between her teeth before answering. 'Well I can't leave the bank early either. I'd need to have asked well before today.' She flicked over a page without turning to face him. 'Not paying for a check-up wouldn't be the worst thing at the minute anyway. Freya's fine. And you know, reminding me *on* the morning isn't exactly helpful.'

The background murmur of the stern morning newsreader mentioned redundancies in some big company. Dad muttered something, one hand braced against the worktop.

'Did you have any homework you should have done over the holidays?' my mum asked.

I shook my head and chewed Shreddies, staring into my bowl.

Reminding me on the morning isn't exactly helpful.

I imagined saying it and hid a smirk. She flicked another page in her catalogue.

'Well, were any of those books you've been reading at least for English? I think you should have been getting a head start on that, you know.'

Flick.

'This year's really important, son. Need to get plenty of extra-curricular things on the Uni applications too.'

Flick.

'And you can't wear that blazer to school anymore. It didn't even fit you last year.'

'Right, right. He gets it.' Dad had finally looked back over his shoulder towards us.

Flip. The catalogue and the conversation were closed. I knew Dad's euphemism for 'shut up' must have reminded her of all those other times he used to defend me. Not even eight a.m.

and I was already causing problems. It had been a while. A new reason not to mention what had happened last night.

I don't think Dad was even aware of the memories he'd stoked. Just sipped the last drip of milk and dumped his bowl in the sink, leaving Mum to reignite. I shovelled the rest of my cereal down and leapt up, grabbing the tie and throwing it round my neck as I left the burning room.

'Still haven't finished the model, Nathan?' Dad muttered as I shoved my feet into last term's school shoes. 'Just as well we didn't buy you that new Eiffel Tower one.'

Drichton should be somewhere you visit on a day trip, not somewhere you live. And not somewhere with haunted midnight wails and ... whatever that thing was. The village wasn't dilapidated enough and there were no castles or crumbling mansions with mythical histories. Everyone with an idyllic front garden had it maintained for the Garden of the Year competition. There were twee little second-hand shops and everyone who lived here always seemed cultishly happy. It was a village you'd see beside a model train set, and my family members were the shabby pieces that didn't match everything else.

Five years of practice was more than enough to have the walk from my house to the bus stop timed perfectly. Well, not an official bus stop, just a random lamp post on the other side of the bridge at the end of Dyrne Street that the school minibus stopped at. Some days it was late. It was never early.

Hannah McKay walked ahead of me and I adjusted my pace so I wouldn't catch up with her. How awkward would that be? She was in the year below me and was one of two other Ballahan High pupils who lived in Drichton. The other was Jonnie Knight, a complete fucking idiot in my year at school. The three of us would be the only life in Dyrne Street this early in the morning; that's if Jonnie even bothered to turn up.

I inspected every house as I passed, waiting for the shadowed figure to appear at a lace-curtained window or float out from behind a perfectly manicured rosebush. Then, glancing over the street towards The Book Cover, I could tell it was different, like walking into your bedroom and knowing someone has moved something. I took a detour across the road - I could afford the extra twenty seconds and it would help put a few more feet between Hannah and me. The Book Cover sat between a narrow little lane that led off to the river and The Bridge Hotel. That was a favourite with families and grannies visiting for the day and looking for a traditional 'bar lunch'.

After a few steps I could see what was new: an A4 sheet of lined paper blue-tacked on the inside of the glass door. 'PART TIME ASISTANT NEEDED. ENQUIRE WITHIN.' It was handwritten in big purple felt-tip pen with smiley faces drawn in each of the corners, as if whoever wrote it was proud of the spelling mistake. It must be the woman who owned the shop – I'd never asked her name – in her early fifties maybe, with short, tufty, maroon hair. I couldn't figure out why she'd need an extra person to work there. I was always surprised the shop even managed to stay open - usually when I was in there for a new book, I'd have the place to myself. Sometimes I'd even read a whole first chapter of a novel before deciding if I wanted to buy it or not. The woman would wander between the counter and the back area, letting me read what I liked.

I'd been shouted at once for doing that in a big book shop in Perth. I *had* been sitting on the floor with my legs crossed eating a sandwich, mind you.

I read the poster again. After Safeway, I swore I didn't want to work another part-time job until I was at uni. The thought of those twenty-year-old supervisors asking me to do announcements over the PA system still made me feel sick. It wasn't even the speaking that bothered me. It was the smothered giggles I could hear behind me when I did it.

Maybe this could be fun, though. I hadn't been in The Book Cover for a few weeks since I was working my way through my *Mysteries Unsolved* series but I normally paid a visit every fortnight or so. And I wouldn't have to travel far, would I? I imagined myself behind the counter, selling the books instead of buying them.

Movement caught my eye and something shuffled past the empty doorframe in the back of the shop. I jumped back from the glass, tripping off the step, and jogged along.

Arriving at the bridge my feet slowed and I looked down the little gravel road on my left. St. Germaine's was the Catholic Church: a tiny, granite building about fifty yards down the pebbled path with a statue of, I presumed, St. Germaine looking down over the green entrance doors. I didn't stop. I wasn't even looking at it for a specific reason. It was just a habit. We didn't go to church except at Christmas or on those few occasions we'd visited Aunt Brenda and Uncle Frank or Granddad down South, even though Mum asserted we were Catholic at every given chance. Dad would come with us but he'd never grown up with Bibles or pictures of Jesus hanging in his house – my mum would have more of these if she could – and always tutted and swore whenever the latest church scandal was on the news.

Other than the book shop, this little building was the only place in the village I was interested in, but not because I was like my mum. I'd always been fascinated by the little door at the side of the altar. We caught tiny peeks through it when the priest and the altar boy used it at the end of mass but I'd decided it led to another dimension and had written stories about it in my mind. *I* never was an altar boy. Dad wouldn't let me do it. I'm not sure if that was for my benefit or the priest's.

Maybe a priest would be able to answer questions about ghosts. And other things that had happened to me.

I heard the grumble of the bus lumbering towards us. Jonnie, jacket half hanging off, pushed away from the lamp post he'd been leaning against, ready to bombard his way on and towards the other morons sitting in the back row. I made sure to sit right at the front. In my head I sang the Blondie song *Maria*, repeating the couple of lines I knew over and over. I'd have to tape it from the radio at the weekend. What was she singing in the chorus? 'A million and one *kinda* lights? *Candle* lights? *Ken doll eyes*?' And that's when it came chiming through the driver's tinny radio.

'*She moves like she don't care…*'

That happened to me a lot; my thoughts tumbling out into reality.

I glanced around, as if thinking for a moment that I could tell someone. But who here would care? I turned back to face the back of the driver's head, gripping the straps of my bag. Seconds later, Jonnie yelled something and the other boys bellowed laughing. *Maria* was foghorned out and I never did hear that line in the chorus.

3

The pane was cold against my forehead as I stared out at the courtyard. The bell had just rattled and a little group of new First Years were toddling en masse to their next lesson. My breath misted up the glass every few seconds and the First Years kept vanishing and reappearing through it. It reminded me of my first few months here. I might not have reappeared from behind the mist, though. I hadn't bounced from class to class with my Primary schoolmates. There were none. Everyone at Ballahan High had been a strange creature to me; all from mysterious primary schools I'd never heard of.

Maybe I could incorporate the steamed-up window into the story I was supposed to be writing. I lifted my head, leaving a greasy smudge on the glass, and caught Mr. Young's watching eye. He plunged down again, continuing to mark at his desk. Wasn't the reaction supposed to be the other way around? Twenty minutes left to finish before the dreaded swap. My short story with a twist in the ending was almost done, except I'd changed my mind about my twist halfway through, stupidly ignoring Mr. Young's advice about how the clues and hints should lead us towards the climax. I'd written about a couple who, every year, received a Christmas card addressed to the old man who used to live in their house until he died. Whoever was sending the cards didn't know he was dead so just kept posting them year after year. There was never a return address so the couple couldn't ever write to the sender to give them the bad news. I'd dreamt up the idea last Christmas when I thought about some of the cards that might have been sent to Granddad's house. Well, his old house.

In the margin of my jotter I traced the outline of the silent silhouette I'd seen last night and wondered If I should have a supernatural, creepy ending to my story. Or maybe Mr. Young wouldn't like that. Maybe it should just turn out a bit more realistically with something sombre and gloomy. If I was clever enough it could have both endings and be ambiguous, like the novels and poems we always analysed in class. I added a new paragraph describing the couple's kitchen to keep the story going for a little while longer, holding off on the denouement. Mr. Young had just taught us that word.

'OK folks, time's up.' He stood and glided round to perch on his desk right in front of me. He'd been my teacher last year too. I smelled his aftershave, familiar and warm; some sort of spice that reminded me of a cake I'd had once. I'd like to wear aftershave like that when I'm older.

'Who's managed to finish?' Three or four hands rose. 'Oh, come on, we started this before the summer.'

Mr. Young never shouted. I hadn't heard him do it, at least. He was one of the newer teachers maybe only out of school himself by six or seven years, I'd guessed. Every reprimand had a half-smile behind it and pupils who didn't hand in homework never seemed to be punished. I'd always handed my work in on time or early so I didn't know. Maybe I should forget it next time to find out.

'OK, group feedback time.'

Wouldn't be a first day of term without some forced social activity. This couldn't be too bad, though. It was Advanced

Higher English so there weren't any real pricks in the room and anyway, Stacey was here. Her wavy, honey-blonde hair that I always thought was pretty had been straightened and attacked with a series of red stripes. I wondered if Gillian or Nick had undergone any summer transformations too. Stacey had been the tallest girl in our year since we were twelve and had always made it easier for us to get into fifteen-certificate films on our weekend cinema trips when we were still only thirteen and fourteen. She was always pretty good at bantering with the box office staff and wore red lipstick and high heels. Nick and I must have just looked like the tag-along boyfriends, lurking behind the girls and saying nothing more than our mumbled pretend dates of birth. After a while, though, my parents put a stop to it. Dad had found some of my saved ticket stubs and realised what kind of films we were managing to sneak into.

'Find yourselves two or three others to team up with.'

A space waited opposite Stacey and she nodded to me.

'Nathan, here.'

I shuffled my chair into position and slid my jotter along with a grimace. The other two at our group, Heather and Kenneth, had already begun reading one another's stories and after we'd all finished we did a pass-the-parcel swap. Stacey's story hadn't been too bad, although compared to the other two it was Novel Prize stuff. Kenneth's story was essentially the written script of any first-person shooter Playstation game and Heather's was fourteen pages of enormous, circular handwriting about five girls being chased around a haunted house by some demon or murderer or… something. I was glad I didn't go for the ghost angle with my story – I could see how stupid it looked now.

After some pitiful praise-sharing – 'you're good at description' and 'you wrote a lot' – our book panel ran out of compliments. The other two groups in the room still rambled on, laughing with one another, and Kenneth and Heather soon turned their chairs towards them.

'So what did you do over the summer?' Stacey asked. She was wearing a black choker ribbon and started playing with the plastic jewel hanging from it, probably noticing that I was looking at it.

'Just, you know, hung around, visited family, stayed up late… and slept in a lot.' She didn't laugh at what I'd meant as a joke. 'How about you?'

'Well, you know we have that holiday home in Portugal, eh? So we were out there for most of July. Mum and Dad let me come home early to go to Charlene's birthday party, though. It was so cool; her house is massive. You should have come.'

I nodded and shrugged at the same time, as if I'd been invited but had been busy with other wild parties.

'I started my new job at the salon in Perth too, so really I came home from Portugal for that as well.' So that explained the hair. 'Did you see Nick over the holidays?'

I thought about pretending I had but knew I could be caught out too easily as soon as she spoke to him. Maybe she already had and this was a test. 'No. I think he was busy this summer. Away somewhere.'

'Don't think he was.'

The conversation ended like an unexpected roadblock. I thought about swerving around it by telling her what I'd seen last night, but Mr. Young cut me off before I had the chance.

'So… anyone think they read a piece in their group we might

all want to hear? I really want to find out what ideas you've come up with.'

Staring back down at the desk, arms folded, I thought someone might mention my name. Instead, one of the other groups volunteered a teenage-witch film rip-off to be recited. A smattering of applause while I looked at Stacey, clapping along. Maybe my story needed more action. I could kill off the couple in a mad bloodbath. As the clapping subsided, I looked to Mr. Young who smiled far too widely and scratched his wrist. I knew he must be thinking of how best to compliment it.

'… That's a good first draft.'

He finished the period by handing us each a new spiral-bound notebook. Mine had a shiny green cover.

'This is for creative writing from now on. You should always be on the lookout for ideas. Listen in to conversations. Watch people on the street. Notice the unusual things around you that you'd normally ignore. Write every spark down in here, even if you don't know how it's going to become a full story yet. I want to see these notebooks full by the end of the year.'

Once the bell had rung, I cradled my green book to my chest, ready to thank him after the others disappeared. Maybe he could be the one I'd talk to about what happened last night. But Mr. Young escaped the room before I did, leaving me to pack my bag and close the door behind me.

Stepping into the corridor, I called out to Stacey just a few feet ahead, but she kept walking without looking back. I turned and scarpered in the opposite direction before anyone could laugh at me.

✩

I wanted to stop at The Book Cover on the way home to ask maroon-hair lady more about the job and how I should apply, but Jonnie had hopped off the bus with two of his pals and the three of them swaggered down the street behind me. I didn't fancy giving them something to laugh about as I walked into a book shop. I could just imagine them having a group fit by the glass front, sticking up their stubby fingers and grunting at the geek. Don't think it would have helped convince the owner that I was a great candidate. And I knew I couldn't be so bold without asking my parents first.

Shutting that frosted glass door behind me and hearing it rattle through the empty house marked the beginning of my two-hour window alone. It must be what a swimmer feels like surfacing at the end of a race, able to breathe properly again before the next heat begins.

A thud upstairs. Creaking floorboards.

'Freya!' Might as well feed her now.

Another thump, but this time it was from the kitchen straight ahead of me. Meowing, Freya came trotting towards me, rubbing her stripy head against my shin. I stared down at the oblivious cat. She hadn't been upstairs. Electricity crawled over me. It took a minute before I shouted again.

'Mum? Dad?' An invisible hand squeezed my throat.

The silent house was a frozen still around me.

'Dad? Are you home?'

Freya meowed again.

Giving her a hurried rub on the head, I crept forward, feeling like one of those stupid people in horror films walking towards an unexplained noise, instead of away from it. But there were no high-pitched strings or creepy piano notes tinkling. No thunder and lightning outside. It was four o'clock on a Monday afternoon in the middle of August and I was in my own house. Mr. Young had said pathetic fallacy was a clichéd storytelling technique anyway. It was then, as I neared the stairs that the smell came. Chemical and sharp. It made me think of childhood scrapes and plasters. A hospital smell.

I tried to march up the stairs, but only managed to wobble with one hand on the banister. I pictured the shadow figure standing in my bedroom doorway, waiting for me. Each step felt colder under my feet than the last and I remembered how cool it had been last night when I stuck my head out the window. I called out for my parents again, thinking maybe they'd just ignored me at first – my mum hated me yelling at her from a distance, expecting her to shout back – but my voice was met with emptiness. As I stepped to my room the hanging dreamcatcher on my door looked like it was swaying a little. Not realising I'd balled my hands into clammy fists, I shoved the door open then jumped back a step. No one was there.

But someone *had been* there.

My bedside drawer was open. I never left it like this. Bits of paper and old cinema stubs were scattered on the pillow. The sickening feeling in my stomach from last night plunged back. I stepped inside and found what had made the thud I'd heard. It was behind the door, broken on the floor, glittering up at me. A stone from the crystal-growing set I'd bought when I was twelve or thirteen. I knew they weren't real or worth anything, but I'd been obsessed with it back then and still kept the big, green, spiky piece on my bookshelf. And here it was broken in two, surrounded by little shining fragments and shards like smashed glass at a crime scene.

I didn't clear it up straight away, just looked at it for a while, stuck still. Someone had been in here, moving things. I sat on the carpet with my back pressed against the wall like my spine was sewn into it until I heard my mum come in the front door two hours later. Even then I didn't move. Instead, I pulled out the new notebook from my schoolbag and rubbed the shiny green cover with still-shaking fingers. Mr. Young had said it was for story ideas, but maybe I could use it as a diary too. Most writers must get ideas from their own lives.

4

I didn't have nightmares that night. I had a half-sleep of sweat and heat; a tangle of pillows and an aching back and birds twittering and muffled grey light. One of those nights, or mornings, really, when you lose judgement of time and how often you wake up from the unconsciousness. And whether you were really waking up at all or just dreaming everything. I knew I had dreamt at times but there was no order to any of it and no chance of writing it down. The one thing I remember clearly is looking over a banister down a spiral staircase with green carpet. There was a hand holding the banister a floor below me. The rest was just random places and snapshots and glimpses of people – some real, some invented. Some forgotten. But no one standing in my doorway.

Dad wasn't in the kitchen when I staggered down. More and more often over the past couple of weeks he'd started leaving to get to the video shop before I'd even had breakfast. He wanted to look at accounts and figures – at least, that's what I'd heard him saying to Mum. The shop was in Ballahan, about ten miles away and in the same town as my school. I'd thought Dad might have asked if I wanted a lift. I'd be there far too early but maybe the car journey could have been a good time to tell him what had happened in my room yesterday; mention it with a laugh as if it hadn't bothered me. But then he might have been annoyed that I was just getting around to telling him that someone had potentially broken into our house. Probably best that he'd gone without me.

My mum sat in her usual position in the kitchen. She flicked through a newspaper today. I took Dad's place in front of the little TV, eating as if I was in a rush and too busy to talk.

'Dad's away early,' she said.

'Mm.'

Obviously.

'Were you doing homework last night? We didn't even see you.'

'Mm.'

I thought about asking her if she'd been in my room, but it was pointless; I already knew it hadn't been her. She avoided my room like it was under quarantine. Unless I was having a nightmare.

The next few minutes were filled with the sound of my spoon clinking the bowl, toast crunching, newspaper pages flapping, the TV murmuring, needless coughs. It was just how it used to be on those mornings at primary school. The mornings after something had happened. The mornings when Dad wasn't there, although he wasn't quite beaming with pride when he *was* there. Neither of us would speak: her wanting to pretend the thing hadn't happened, me praying for her not to ask why the thing had happened.

She folded the newspaper and plonked it onto the table.

'Time for me to go. And you.'

She pushed the chair back from the table and stood. I needed to ask now.

'Mum… you know the book shop?'

'… Yes.'

'There's… well they're… there's a job. A sign in the window.

28

They need an assistant.'

She tidied around me, throwing cutlery in the sink and shoving cereal boxes back in cupboards.

'I wanted to apply.'

'Another job? The last one didn't really work out well, did it? Took too much of your study time up. Thought that's why you packed it in?'

That's what I'd told her. I think she was always on the lookout for such big lies from me that the little ones went unnoticed.

'I know, but I'm not taking as many subjects this year, and it's only around the corner. And it took much longer to get home from Safeway since it was in Ballahan.'

'I don't know if it's a good idea, son.'

I hated when she put that at the end of her sentences, like the little bag of soggy salad they put in with takeaways to pretend they're healthy.

'Well, I'll need new books this year for English. I might be able to get them for free if I work in the shop.'

She shrugged then grabbed her coat from the back of a chair.

'I'll talk to your dad about it,' she said without looking at me and left.

It's amazing how quickly you can forget you've been away from school for seven weeks. After the second day back I felt like nothing had ever been any different. The teachers had already stopped asking how our summers were; I'd had my first spitball fired at me through a snapped biro; every dent and swerve in the road on the minibus ride home felt familiar. I'd gone another day without seeing Nick, too. Sometimes we convinced ourselves he'd stopped coming to school halfway through Fourth Year and had only been sneaking in every now and then to see us at lunchtimes or between periods.

I pretended to tie my shoelace as I bent over at the village-end of the bridge, fiddling around with nothing. Hannah's boots and Jonnie's trainers passed by and wandered off home ahead of me. The idiot hadn't brought any of his goons back with him today. I stood back up and walked towards The Book Cover, giving St. Germaine's a fleeting look. The priest stood at the little side entrance, hands tucked in robes, talking to an older lady and laughing. I never thought of priests as having a sense of humour before. They were just extra characters from horror movies or Agatha Christie novels; tiny plastic figures in the model village. I couldn't even tell if he was the same one who'd given the last Christmas service or not. I was more interested in the building and the weird rituals. They should give you an instruction book at the door to explain the rules. There might be a section on DIY exorcisms.

The door to the Book Cover was wedged open with a chunky wooden doorstop and I stepped inside. I still remember feeling lucky we had a bookshop just minutes from our new house when we'd first moved to Drichton. Made the move a tiny bit easier. Enjoying reading had been normal at primary with our little class library shelves and our private reading time whenever we finished classwork early. At seventeen it wasn't so cool. I'd been jeered at more than once after taking a book out in the school canteen or a stairwell. I never took the *Mysteries Unsolved* books to school, though. Imagine. Might as well build a giant neon sign to hang around my neck with the words 'slag me off please' blinking at everyone.

The shop had two rotating stands near the door filled with new, shiny novels with colourful covers – the ones with the fresh print, shopping centre scent in the never-opened pages. The rest of the cramped little place was filled with its four or five almost ceiling-height shelves with worn second-hand books. Those were the ones whose pages smelled of attics and that, you knew, had the best stories. One wall was entirely dedicated to children's stories. There was even a cardboard box on the floor near the counter with books for a pound or even fifty pence. My mum always urged me to look through that before venturing towards the other shelves.

The counter faced the entrance and had a little doorbell screwed into the desk. 'Ring for Assistance' was inked on a sellotaped piece of paper. No spelling mistakes on this one. The counter probably didn't need manned all the time, even with the shop always having its door wide open and zero security cameras. Come to think of it, I don't know if I've ever noticed any CCTV in the whole village. I doubt there'd been a crime reported for years. Maybe a hanging basket sabotage during the annual gala competition.

After touching some of the book covers by the till for a few minutes, procrastinating for as long as possible, I held my breath, ready to press the bell. Just as I reached forward, though, the little woman with her tufted maroon hair appeared from the doorway a bit farther along the back wall, smiling as soon as she saw me.

'Hello! How you doin'?'

'Em, good, yeah, thanks.'

'Time for somethin' new?' she asked, stepping behind the counter and dumping a pile of paperbacks she'd carried out onto the floor with a thump.

It took a few seconds of searching her face and doing some sort of weird, nervous laugh before I understood.

'Oh. No, I'm still reading something just now. Not buying anything new yet.'

Waiting for the next part, she nodded and smiled back. Dark lips stretched over china white teeth, although the bottom row was all crooked.

'I was just going to ask about the, em…' I pointed behind me to the sheet of paper stuck on the door. 'The, em, job.'

'Uh-huh.'

'I was wondering if, em, if you still need someone. And–and when you need someone to work… or how often, and stuff.' If eloquence was a prerequisite then I was fucked.

'Well…' She leaned forward on the counter, clasping her hands. An opaque, green stone on a silver chain dangled from the folds in her neck, tapping the desk. It looked a bit like my crystal. My shattered crystal. 'I'm needin' someone to do Saturdays. Maybe a Sunday as well, dependin' on my bookin's.' I nodded, pretending to know what she meant. 'Durin' the week's fine, I'll still be doin' Tuesday to Friday. I keep it closed on a Monday. It's just that most of my bookin's are at weekends – that's when seems to suit most people, but I can't afford to close the shop, not on a Saturday. That's obviously when folk are up visitin' if it's a nice day.'

She didn't explain what her 'bookings' were and I didn't ask; just focused on my plastered grin while she went into even more detail about when the shop opened and closed.

'So you must like books. You're in here all the time, eh?'

'Yeah. Yeah, I like reading… it's… good.'

'What's your favourite then? I reckon you can tell a lot about a person from their favourite book.' She beamed rosy-cheeked at me. I hadn't realised yet that she was basically interviewing me. I thought this was just chit-chat.

'I-I'm not sure. Em, I can't think of one.' Heat blazed through my neck and cheeks, even though I did have an answer.

'Aw, come on, there must be one of those books you've bought that you've enjoyed the most; one that you kept thinkin' about for ages after you finished it.'

I think it was then that I realised I ought to try and impress her.

'Well, I always really liked this book called *Empty World*. It's by John Christopher. I got it in the, em, bargain box.' I nodded towards the cardboard box in the corner and wondered if I should be telling her that I only buy from the cheap section?

'Oh, I don't remember that one. What's it about?'

'It… it's about a plague that spreads across Britain and this boy, I can't remember his name, ends up being one of the only people left alive and he has to travel around looking for other survivors. It sounds a bit far-fetched but I kept imagining how I'd react if it happened to me. I read it in about two days.' I was worried she'd think I was making it up when I couldn't even remember the name of the main character, but she raised her eyebrows and nodded like she thought it sounded interesting.

'There's one I read a bit more recently, too,' I went on. 'It's called *Down a Dark Hall*. I think it's a bit old now but–'

'-Oh, I know that one. That's a scary one isn't it? Aye, I'm sure I've read that.'

That's when I remembered the image from my dreams the night before: the view over the edge of a banister looking down a spiral staircase. It had been the cover picture on my copy of the book. I wanted to tell her that I'd just dreamt of that and how strange that was but stopped myself.

'Yeah, it is a bit creepy. It's kind of a horror book. Well, horror for kids anyway.'

My stammer had receded back down inside me, although it wasn't a proper stammer anymore like when I was younger. I just stuttered a little still whenever I felt nervous. A speech therapist had told us that could still happen.

'You like that kind of thing, though, horror and ghost stories and the paranormal.' She said this as if we were old friends and I couldn't tell if it was a question or a statement.

'Yeah. I do.'

'So, have you had a job before? My name's Iris by the way.' She said this just as I was wondering it.

'Oh, I'm Nathan.' I felt like I should shake her hand but kept them both held in my jacket pockets where I'd shoved them as soon as she'd come over to talk. 'I worked in the Safeway in Ballahan for a while. Next to the school.' I avoided elaborating on my definition of 'a while'. 'Mostly stacking shelves but I was put on the tills a couple of times and I was pretty good at that. I picked it up quite easily.'

'And you live just around the corner.'

A question?

'Mm.'

'Just you and your mum and dad?'

'Yeah.'

'No brothers or sisters?'

I looked down at my shoes before deciding to shake my head.

'Only child here too!' She raised a hand like she was pleading

34

guilty to something.

I rifled through what questions she might ask me next: dealing with customers, counting money, being responsible with keys, what grades I got for my exams last year... And the worst question: what I wanted to be when I was older.

'Well, Nathan, if you're happy, I'm happy.'

I stopped rifling. What did she mean?

'You're happy for... for me...'

'To start, uh-huh.' She was nodding and beaming that wide fuchsia smile at me again. 'You're the only flippin' person who's come in about it! I've asked everyone I know if any of their kids or nieces or nephews were interested but nobody had anyone for me. Maybe I've got a reputation!'

I looked down to the pile of books Iris had dropped on the floor. I'd be surrounded by them, maybe even choosing what to put on the shelves. I'd be good at that. And I started calculating the extra hours – paid – I'd have out of the house, away from the static silences and kitchen questions.

'Wow. Thanks! Are you sure?'

Iris raised an eyebrow again. 'When someone offers you a job, you don't ask them if they're sure! You take it before they can change their mind. Right, when can you start?'

'Um, whenever you need, really.'

A mirage of my mum frowning over the top edge of a newspaper flashed in my head.

'OK, what about comin' in this Saturday mornin' and we'll have a wee trainin' day? I usually open at ten so try to get here just after that.'

'That's great, yeah.'

'Perfect. In fact, while you're here, can you take somethin' down to the Post Office for me before it shuts?'

Without waiting for me to answer, she tottered off back through the doorway she'd first appeared from. My hands had freed themselves from their pockets and I stretched my jaw, easing my face out of the giddy expression it'd been frozen in. Swishing through the curtain, she reappeared and handed me a brown envelope. I made sure to grin again.

'Hopefully you can get there before the last collection.'

'I'll run!'

She ushered me off and as I paced down the street I started thinking about Saturday morning already. What should I wear? Should I bring a pen and paper to write things down? What if she changed her mind?

Glancing back over my shoulder, the little shop looked bigger than before.

And my mum's car drove towards me.

5

I clutched Iris's envelope in both hands, the address a secret against my chest. When I told my mum it was a writing competition entry from school she looked half-impressed, half-surprised. It probably didn't make sense that I'd be posting it myself, but she didn't question it and when she drove off I jogged along to the Post Office, thinking of five other excuses that would have worked better.

For once, I was glad she was already home when I walked in the house five minutes later. It made the walk upstairs easier, hearing her singing quietly in her room, and when I opened my bedroom door everything was just as I'd left it that morning. I spent the next couple of hours before Dad came back in time for dinner thinking about whether I really needed to tell them about my new job. Maybe they wouldn't notice I was out of the house every Saturday; we didn't exactly spend quality family time together. I could say I was on days out to Perth with Gillian or Stacey or Nick if they ever asked and I'm sure they'd believe it, for a while at least. But it was all pointless. What would happen when one of them wandered by The Book Cover one weekend to see me standing behind the counter handing some old granny her change and her new Maeve Binchy in a plastic bag? I knew what their faces would look like. I'd memorised those expressions.

My mum hadn't even sat at the table to eat when I blurted it out.

'I got that job at the book shop.'

'What job?' Dad asked.

My mum uttered something as she stomped over from the sink. A 'what?' or an 'eh?'.

'There's a part-time job at the book shop,' I answered, looking at Dad. 'I asked about it today and the woman just gave me it on the spot.' I didn't tell them that no one else had applied, thinking it would make me look better.

'I told you I was going to speak to your dad about that!' She thudded into the chair opposite me.

'I know but…,' I chewed the inside of my cheek, thinking of an excuse, 'I overheard Hannah McKay on the bus saying *she'd* already asked about the job. I didn't want it to be too late by the time you talked to Dad.'

I gulped down a spoonful of soup, impressed with how quickly I'd come up with that.

'Good thinking,' Dad mumbled with his mouth full.

'Colin.'

He raised an apologetic hand and we slurped without speaking for a few minutes.

'If you were going to get a job,' said my mum, 'I just think it might have been better if it was in a bigger place, maybe in Ballahan. Back at the supermarket or somewhere. At least you'd be working with other people. Younger people.'

'The book shop will be easier for him to get to.'

'I know, Colin. Might not be very stable though. Isn't that woman a bit… scatty? Don't you think? Bit odd.'

I nearly laughed and spluttered a dribble of soup back into the bowl. There it was. Nothing to do with me having time to study or being more sociable. She just didn't want me hanging

38

around with anyone out of the ordinary.

'Iris,' I said, stirring the remains of my soup.

'Eh?'

'The woman who owns the shop. She's called Iris.'

More empty time of clinking spoons.

'Well at least she gave you it right there and then,' my mum muttered once we'd finished. 'Must have impressed her.'

She stood up to gather our bowls before I could see whether she was smiling or scowling.

☆

Focusing on the pain in my thigh helped me avoid looking at everyone in the corridors. The sharp corner of the careers appointment card Mrs. Turnbull had given me during registration dug through my pocket with every scuffed step. I'd barely glanced at it before slipping it away. During RE, I'd covered one side with a cartoon cat and the other with a doodle of Mr. Young, obscuring the details of the meeting. They asked us every year about our 'career aspirations' and where we saw ourselves in five years. And I was used to my mum always whirring on like an answering machine recording, repeating her lectures about University and what I was going to do with my life. That was more recent, though. She didn't ask me what I wanted to be when I grew up for a long time after primary school and Miss Harvey.

Thinking about that had made me slow down.

'Hey, Nate.'

A hand tapped me on the shoulder. Gillian twirled in the corridor to wink as she swooped past me in the opposite direction. She'd decided on this new nickname at some point last year and I never corrected her. I didn't really like it but at least having it to share was a secret string connecting us.

'Hey.'

She wasn't wearing her glasses but I didn't get the chance to ask why as she swivelled away again and her curly brown hair bounced off through a set of swinging glass doors. No cinema invite, then. No mention of where Nick was these days. Gillian had been my Home Economics partner in first and second year since the teacher had put us together alphabetically – I was a Love; she was a McCartney – so we'd had a friendship thrust upon us making apple crumbles and vegetable samosas together. She never kept her creations at the end of classes so I'd take hers *and* mine home. She was also the first one to invite me along with her, Nick, and Stacey to the cinema, come to think of it. In Fourth Year, during the trailers before *My Best Friend's Wedding* I asked her out. She'd touched my arm and told me she didn't think it would be a good idea and I spent the rest of the film holding back a snooker ball in my throat and pretending to laugh at all the funny parts.

As I watched her forbidden non-school white trainers turn a corner someone barged into me, dislodging me from my stupor back into the flow of teenage bodies bumping off one another down the corridor.

In the Art room, we were left to work alone on our newest pieces. I was experimenting with charcoal, although everything I'd attempted so far had turned into smudge-collages. I swung back on the stool, gripping the edge of the desk and looking out to the empty asphalt 'playground' for inspiration. The bookshop wandered back into my mind. It was only a couple of hundred feet from my front door, and I'd been in it a thousand times before. But Saturday was approaching like a newly invented day of the week. Maybe this was what it was supposed to feel like knowing you were going off to university... to stay in prison-cell halls with ten strangers you're expected to become best friends with.

I leaned forward and scrawled with the crumbling charcoal bars, trying to etch the silhouette of a man in a doorframe. Art was the one other subject I enjoyed outside of English and Mrs. Pamela had once told me I had 'a flair for line studies'. I always remembered that. But my charcoal shadow man was another messy, black blob. I scrunched my charcoal paper up and threw it towards the bin, missing. A boy behind me laughed.

Somewhere else in the room someone had opened a pot of glue. The PVA smell floated to me bringing the Primary Seven classroom memories with it.

I couldn't march the memory away this time.

I remembered where every single person sat.

We'd been gluing felt shapes onto coloured card and they were all lined up along the shelf under the windows to dry. We'd taken our little blue jotters out from our trays and all had our pencils with silly rubbers on the ends. Miss Harvey had asked us to write down what we wanted to be when we grew up and to draw a picture underneath of what we might look like in this magical dream future. The funny rubbers and pencil trolls around the room all wobbled back and forth, grinning at me. But they were all scribbling crude fire engines and stick figures in long, white coats. I thought we were supposed to be using our imaginations. When she asked me to read mine aloud, I did, without stammering.

'I want to be dead.'

I was beaming, waiting on a 'haha, great idea', or an 'oh, tell us why you wrote that, Nathan.' Instead, I was met with frowny, big-eyed, pink faces staring at me and Miss Harvey looking like she was going to puke into the bucket.

They phoned my parents that afternoon. Soon after that I had to meet with an educational psychologist or a children's counsellor – I can't remember which and I can't ask about it since my mum would faint if I even mentioned it. It was sorted soon enough after I repeated a hundred times what I had meant in the task: that I wanted to die and become a ghost so that I could come back and be invisible and play tricks on people and make everyone laugh. I said I got the idea from *Roald Dahl's Book of Ghost Stories*: the book I'd been reading from Miss Harvey's little fucking bookshelf. I'd even drawn my little bedsheet ghost in the jotter.

They moved me to the other class anyway and every time I saw her, she busied herself with some other pupil, trying not to look directly at the suicidal eleven year-old she'd punted from her set. I wonder if someone had ever removed the Roald Dahl book from her shelf.

Even now, whenever my mum gets a report card or a letter home about the next parents' night, I watch her and I see the sickness. Her skin reddens and her fingers jitter over the paper. She only exhales when she knows it's safe and I haven't done something weird again.

The careers appointment card and its impending questions about my future dug into my thigh again. I knew I wasn't going to attend. I'd known since I'd been handed it in the morning. I'm using the card as a bookmark in this notebook now.

6

The house ignored me. Every day after school I'd started lingering for sixty seconds in the hallway waiting for another thud or moaning voice or silhouette watching me. But the floorboards and the walls and the doorframes were defiant. The only thing that watched me was Freya, staring with gold coin eyes. I'd even been sleeping with the window open like some ritual to invite a god into my room. But the August nights when the sky didn't darken to anything more than indigo didn't give me anything. Just the river babbling beyond the garden. Maybe leaves blowing around. Never anything that made me feel that stomach lurch from the first time.

Shuffling into the kitchen on Saturday morning, the empty table made me realise these days would be different, as long as Iris let me keep the job. Dad would be at work since the video shop opened earlier on Saturdays and my mum had already left the house too. She'd either be at the antique shop bargaining over some new vase she had to trade, or haggling at a car boot sale, or even bidding at one of the auctions – whichever she'd calculated had the best chance of making a profit. Not that there ever seemed to be much to show for it. At least wherever she'd gone she wouldn't have to see me starting my new job: the job she hadn't wanted me to take with the 'scatty' woman.

My legs splayed out under the table and I slumped back in the chair, chewing my cereal slowly without having to focus on what to say next or avoiding questions I didn't want to answer.

Thirty minutes before leaving – much more time that I needed – I pulled on my brown cords, frayed at the hems, and wore a blue jumper over my school shirt. I even put on my black school shoes, thinking they gave the impression I'd tried to look smart. I hadn't asked Iris what I should wear and there wasn't a uniform like there had been at Safeway. Whenever I'd seen her in the shop she'd always looked comfortable, wearing scarves, shawls, cardigans, flowing skirts and billowy tops. And always jewellery – some gemstone hanging around her neck or elaborate bracelet that jingled when she served me at the counter. But then she did own the place. Maybe the rules would be stricter for me. And I didn't think I could pull off the bohemian fairy look.

Arriving at the shop at ten exactly, the door was already open and I almost knocked with a nervous fist before stepping in like I'd done a hundred times before. I looked around at the shelves, the rotating stand, the counter, the bargain box, a pile of books in the middle of the floor, and the little doorbell by the till. It looked different, like I was little and trying on my mum's giant glasses again. I bobbed up and down on my tiptoes, hearing my own heartbeat.

'Neil? Is that you?' Iris chanted from somewhere.

'Em… it's Nathan,' I called back, not sure where to direct my voice but assuming it was the little doorway to the right of the counter.

'Och, Nathan, Nathan, that's what I meant! Come through here!' A forearm and ring-adorned hand popped out from behind a curtain, waving me over.

The off-white drape was attached to a wire, taking the place of an actual door, and had been pushed aside, letting me

44

through. The floor of the cramped, dim back area was scattered with some cardboard boxes and big plastic containers, full of books. A tiny toilet behind a half-closed door was on my right. And in front of me stood the foot of a wooden staircase leading up to a small landing. The stairs doubled back rising over my head, so I couldn't see where they led. As I pivoted left, Iris's purple-skirted, round backside was facing me, bent over.

'Nathan, love, how're you doin'?'

It still muddled me for a second anytime someone referred to me as 'love' since it was my actual surname. I couldn't figure out if people were just using it to call on me like a nickname, or if it was meant as a term of endearment. Neither happened very often.

'Em, good, yeah, thanks. How are you?'

'Aye, fabulous. Just tryin' to shove some of these out of the way for you.' Another cardboard box scraped along the dusty floorboard.

'Oh, em, want a hand?'

She gave a strained old-person groan as she unbent herself and turned, scarlet-faced to meet the height of my chin. 'No, no. All done.'

It seemed like this was the 'staff room'. And storeroom. And kitchen. All in the narrow space of a few square feet. Or maybe it was bigger than that – English was my thing, not Maths. Boxes were piled up beside me against the back wall and a small sink was built into a mini-counter with seven or eight cups resting upside-down on a tea-towel beside it. I wondered why there were so many.

'Right. Let's get started.' Iris sighed and smiled, clamping her bejewelled hands onto wide hips.

First, she talked me through the process of sorting out donated books. She'd put the most up-to-date, interesting ones that weren't too shabby out on the shelves, depending on how much shelf-space there was. Other, ancient tomes with ripped pages and missing covers were either binned straight away or stuck in the boxes piled up at the very back of the storeroom.

'You never know when folk might come in askin' for books on weird and wonderful topics.'

Prices were up to her, which she'd scribble on the inside of the front covers in pencil. I'm not sure how she made them up and I guessed there wasn't a real system. The proper, new books she'd order in were different. There weren't many but they had to be put in the rotating stands near the entrance; stuff like John Grisham, the *Bridget Jones* books and celebrity autobiographies. They had the prices printed on the back cover. She'd decide when they'd been there for too long and had to be reduced with a big red sticker and retired to the ordinary shelves. She'd make little displays in the long window at the front of the shop too – spooky kids' books for Halloween or a bunch of Stephen King novels whenever he had a new one coming out. I thought I'd be pretty good at setting those up if she let me.

Next was the clunky till – an old, unwieldy thing that didn't always seem to work properly. Sometimes the drawer jammed, sometimes the little LED screen didn't show you how much change should be given.

'I'm pretty decent at Maths so I should be OK adding up prices and change if I need to.'

'Oh, very good!' Iris replied. 'You can sort my bills too!'

The rest of it was obvious stuff – being friendly to customers, trying to offer help if they were looking for anything. The shop's pretty small with three sections on the main shelves: Fiction, Non-Fiction, and Children's. She also wanted me to try suggesting some of the new books which cost more. I clenched at the thought; trying to be a real salesperson and talk people into spending more money. Then she mentioned keeping an eye on groups of kids that might come in. I thought it was kind of weird considering I was a teenager myself. I pictured Jonnie and some of his idiot pals barging in and pissing about and me trying to speak loudly enough to tell them to get out. It was a stupid thought – Jonnie would never come into a book shop – but still, I kept thinking about it so much for a while afterward that I'd stopped listening properly to what Iris was telling me.

A few customers drifted in and out over the next hour or two. Most just had a quick look before leaving, smiling on the way. One woman bought second-hand books. I only recognised *Little Women* and *Lord of the Rings*, which Iris asked me about afterward. I said I hadn't read *Little Women* although I'd seen the film that had come out a few years ago and liked it and that I'd read most of *Lord of the Rings* but thought it dragged a little. It had been Dad's favourite when he was young, though, and Granddad's before that. I'd wanted to impress Dad by sticking with the trilogy until the end. When I told him I'd finished, he brought home a 70s animated film version from his shop. We watched it together, commenting on all the parts they'd missed out from the novels. Dad must have seen it before, though, and kept saying lines in sync with cartoon Gandalf and Frodo. I'd tried to learn some of his favourite phrases too.

'So are your mum and dad happy you've got a wee job then?'

'Mhm.' I nodded far too hard.

As Iris used the till and talked to the customers, I hovered beside her, watching, trying to memorise what she was doing. She spent more time in the afternoon asking me about books I'd read, occasionally delving into school territory. I started with the brief, vague responses I'd give my parents any time they'd ask about school, but gradually started elaborating, telling her about Mr. Young and what we'd be reading in English this year. I even asked some questions back.

In between batches of customers, we looked through the newest couple of carrier bags of donated dusty books in the cramped little area behind the curtain. I knelt on the floor as Iris plonked herself down on the staircase that she still hadn't shown me the top of. As she examined each book, filling the air with the smell of its age, I noticed that today a different stone hung around her neck – a purple one this time.

'See your necklace? Is that an amethyst?' I thought I should ask before she wondered why I was staring at her chest so much.

'That's right.' She lifted the little violet iceberg up between two fingers. It glinted under the bare lightbulb. 'Are you interested in crystals, Nathan?'

'My mum used to get me this magazine about gemstones every month. I had to beg her for it and said it would help me with Geography at school. It was in the newsagent in Ballahan – they didn't even have it in Drichton – and it always came with a free stone. One of the first ones was an amethyst. It's not as big as that one, though.'

'Fantastic. Have you kept them?'

'Mhm,' I grinned. 'One of the issues came with a plastic case to keep them all in a sort of grid.'

'Ooh, plastic's not great for them. Better vibrations from wood.'

'Oh.' I nodded, pretending to understand. Iris added another book to the reject pile between us.

'And do you know what amethyst is for?'

For? I felt myself frown like a cartoon.

Whispered voices from the shopfront drifted through and Iris pushed herself up, making that straining noise again. I dived up to follow her out.

A girl from the year below me at school twirled one of the book stands around. It wasn't the encounter with Jonnie I'd dreaded, but I still felt my chest pulsing. Her mother, I assumed, drifted between the other shelves, one hand holding the strap of a handbag in place over her shoulder, the other fingering a row of book-spines, skimming along them. Emily, I think the girl was called. Her cheeks were smooth and shiny and her blonde hair was tied up in wrapped-up plaits like that Heidi character. She was wearing a denim jacket with a few little badges pinned to the front, too small to read. I knew she didn't live in Drichton but her mum might have been one of those people who just liked coming here for a pointless visit.

'Hello!' Iris beamed at Emily, who glanced up with a quick smile. Trailing behind, I stared at the worn, brown carpet, willing the girl to wander away round the shelves with her mum or better still, leave altogether. She didn't pick up on my brainwaves though. Unable to avoid looking up any longer, I lifted my head just in time for both of them to step forward to the counter right in front of me. Her mum plonked a book down and raked through her handbag.

'Just this, please.'

'How about you do it this time, Nathan?' Iris gave me a heavy nudge with her elbow. Emily returned to turning the bookstand, scanning over the covers. She must have recognised me from school and had no desire to talk to me.

I thought about pretending I still wasn't confident with the ancient till yet but realised it would only cost more time and awkwardness. Instead, I budged forward, smiling in the mother's direction without looking at her. I checked the pencilled price and managed to use the till without jamming the drawer. The woman took the paper bag from me with an exaggerated smile that you might give a toddler who's just managed to use a spoon.

'Bye now.'

I waved back like an idiot. Emily folded her arms then followed her mum. But as she stepped out the door, she turned back with a quick thumbs up before disappearing. I exhaled and leaned back against the wall then glanced towards Iris to find her watching me with a wry smile creasing her eyes.

'You'll probably see a lot of your pals from school in here.'

Before I could respond to tell her that Emily wasn't my pal, Iris glided back through to the storeroom and I heard the click of the kettle.

Not long after, sitting on two little stools behind the counter and finishing the dregs of our tea, she yawned and told me that I could head home. I checked my watch, knowing that she didn't close the shop for another couple of hours.

'Are you sure you don't want me to help you tidy up? Or take out the rubbish? I could help count up the money from today.' I'd anticipated arriving home later than this.

'No, no, on you go. You've had a long first day, love. Wasn't very busy, makes it seem longer.'

'No, I had fun,' I blurted out, immediately regretting it.

Iris laughed. 'Well, that's not bad, is it? Workin' and havin' fun! So I take it you don't want to pack it in just yet?'

'No, definitely not. It was good to be…' I shrugged off the rest of the sentence, standing up and checking my watch again. When I looked back to Iris, she was sitting with her hands clasped in her lap, watching me, head tilted to the side as if she was examining an abstract painting in a gallery.

'Do you have dinner with your mum and dad or just on your own?' She wasn't smiling anymore, but she didn't look sad either. 'It is just you isn't it? An only child?'

'Mhm.' I scuffed one foot on the carpet and wondered why she was asking me this again. 'I just eat on my own usually. There's stuff in the freezer so I can just pick something. I think I'll get my model fini–'

'You don't like sittin' with your mum and dad.' She cut me off, unflinching. I couldn't tell if it was a question or not and I remembered she'd spoken that way before. I looked back, fiddling in my pockets, mouthing half-formed words, trying to pick one to begin with.

'Right, you get away home, love.' Her chatty voice had switched back on and she stood, stepping past me. 'And I need to get ready.'

'Ready?'

'Yip. Got an appointment.'

At school, Gillian had told me never to ask any more questions if a woman ever mentioned an 'appointment'.

'… OK. Will I just come back same time next Saturday?'

The phone in the storeroom rang. I'd noticed it earlier – one of those clunky cream things with a dial you had to turn for every number. We'd had one in the old house when I was growing up.

'What? Oh, aye, aye. We'll have another wee day together and then take it from there. Off you go and I'll see you later.' She disappeared behind the old curtain, hurrying to pick up the phone that was still drilling out. When she answered, I stood locked to the spot, hands limp by my side, listening.

'Hello, The Book Cover… yep, it's me Iris… uh-huh that's right, I'll be here.' Her voice was muffled, but I could hear the tone of it had changed. It was lower and more serious, like my mum whenever she spoke on the phone. '… the main road through Drichton, that's right… no, no, not to worry, you don't need to have done it before.' Maybe there was an order of books coming in late. Seemed odd, though. A floorboard creaked behind the curtain. I spun around and jogged out the door.

Farther down the street I slumped into the grocer's, wasting time hanging around the shelves full of middle-aged women's magazines before buying a bottle of cola. As I left, after realising I was probably starting to look like a shoplifter, I glanced back to The Book Cover.

Iris stood on the pavement outside, arms folded, facing the road. I almost waved, but she was far enough away that she wouldn't have seen me. And anyway, she was too busy staring across the street to a red car that had just parked. A woman wearing a bright yellow cardigan stepped out. I guessed she was in her thirties but I couldn't be sure from that far off. She clutched a handbag with a jacket folded over her arm and crossed the street towards Iris. As she walked with her head tucked down, she reached up to rub her eyes. Iris reached her arm out and touched the woman on the back, steering her into the shop entrance like a shopping trolley.

Maybe it was a customer coming to get a book before the shop closed and Iris had noticed she'd hurt herself. Maybe she was some sort of inspector or book supplier and Iris was trying to impress her. Then I wondered if she was interviewing someone else for the job; she'd realised already that I was the wrong choice. Maybe I'd been too nervous in front of Emily and her mum.

Then the door was pulled shut behind them. I plodded home, memorising what the woman had been wearing like this was a case study in *Mysteries Unsolved*. An hour later I wandered back, ready to pretend I'd left something in the storeroom – my wallet or a housekey. But the door was locked. I peered inside, ready to knock on the glass. But as I raised my hand, I saw the reflection over my shoulder. The red car was still parked across the street. I stepped back towards the kerb and craned up. A light flickered from a window in the roof.

7

That same week I had my first dream about Iris. I was in The Book Cover in the middle of the night and the streetlights were red, giving everything a horrible maroon tint. She was making me serve Emily, the girl from school, at the till. Then Hannah McKay. Then Stacey, with her hair the pretty way it used to be, and Gillian, then other girls from school, even ones whose names I don't know but whose faces I recognise from the corridors. Each time Iris pushed me forward, nodding and winking. Even though I was just taking money from them and giving them books, it was a test to see if they would say they'd go out with me or if they'd kiss me, and as the dream went on Iris started prodding my back with the sharp rings on her fingers.

The whole time, Jonnie Knight was outside the window, standing on the pavement, laughing at me. But sometimes it didn't look like Jonnie. Instead, it was the shadowed figure I'd seen in my room that night. And my mum and dad kept walking past, back and forth, without looking in my direction or trying to help me, like they just wanted me to get on with it.

I woke up when I heard the wailing voice in the dream and thought I'd been sick in my bed. It was just damp from sweat. I must have been talking or shouting out because my mum peered round the door. We didn't speak. She just watched me for a minute and then left.

After a second Saturday spent with Iris, she'd left me alone, giving me an extra set of keys to open and lock up. Even my mum was struck by that: 'Ooh, she's trusting you with a lot.' Or maybe it wasn't a compliment.

While I was alone in the shop, my mind shifted from my own unexplained events to concocting ideas about the woman in the yellow cardigan. It sounded like the name of an old mystery novel that Iris would move to the bargain box – *The Woman in the Yellow Cardigan*. I kept running the images through my head, trying to remember her face. Had her car already been there when I left the shop? How had Iris reacted? Had the woman been crying? Had she been about to turn back for a minute? But every time I replayed it, it changed and warped like my cassettes that I had recorded over too many times and I wasn't sure if I was just adding in new parts that never happened. I assumed the woman was the same person Iris had spoken to on the phone just as I had left that afternoon but maybe they were unconnected. And if so, then *The Phone Call* was a new and separate mystery novel altogether.

Now that I had independence here, I'd started exploring the storage area more over the past couple of weeks. I wasn't rifling through files or prising up floorboards, but when there weren't any customers, I took quick looks in the drawer and the little cupboards in the kitchenette. I moved boxes around and flicked open the flaps of each, poking around for anything interesting. I don't know what – a massive hoard of cash or drugs shoved behind a bunch of old atlases and Dickens books? Of course, anytime I heard a noise from the shop front I jumped straight up and grab a mug so that if it was Iris, I could pretend I was just having a quick cup of tea. It was never her, though.

The only place I hadn't searched was upstairs. And I'd seen a light through a window in the roof that night with the woman in the yellow cardigan. Iris hadn't shown me or told me what was up there and I hadn't asked. I assumed that if she hadn't mentioned it, there mustn't be anything. Just a big empty attic. But it didn't make sense to have all the boxes and carrier bags full of books piled high down here in this cramped little area if there was a giant empty room upstairs. And if there were more books stored upstairs, why hadn't she shown me? Even though I'd already been prodding around downstairs, venturing up there still seemed forbidden, like there was an invisible electric fence beyond the first step warding me off.

I decided I'd give it a few hours. If Iris hadn't appeared by closing time, I'd creep up there. In the meantime, I dawdled back to the shop counter, sitting on the little stool behind the till to read. Despite the teeming shelves I could have chosen from, I'd brought my own book from home – another *Mysteries Unsolved* volume. Pretty appropriate. *Healers and Shamans* edition this time. I'd never been as interested in this one when I was younger but it was the next volume in the series I was due to move on to. When I'd opened it the night before, I'd noticed there was a section on crystals. Apparently they could be used for healing illnesses or helping things in your life. I'd never known anything about this – it was never in my gemstone magazines – but after Iris had said that weird thing about her amethyst necklace being 'for' something, the idea had been tumbling around my head. I thought it was a strange coincidence that it was in my book. Maybe I could show her the chapter next time I saw her and ask if it had been what she meant.

'Hello!'

Mysteries Unsolved jumped from my palms and my back thudded against the wall.

'Oh sorry! Did I give you a fright? You must be Nat'an.'

The Irish accent belonged to a tall woman with dark, curly hair tied back in a scrunchie. Brown eyes, much darker than mine, and a freckled face smiled down at me.

'...Yes.' I clambered upright.

'I'm Marcy. Iris told us about you.'

She offered a soft hand which I shook limply, making her wooden bangles tap and clatter together.

'Is she not around today?'

'Em, no. It's–it's just me doing Saturdays now. On my own.'

'Aah, I think she might have mentioned somet'in' about that. Oh well, how are you gettin' on?'

'Fine, yeah, thanks.'

'I take it you like readin'?' She nodded towards my upturned book on the carpet.

'Yeah.'

'Ah, just like Iris then. She must've sensed a good vibe from you.'

I stood there like an idiot, trying to figure out who the 'us' was that Iris had been telling about me. Maybe it was just an Irish slang thing.

'Sure I'll catch her another time. If you see her before I do, tell her I popped in. I'll let you get back to your mystery.' She tapped her hand on the counter, her bracelets clacking again, before swirling around and breezing out the door.

I watched her multi-coloured dress flutter after her, still wondering what Iris had told people about me. It made sense that she would tell her friends that she'd just hired someone to work for her, I supposed. Then I began to wonder if Marcy had been the woman in the yellow cardigan. I tried matching their faces in my head like a game of pairs. But I lost every time, no matter how much I forced the comparison. I stayed in the front of the shop after that and didn't leave the counter until half five. The stairs suddenly felt dangerous. Marcy had been an alarm.

My parents argued that week. Not a shouting kind of argument, which they hadn't had for years. They'd avoided those altogether by ignoring one another most of the time; each becoming voluntarily invisible to the other.

I think the 'disagreement' started with me. Surprise, surprise. I was only waiting for my microwave pizza.

'She's just handing you cash?' Mum raised an eyebrow. 'Doesn't she know you've got a bank account?'

'Didn't ask,' I mumbled back.

The three of us being in the kitchen together was normally a morning occurrence, but tonight we'd all ended up in there, like planets aligned at the wrong time. I think it was the most my mum had asked me about the book shop yet. She'd even told me about a job at the sports centre in Ballahan, as if it wasn't too late to just ditch Iris.

'Sounds a bit dodgy to me.'

'What does it matter? She's paying him decent money,' said Dad. 'Better than the supermarket anyway.'

I turned back to the humming microwave, watching my pizza trundle round in the slowest circle possible.

'I suppose you having your own job makes things a bit easier for us,' my mum said behind me. 'No more pocket money.'

Wow. I didn't realise they begrudged that tenner for the bus to Perth and a cinema ticket every once in a while.

'Nathan's pocket money is hardly at the top of our list is it?' said Dad.

As I tried to figure out what he meant, a knife and fork clattered to the floor.

'Freya! For God's sake!' Dad shouted. 'Get the cat off the bloody table!'

I jolted around to see Freya scarpering out into the hall. Dad grabbed the cutlery and smacked it back onto the table.

'Oh, get a grip! Don't take it out on her,' my mum said.

'She shouldn't even be in the bloody kitchen!'

'Well you need to do something about it yourself if you don't want her in here. Shut that window. Stop leaving the door open. Don't leave it up to Nathan and me if it's bothering you that much.'

Dad huffed and turned to face the TV, standing far too close to it.

Ping! As I yanked the pizza out, burning my fingers, I felt my mum brush past me and listened to her slippers marching upstairs. She'd obviously just waited a few customary seconds before storming off, trying not to draw too much attention to what was happening, as if that was possible.

Sinking into a chair, I looked up at Dad, waiting for him to turn around again. It was usually at this point that we'd talk to each other. Not about my mum or whatever they'd just argued about. Not even anything worthwhile. Maybe whatever was on TV, a model I was in the middle of building, the film I'd seen at the weekend – none since before the summer, even though I'd spotted Nick a couple of times at school now and waved. But the natter of the football commentary was the only thing that filled the kitchen. I wondered for a minute if he hadn't realised I was still there so started chomping and scraping the plate across the table a bit.

He turned the volume up.

I gobbled down the pizza and planned my exit.

'Where the hell are my catalogues, by the way?' I jumped as my mum reappeared in the doorway. Dad turned his head just an inch, as if he'd forgotten to be mad for half a second then remembered. 'I need to buy him new shoes and the damn catalogues keep disappearing.'

I was 'him'.

After Dad shrugged and Mum vanished again, I homed in on the front door. Squeezing it shut behind me and exhaling, I jangled the book shop keys round one finger, watching Iris's little quartz keyring spin round in circles. I hadn't brought them because I was planning on sneaking into the shop. They just gave me power. I knew that I *could* go in if I wanted to.

The sky was filled with the kind of light that could either be late evening or really early in the morning. I wandered off towards Dyrne Street. Everything was shut. Of course. Living in a town this size meant that all life just stopped after seven o'clock. No one was outside, except in their own gardens maybe. It looked like a film set, abandoned by its crew overnight. A couple of cars crawled by, with the drivers peering out towards me, probably trying to figure out who I was and which house I was from. Everyone here was connected and familiar to one another somehow, all tangled together like a giant ball of knotted string.

I should've put a jacket on; the warmth of summer nights had dissipated and autumn had settled in. Instead, I was wearing a stupid thin sweater I'd had for years. Didn't really fit me anymore. Not because I'd had some growth spurt. More because I used to be much chubbier. My mum had become obsessive about what I was eating for lunch at school – usually at least one bar of chocolate and can of juice with every sandwich, not that I told her that. Dad had called me 'healthy fat'. They started buying me rolls and stuff to fill them with at home instead of giving me lunch money. Some days I take them and some days I just don't eat.

I shuddered as I walked down the empty street. The goosebumps rising on my skin brought an older memory to the surface. I was eight, I think. It would still be a few years until I'd tell Miss Harvey I wanted to be dead. This day I just wanted to do something different. Wanted to see the houses on the other side of the playground fence up close and find out who lived in them and what I could see through the windows. When the bell rang at the end of breaktime and everyone around me ran back towards the school building I watched them go.

Then I turned around and left.

I was small enough to wriggle like a cat through the little gap in the mesh fence right in the back corner of the playing field. I followed the concrete path over the tiny bridge and entered the new, expensive housing estate I'd only seen through wire diamonds. Wandering around in my 'playtime' shoes with a Ripple in my pocket was like being in a lucid dream – not that

I knew what lucid dreaming was at eight years old but Iris had left a book on it under the counter last week and I read it all during my Saturday shift. A woman with a pram had passed me and looked down at me without saying anything. An old man cut his grass, sweating and stopping each time he reached an edge of the garden to stretch his arms and rub his back. He didn't pay attention to me. I was in complete control, exploring somewhere unknown and unreal. I was free.

Like most dreams when you become lucid, though, it ended soon enough. I thought I'd been gone five or ten minutes. Turned out to be almost an hour before I strolled back to the school, the notion of rules and trouble finally descending on me.

It's not even the policewoman or the head teacher that I remember noticing first when I toddled back through the school door. Nor Dad. It was my mum's face. A mix of angry eyebrows and squinting eyes and sighing lips. I didn't know if she was relieved or sad or happy. Or just angry because it was typical of me and she knew I'd be back and I'd pissed her off by taking so long. Dad ran at me, wrapping me up in his arms before shaking me. Only then did I notice the police officer who stood with one hand in her pocket and the other rubbing her forehead. The headmistress was clutching her hands over her heart and uttering what looked like a prayer to herself, crying more than my mum. And looking sicker. That night was the first real argument I remember. Mum hysterical. Dad defensive. Me saying as little as possible. The school fixed the fence after that.

The pebbled path stared back up at me. I realised I'd stopped moving. I looked up at St. Germaine's blank, stony orb-eyes gazing down in my direction and waited there for a while, reliving my primary school escape, watching it like a secret video on the TV in my room at night.

By the time it was dark enough that I was struggling to see back up to the main road at the end of the gravel path, I left the church behind and drifted homeward. Still in a half-daze, the chatter sounded miles away at first. Tuning back in to the world around me, I stopped again. Yellow light was glowing on the pavement outside The Book Cover. Had Iris left the lights on by mistake? But then I saw that the door was open, spilling out sounds and moving shadows. I stepped back, hiding myself in the doorway of the Bridge Hotel like Harry Lime in *The Third Man*.

One by one, people filed out of the shop. One, two, three, four. All women it looked like from where I stood. A couple of them were older, with white hair. And then a familiar brunette skipped out at the end of the line: Marcy. I could hear her laughter over the hushed chit-chat of the others who all began to disperse to various cars parked up and down the street. A few seconds later, the warm shop lights blacked out and Iris stepped from the door backwards, pulling it shut behind her, locking it with a clink. I pressed myself further back against the hotel doorway, praying her car wasn't parked at my end of the street. But her footsteps tapped along the pavement in the other direction and one car door after the other slammed shut. I waited for the engines to grunt to life and listened to the sound of each one rumble off, abandoning me to the silent street again.

8

At noon on a Saturday, Iris burst into the shop, shaking off rain and rubbing her hands through her short, purple hair – a different colour since the last time I'd seen her a couple of weeks ago. I sat back on the stool behind the counter, watching her. She wasn't just the eccentric book shop owner anymore. She was the woman hugging scared strangers in the street; the woman holding secret meetings at night in the middle of shitty Drichton; the middle-aged woman who I'd been spending more time with than my friends from school.

Were they still my friends?

'Everythin's OK?' She nodded while asking, as if encouraging me to agree.

'Mhm.' I nodded back, trying to absorb every detail about her like Sherlock Holmes, as if I could understand more about her from little clues in her appearance. All I could focus on was a little brown leaf stuck in her hair but I didn't say anything about it.

'Have you had a look at the new books I put out durin' the week? Anyone bought any today?'

'I saw them, yeah… No one's bought one yet, though.'

Then I noticed her duffle coat was buttoned up the wrong way – one extra hole at the top, one extra button at the bottom.

'Has it been busy today? No doubt the rain's puttin' people off.'

'No, it hasn't. Been busy, I mean. Yeah… the rain.'

She nodded again, hands on hips. 'Right, I'm just goin' upstairs for a minute. Want a cup of tea?'

I shook my head, already too busy wondering what the hell was up there.

She turned to move off through the back doorway, but stopped halfway, before swivelling back like a bloodhound picking up on the tiniest whiff of a scent.

'Nathan, are you alright?'

Immediate alert. It was the question of curious teachers, or sometimes Gillian. I nudged my book further underneath the counter, worrying that maybe I shouldn't be reading while I was working.

'Yeah, why?' I could hear my defensiveness, the tone my mum said she didn't like. Iris edged closer to me.

'Is there somethin' on your mind? You don't seem yourself.'

'Well, I've just been thinking about some stuff at home.' The on-the-spot cover-up came easily. 'Weird stuff that's been happening.'

'Uh-huh.'

'It's… I saw… a while ago I saw something in my room. And heard something outside. A voice.' I remembered how it had felt that night; the feeling that what I'd seen and heard wasn't imagined or exaggerated. And I was still scared of it.

I poured the story out: the distant wail, the shadow in the doorframe, the churning feeling it gave me, the empty garden, and then what had happened a few days later – the thud and creak upstairs in my room, the hospital smell, the broken crystal. By the time I finished I was squinting out of the window with my mouth open. I didn't mention the other things I'd been preoccupied with – the woman in the yellow cardigan and the collection of people who'd poured out of the shop that other night.

'And what did your parents say when you told them?'

'... I didn't.'

'Oh?'

'I don't think they'd believe me.'

Iris screwed up her brow.

'... I used to make stuff up a lot. Get into trouble. Not for years but still... we don't really talk that much.'

She tapped my arm. 'We definitely need tea for this. Come on.'

I followed her through to the kitchenette where she plonked her bulging handbag onto the floor, unbuttoned her coat, only then noticing how she'd done it up wrongly, and filled the kettle. I leaned back against the doorframe, my breath fluttering in my chest.

'Have you ever experienced strange things before, Nathan?'

Heat simmered up my neck. A slideshow of every 'strange thing' I'd ever experienced or said or done flickered behind my eyes. She must have seen it too.

'Someone's tryin' to get your attention, Nathan.'

'What?' I stood straighter, peering back through to the front of the shop for the customer I hadn't heard.

'No, dafty.' She laughed. 'Someone from spirit.'

The kettle rumbled. Was Spirit a place? An organisation? I'd never heard of it. Then my heart fired blood like bullets. I stared back, saying nothing for the next few minutes. I must've known, somehow, even then, that this was the first footstep into some dark and thrilling place.

'Spirit – the afterlife. Someone who's passed over in that

house or someone with a connection to you is tryin' to communicate with you, love. That moanin' voice you heard wasn't outside at all. Sounds from spirit are disorientatin'. They're not comin' from a physical space around you. They're from another plane altogether. The voice sounded distant, eh?'

'Mhm,' My puppet head nodded. The kettle shook and bubbled.

'Aye. You just assumed it was outside, but it wasn't. It *was* coming from far away, but not physically. And you weren't just imagining that figure.'

Something bloomed inside me. I remembered a science experiment we'd done at school once, setting fire to a gas inside a glass flask and watching the swirling blue-green flames blossom inside. That's what I felt. Coloured flames unfurling.

Click. Iris turned to pour us two steaming cups of tea.

'Do you understand what I'm talking about?' The cheeky smile at the corner of her lip told me she knew that I did. I'd always been drawn to anything like this; I just wasn't sure what 'this' was. But the *Mysteries Unsolved* books, *The X-Files*, my gemstones – they were all charms on an invisible chain I carried around with me. I had others too.

'Yeah, I do.'

She paused, the smile spreading.

'I knew it when you first came in to ask about the job. Could sense it in you. You were meant to see my wee sheet of paper in the door when you did. Cosmic timin'.'

I smiled like I'd just been told a secret, one that overtook every other secret I'd ever kept.

'And what about the stuff in my room that had moved?' I wanted more, hungry on the taste of Iris's words. 'A drawer was open and things had been pulled out, like someone had really been there.'

'Aye.' She laughed. 'Spirit can move things without physical touch. And you said you smelled something funny right before you found the broken crystal?'

'Yeah, like a doctor's surgery or the dentist.'

'You get smells too. They bring them through. I sometimes get that antiseptic smell, especially if it's an older person who's maybe been in hospital or was ill for a long time before they passed over. They'll give you signs, try to get your attention.'

'... Get my attention for what?'

She took a sip of her tea, leaning back against the counter. 'Well, that's what we're going to have to figure out.'

I liked that she used 'we'.

I see scenes like this in films and read them in books: when someone learns about some magical portal to a new world or an alien appears in their back garden or they discover secret superpowers on their sixteenth birthday. And I never believe their reaction. There's no long adjustment period. They don't lose their minds screaming in disbelief. They don't ask a hundred questions and reject all the answers. And it might seem like I should've reacted like that. Maybe I should've asked Iris what the hell she was talking about or laughed at how ridiculous it all was and told her that what my mum had said was true – just a scatty, mad woman.

But I didn't. I did the thing that the characters in films do. I opened my brain and let it all pour in while I smiled and stepped into the portal. Not because I'm stupid or because I thought it would be fun to go along with it all. I accepted it because of those blue-green flames inside. I already knew it was true. I knew what was happening to me before I'd even met Iris. I just couldn't say it out loud because I had no one else around to believe it with me. Those were always the books I'd pick out from the bargain box and they were the films I'd want to see when I used to go to the cinema. The ones with ghosts. But Iris had a new word for it, the right word. 'Spirit'.

'Iris… what else do you do here? I mean, it's not just a book shop, is it?'

She chuckled again and squinted at me, as if she was congratulating me for solving the clues to a riddle.

'I lead a spiritual circle, Nathan. Do you know what that is?'

I shook my head then gulped my tea. I think she was enjoying telling me as much as I was enjoying hearing it.

'I've got a group who meet here on Wednesday nights, upstairs. I'm helpin' them develop their awareness of spirit and their… well, their skills. You met one of them – Marcy, the Irish woman. She's lovely, eh?'

'Yeah!' I was nodding madly as if Marcy was my best friend.

'We have hour-long sessions – meditations, readings, energy work and loads of different things.'

I sort of understood what 'readings' might be and had no idea what 'energy work' was, but every new sentence from Iris was another page turned in my book. When she asked me if there were any coincidences or other strange events I'd been experiencing recently, I listed a handful of things I'd been writing about in Mr. Young's notepad: singing songs in my head just before they came on the minibus radio; dreaming about the cover of *Down a Dark Hall* the night before Iris asked me about it; coming across the crystal chapter in *Mysteries Unsolved* days after she had talked to me about her amethyst.

'There you go. That's spirit.'

'How? What's happening to me?'

'Well spirit's always workin' with us. Sendin' us wee messages, puttin' things in place, helpin' show us how we're all connected. You just need to be open to it. Need to recognise the signs and accept them.'

I still didn't understand a lot of what she was telling me, but it felt like a new technicolour world had exploded open for me. I was Dorothy stepping out of my black and white house into Oz.

'You know what you are Nathan?'

I stared back, eager for the answer.

'You're clairvoyant. You can see spirit.'

'... So I'm a good witch, not a bad witch?'

'Eh?'

'Nothing.' I grinned.

Although I had nightmares a lot, sometimes I had strong, vivid dreams too, happy ones, usually about travelling somewhere amazing I'd never been, like New York, or going to another high school with all of my old friends from primary school or meeting someone new at school I really liked and who liked me back. But they were always tainted as soon as I woke up, feeling the plummeting realisation that none of it had been real. The happiness would fade off like a friend walking away from you without looking back. Leaving The Book Cover that Saturday, though, I didn't wake up from the dream. All the way home, it was still real, like that day in primary when I'd snuck off on my own, only this time I didn't have to come back.

Turning the corner to face my house, I mouthed the words Iris had used and looked up to my bedroom window.

Clairvoyant.

I had been called lots of names before. This was the first one I wanted to remember.

9

'Are you there? This is Nathan.'

I sat on the bed with my legs crossed and the window wedged open, thinking this would help.

'Give me another sign.'

I was almost whispering, aware of my parents through the wall. The last thing they could handle was finding their weird son talking to ghosts in his room. Maybe I could tell them I was reciting poetry for my English homework, which is what I should have been doing. But did I even need to speak aloud at all? Maybe just thinking it in my head would be enough.

After leaving Iris, I'd bounded home and dived straight to my room, already trying to summon the spirit I'd seen and heard that night in August; the presence that had been in my room moving things, trying to contact me. But I suppose it was like trying to play Beethoven after just one piano lesson. I thought I might at least hit a few notes, though. After it had fallen dark outside and the voice hadn't called on me again, I started making a mental list of the questions I would ask Iris next Saturday. The English homework stayed folded up in my bag.

☆

Jonnie looked a bit like a Jim Henson puppet. Not one of the cute ones that spoke like a baby but one of the hump-backed, veiny creatures from *The Dark Crystal* or *Labyrinth* with a disproportionately small head. It's what I thought as he slugged towards me in the Art corridor, sniggering with two of his fellow goblins, muttering something and flicking glances at me. He'd never do this on his own in the street in Drichton. I pulled the straps of my bag tighter over my shoulders and focussed on the floor, wishing someone else was with me, maybe Gillian.

And as I looked up, she was there, rounding the corner a little further behind the boys.

Apart from our shoulder-tap in the corridor, I had only spotted her a few more times than Nick and she hadn't heard me when I'd called out to her outside the school gates a couple of days ago. I shuffled towards her, saying her name far too early for her to hear me. She was with that camp, skinny boy, Crystofer. That spelling always irked me. I'm sure he changed it himself in Third Year.

'What did you say, Nate?' she called, scrunching up her nose.

'Just saying hey.' I was sure Jonnie had barged his way through the double doors behind me and faded off. 'You're not wearing your glasses.'

'Yeah, I got contact lenses over the summer.' Her hazel eyes looked bigger.

'I noticed last time I saw you but…'

But she'd walked past me without even stopping to talk. I scratched a pretend itchy spot on my nose and swallowed the familiar rock creeping back up my throat.

'We're going to Safeway for lunch I think.' Gillian glanced towards Crystofer as if for confirmation. He closed his eyes and nodded. 'Probably meeting Stacey and that there. You coming too?'

I wanted to say yes and go with her and ask what other new

things she'd done in the summer, but I assumed 'we' included Crystofer, who at this point was standing cross-armed, eyeing me with an arched brow.

'Nah, it's OK. Think I'll stick around with Nick in the Computing rooms.' I didn't even think he still went there. She probably knew.

'Cool. See you later then. History last period? I've joined your class I think.' With a quick smile, Gillian and her new pal strolled off behind me. A few seconds later, though, she turned around, walking backwards, adding, 'We might start doing the cinema again in Perth if you're up for it?'

I think the surprise must have flashed from my face like a siren. '... Yeah, yeah. Just let me know when. Bye!'

She flipped back around, whispering and giggling to Crystofer. Stupid name.

I spent lunchtime ambling round the science block on a loop with a sandwich and a doughnut from the canteen. For most of the day I had been replaying snippets of things Iris had said on Saturday. After a while on my own, though, I started thinking of joining my group of semi-friends at the supermarket. But every minute spent debating how to change my story about Nick and how long it'd take to get there and who I'd speak to first when, and if, I found them in the car park was another minute taken from any time I'd have left with them. So I ended up slumped in an alcove, leaning against a fire exit, thinking about who the spirit in my house might be.

By half-past three on Saturday, it was obvious my questions for Iris weren't going to be answered. Every time a figure passed the shop window my chest would tickle like when you're unwrapping a present. But each time it was never the gift I wanted – just people from the village or strangers wandering by, some of them stopping to come in and look around, usually leaving with a cursory smile, bookless.

All day I'd pictured Iris walking in, pulling up the other stool beside me, and carrying on our conversation from the same sentence we'd finished at last week. I'd imagined what colour of gemstone she'd be wearing around her neck, and what else she would tell me about spirit and the voice I'd heard in my room and her 'circle'. But the dream-feeling I'd had a week ago was just sand sifting through an hourglass now, the way I was afraid it would be and the way I was used to.

As the next shadow passed the window, I knew already that it wasn't Iris; it was slimmer and too quick. I held my chin in my hands and leaned on the counter, glancing back down to my book, *Beloved*. I'd read the start of it during the summer and found it too difficult to follow but it had a ghost in it and I wanted to impress Iris in case she had read it too.

'Hiya.'

I looked up to see Emily again, this time without her mum and without her Heidi plaits. Her blonde hair was down, reaching the shoulders of that same denim jacket adorned with little pins and badges. I still couldn't read them but guessed they had names of bands I'd never heard of.

'Oh, hi.' I stood up and tried smiling.

'Do you have a copy of *The Great Gatsby*?' She tucked her blonde hair behind one ear then whirled a book stand around. 'My mum said I should ask in here before we drive to Perth. You know how horrendously far away that is.' She rolled her eyes but with a sort of smile.

'Yeah.' I laughed, too hard then coughed. 'I'm sure I put one out just last week. Over here.'

I led her to the long shelf against the back wall, skimming my finger along all the 'S's, wondering whether I'd put it under Scott or Fitzgerald.

'Here it is.' I pulled out the frayed little book, catching a discoloured page as it fell out.

'Thanks. I'm reading it with Mr. Young.' Although it was obvious we recognised each other from school, it sounded odd hearing her acknowledge our connection aloud. 'My mum wants me to get my own copy so I can write notes in it or something.' She frowned and looked away, making a face as if it was the most ridiculous idea she'd ever heard of, although I got the impression she was acting this way deliberately. I don't know why.

'Yeah, I did that book with him last year too.' We walked back to the counter together.

'Any good? Or is it like *Of Mice and Men*? I did that last year and wanted to kill myself at the end.'

'Em, well I quite liked it. I mean, compared to most other shit we read at school.' I didn't really mean that last part but felt compelled to take a lead from her. 'And it's pretty short.'

She smiled. 'Yeah. Maybe it won't be too bad.' She pushed her hair back again and I found myself staring at it whilst trying not to. 'And Mr. Young's kind of a babe, so I suppose that could keep me entertained.'

She handed me the pound it cost and headed for the door. Before leaving, she turned back for a few seconds.

'What's your name again?'

'Oh, Nathan. Love.' I don't know why I said my last name.

She nodded. 'I'm Emily. PARKS.' She laughed and turned. 'See you later, Love.'

I think it was the longest conversation I'd ever had with someone from a different year at school. And someone that pretty.

10

Shuffling along the pavement, I must have looked like an escaped criminal. I ducked my head and shoved my hands in my pockets. Some days I obsessed over any pair of eyes that might spot me. It was even worse when I used to go into Perth to meet the others for the cinema. I could never walk properly with so many people around. I'd scuff my feet and trip sometimes and my hands felt stupid and useless just flopping along. And I didn't know where I was supposed to look – at the ground, at people walking past me, straight ahead and vacant like a zombie? It was the same in school sometimes. I tripped walking up the steps to the stage in an assembly once and fell at the shoes of the Headmaster. I was supposed to be reading out a poem I'd won a prize for in a competition. No one could hear me through all the giggling, though. I muttered through one verse then pretended that was the end. I even saw Nick and Stacey stifling laughs at the back of the hall.

The door of The Book Cover glided nearer and I swerved inside. No customers and no one at the counter. I reached for the bell to buzz for attention before realising I didn't need to do this anymore. I walked towards the pulled-back curtain in the back doorway and poked my head through, looking left and right. The toilet door was open and the light was off. The kitchenette was empty. A handbag lay on the counter, though. Craning my neck up, following the wooden steps, I could have just walked up there to find her. I was worried I'd give her a heart attack, though, and there was still something else holding me back too. I stayed where I was.

'Iris! Are you in?' My voice cracked. 'It's Nathan!' I shouted.

A door snapped shut and muffled bumps made their way towards me before I saw the two feet in sequined sandals flopping their way down to the little square landing ahead.

'Hi, love. How are you?'

'I'm good, thanks.' I felt the broad smile stretching across my face. 'Just wanted to come in and see you. I was bored.'

She flip-flopped down the rest of the stairs and squeezed into the kitchenette, patting me between the shoulders as she passed. I liked this.

'Back from school already? Not bored of seein' this place?'

I shook my head, chuckling, and shoved my hands back into my jacket pockets.

We chatted about the shop a little, Iris congratulating me for selling some of the new books in the spinning stands. A couple of overly perfumed middle-aged women had come in that weekend and when I saw them having a look I told them about the new John Grisham book I'd seen my dad reading. Then they'd each plonked a copy down with their shiny leather purses at the ready.

Iris kept making small talk while I nodded and agreed in what sounded like the right places. At the same time, I thought up ways to steer the conversation back to what we'd discussed last weekend and what I'd been fixated on ever since. Really, I was baffled as to why it wasn't the first thing she wanted to talk about. To her I supposed it was old news, everyday, ordinary. To me it was like a new gemstone I'd never seen before, sparkling and hypnotic.

After contriving the *Beloved* plan the weekend before and concocting and ditching a hundred different ways to form an opening sentence using the word 'spirit'. I grabbed the next silent pause by blurting, 'Who was that woman in the yellow cardigan?'

I gulped and shifted my weight from foot to foot thinking I looked casual.

'Eh? Who? A customer?'

'I saw you at night with her.' I was sounding more like a stalker with every word. Iris raised her eyebrows and I swallowed again before hurrying through the rest. 'It was last month, after my first day, I saw a woman get out of a car and come in here with you. It was later on, after the shop had shut. I was wondering if she was in your circle... that you were telling me about.'

'Och, that'll have been someone comin' in for a readin'.' She'd gone back to pulling books out of a box and my face cooled.

'Oh right... em, what's that?'

'Well, that's my other job. That's why I needed you in here on Saturdays – it's when suits most people. I read cards. Well, usually. Sometimes I do it other ways; some folk don't like the cards.' She was chatting in the same flippant tone as before, the way Dad might blether about a day at the shop or my mum would witter about the bank.

'You mean fortune-telling!' I shrunk back as soon as I said it, like someone yelling 'bingo' during a game and immediately realising they had made a mistake.

'Ha! Aye well, that's what some folk still call it I suppose.' She put down the old comic book she had been waving around.

80

'I'm a medium, Nathan.'

Embarrassment was swept away as the dream feeling surged back in a tidal wave.

'Oh. Wow. So you… talk to dead people… and stuff.'

'Basically, aye.'

'How do you do that? Is it just people you know? I mean, do they come to you all the time or what? Is it scary?' My hands had escaped my pockets again.

Iris laughed and folded her arms across her baggy purple blouse, leaning back on a tower of cardboard boxes.

'You're really interested in this, eh? It's captured somethin' in you.'

I half-shrugged, half-nodded.

'Well, you're definitely clairvoyant.' There was my new title again. 'I could feel that energy vibrating from you when you first came in. Why don't I do you a wee readin'?' Iris chirped.

Those blue-green gas flames bloomed and swirled inside me again, like when Iris had first told me about spirit. But they felt darker this time. Just for a second. I swallowed the fear back down.

'… OK.'

I thought she might have waited until closing time for it and that I'd have a while to prepare myself for the idea of her finding out even more about me, but she swivelled around and toddled back up the steps. She was taking me upstairs. Exhaling, I trod up onto the first creaking step.

I pointed back over my shoulder. 'What if someone–'

'–Och, nearly closin' time,' she cut me off. 'If anyone appears they'll ring the bell. Come on.'

I followed her, turning at the landing with a skylight above

81

that I hadn't been able to see before. The stairs led towards an open doorway. A wide space invited me in; a stretching room that somehow felt bigger than the shop underneath. The walls were plain white and the carpet pink. Round the edge of the room were about a dozen neatly placed mahogany chairs, like the ones we used to have in the dining room in the old house. In the centre was a small circular table, big enough for a couple of cups and saucers, and in each corner stood tall, thin, black candleholders that reminded me of the altar of a church I'd been in with my mum's family when I was younger – much bigger than St. Germaine's. The last piece of furniture was a heavy-looking oak wardrobe to my left that grazed the sloped ceiling. Another skylight illuminated the room. It was the window I'd seen the light flickering from on the night Iris had given yellow cardigan-woman a reading. This was where the fortune-telling happened.

'I didn't realise what it was like up here. I never came upstairs.' I said, as if to prove to her that I had been trustworthy.

'No, I knew you wouldn't. I put white light across the stairs.'

I bit my lip and nodded, pretending to understand.

'An energy field, to protect it,' she continued, smiling. As soon as she said it, I remembered the electric fence feeling I'd had on my first day alone in the shop and my skin tingled.

'Right, grab two chairs and sit them at the table.'

The room had a thick smell of some spice, I couldn't tell which, but it was an aroma of age, like some of the books downstairs; the opposite of that brand-new smell of show homes my parents would sometimes take me to 'just to look'. I fumbled with two heavy chairs at once and noticed a small pencil drawing in a picture frame on the wall. It looked like a

Native American with something scribbled in the corner that I couldn't read. Iris pulled open the wardrobe doors behind me and rustled around before coming to sit down. She carried a thick, black silk-covered rectangle.

'Come on,' she laughed. 'Have a seat then.'

I slid into the chair, sitting on my cold hands to stop them from fidgeting. Settling opposite me, Iris unravelled the black silk on the table and spilled the cards in a little wave. They were old and tattered at the edges, like most of the books in the shop. The backs of them were patterned with tiny blue and white flowers.

She waved her hand over for them for a minute, as if she was about to perform a trick. Maybe she was 'putting white light' on them. I stared, mesmerised, a perfect audience member. Then she scooped them up again and handed them to me.

'Give these a shuffle.'

They were bigger than ordinary playing cards and I held them like I was wearing oven gloves, trying to give them a mix around as best I could. I only managed a few shuffles until I dropped one. As I reached down Iris nabbed it.

'That one's meant for you. Means somethin' if they jump out like that.'

She kept it face down beside her. The flames inside me turned purple. They flared and twirled. I was performing part of the magic too. I quickly jumbled the rest of the cards together and handed them back to Iris. She wasn't smiling anymore and had shifted forward in the chair, her back straight and her head bowed over the cards which she divided into three piles on the table in front of me.

I already knew what tarot cards were. I was in First Year when

I'd gone to an antiques shop in another town with my mum and dad and spotted an old yellow box with 'Tarot Fortune Telling Game' printed on top. I picked it up to read the description on the back but my mum yanked it from me and handed it to my dad, shaking her head. He put it up on a shelf too high for me to reach like some dirty magazine at the newsagent. I went back a few weeks later with one of my friends and his mum. She let us wander around on our own and I used my pocket money to buy the cards. I had to ask a woman who worked there to reach them for me. My pal had screwed up his nose at me but didn't question it. But I remember being disappointed when I took them home and opened them, realising it wasn't much of a game at all. The pictures on the cards looked like they were from some old illustrated bible and it came with a thick instruction book explaining what each card meant. I gave up on trying to memorise them after getting to a card called Strength. I still remembered the picture of a woman holding a lion's mouth open, though. I've looked for the pack since but haven't been able to find it.

'OK, Nathan, choose whichever set you're drawn to.'

I squinted at the three piles, trying to figure out which one I ought to be pulled towards. They all seemed the same, though. I kept staring, and I could feel myself frowning, searching for some clue, but as the seconds ticked by, I didn't want to give the impression that I didn't really feel anything. So I jerked my left hand forward, tapping on the cards closest to that side of the table.

'Perfect.' She nodded, gathering the other two piles and discarding them to one side.

Iris lifted the cards and set them down one by one in a row, still with the decorative blue backs facing up. She stopped at six and left the rest to the side again. I'm not sure why she used this amount. Maybe that was just the routine or the way it worked. Or maybe she sensed that was where to stop. Whatever the reason, it sent an electric current vibrating through me.

Then she flipped the cards over. Ornate, delicate illustrations shone like stained-glass windows. Most of the cards showed people, but each was different. One was a woman in a purple gown holding a sword, its tip touching stone steps in front of her. Three or four of the others were men in medieval robes and armour. One card showed a Roman chariot being pulled by two horses – one black, one white. I recognised it from my Fortune Telling Game. I noticed the chariot also had a crab painted on its front. It reminded me of my star sign. All of the cards were also full of intricate backgrounds and patterned borders: waves, heart-shapes, roman numerals, animals, trees, stars, flags, goblets, coins, stars, eyes. I recognised some of the words written on the cards from my Fortune Telling Game: Pentacles, Swords, Cups. And although I couldn't remember the meanings of any of them, the images lured me in, coaxing me to explore every inch, finding new features each time I looked from card to card. Each one was an entire novel in pictures.

'There's a lot here about nature and physical activity.'

I wasn't sure which card Iris had started with, but I leant forward absorbing everything she had to tell me. My mouth was probably gaping open too.

'I feel you used to be outside more often, walkin' and explorin' and goin' on adventures. But you've maybe been lettin' that fade away.'

'I did, yeah, with my dad. We used to go out hiking some-times.' I blurted it out, desperate for her to know she was right.

'Mm, this is him here.' She pointed to one of the cards with a king holding a silver cup in his hand, resting on a throne with dogs by his side. It didn't look like my dad. The king was too statuesque and tanned. There must have been something about it that made Iris make the connection, though. He did like animals.

'Travel's a big part of your future, Nathan.' Her hand hovered over the card with the chariot. 'I see you travellin' a lot, on planes, headin' all over the place. I can see all the trails criss-crossin' over each other in the sky.' I must've been beaming at this point. 'In fact, I feel there's travel comin' soon. Are you goin' on holiday?'

I searched my memory of every awkward breakfast chat in the past few weeks, trying to remember some mention of a holiday.

'Em, I'm not sure. We go away most years, although not for the past couple… So we probably will be soon, yeah.'

'Definitely. There's an important trip on the way. And writin' as well. I see you hunched over a desk, writin' a lot, fillin' whole notebooks full of stories and ideas.'

I'd watched a programme about psychics saying that you shouldn't give anything away, that you shouldn't feed them information by nodding or disagreeing or blurting out names and places. But I couldn't stop the grin at the mention of my notebook. I *wanted* to smile; *wanted* her to know she was right. She didn't smile back but she was looking at me differently. No, not *at* me. Into me. She was a new person here. Everything superficial had been stripped away and a pathway had opened between us like a bright tunnel. The power in her glance made me imagine she could even see me in my room at nights, writing all of this down in the notebook, rifling through page after page with my tongue sticking out that way I couldn't help, and Freya tucked in at my side.

Iris pointed to the purple woman next.

'There's a lady who's holdin' somethin' back. She's closed off.' Iris held her hands in close to her chest, clenching them into fists. 'She's hurtin' because of somethin' in the past that she can't let go of.'

I knew already. My face started to burn, hearing someone else say it.

'Is this Mum?' Her voice was deeper, yet softer.

'I think it... it could be... yeah.' Suddenly I felt guilt, like I was doing something wrong by agreeing. Thinking about it was OK, but saying it, even with a stupid mumble, meant I had crossed some invisible, dangerous line into real treachery.

'You need to help her. There are things she can't let go of. But it'll just take a bit of time and patience. This is one of your lessons. A big lesson on your path.'

Iris was talking some new foreign, alluring language. I could hear my heartbeat, thudding through my chest. Talking about my mum like this was odd, though. It didn't match. Hurt. Help. Time. Patience. Lessons. These words belonged to a different part of my brain from her. I felt the room sway beneath me.

But Iris sounded so sure about it all. She wasn't guessing or hesitating or wavering. She was talking like she just knew; like she was affirming everything that was already true. My parents had never celebrated my 'vivid imagination'. They blamed it for my nightmares. And my lying. And other things when I was younger.

Next Iris tilted her head to one side. She seemed to be staring at nothing, as if daydreaming. I wondered if she'd remembered an appointment she'd missed or an errand she'd meant to run. I glanced over her shoulder, listening for the bell ringing downstairs.

'There's a spirit here, Nathan.'

My neck and shoulders shuddered as if a freezing cold wave had frothed over me. I twitched, hurting my neck and trying not to show it, then breathed noisily through my nose like I did when I was trying to stop myself from being sick. But it wasn't unpleasant. It was euphoric.

'It's a male energy. Aye, it's an older man. OK. OK, I'm listenin'.'

At first I thought she was talking to me and didn't know what I was supposed to say. Then I understood. She was talking to someone I couldn't see or sense. She was talking to 'spirit'.

'He's giving me a name... What? Say it again.... OK. I'm getting Johnston. No, Jonathan. Jonathan.'

BBRRRRRRR!

A surge of static seized me.

BBRRRRRRR!

The bell.

'Geezo, that was some timin' eh?' Iris jumped up and waddled towards the stairs.

'I... I just thought about someone ringing the bell a second ago.'

'Ah, see! That was spirit sending you a wee message! We must've been meant to stop there, love.' And she plodded down the steps.

The reading was done. Cut short. Like a ten-ton egg timer had run out and there was no way to flip it over. I listened to Iris's footsteps thudding into the shop below me and her distant voice talking to someone. Knowing I ought to follow her, I stood on still-shaking legs. Before I could move, though, the remaining blue tarot card waited for me on the table – the one that had 'jumped out' for me. I twisted towards the stairs, listening again for Iris, making sure she wasn't about to come back. Then I pinched the edge of the card, half-turning it over.

Another robed figure. But this wasn't a regal character. A profile view of an old, bearded man's face was hooded in a long, brown cloak. He held a staff in one hand and a yellow lantern in the other. It looked like he was in a cave or a forest – I caught all of this in a quick glance, my ears still on alert for the sound of Iris coming back. The last thing I noticed was the name of the card – 'The Hermit' – printed in capitals along the bottom.

A thump in the storeroom below.

I flattened the card back down on the table, letting go with delicate fingers, as if it was a museum artefact I shouldn't have touched. Descending the stairs, I repeated the name of the card in my head, knowing I'd have to memorise it; knowing it was important somehow.

Iris was rearranging boxes and bags beside the sink.

'I'll fit it right in here, pal.'

In front of me, a tall, blonde man stood holding a big cardboard box. His arms bulged under the weight.

'Want me to help?' I asked Iris, smiling awkwardly at the stranger carrying what I assumed was a box of donations.

'No, no, love, it's fine, I'll start working through all this. Off you go and enjoy your holiday.'

On one hand, I was disappointed. Another day of magic and new discovery was scalpelled off in the middle of my awe. On the other, I could go home and begin researching The Hermit and what he meant for me.

The blonde man winked as I brushed past him.

11

I spent the rest of the evening raking through my room and the loft trying to find my old Fortune Telling Game, or even just the little book that had come with it. I'd decided years ago it was gone forever but thought my eagerness might conjure it back into existence. It didn't. In the end, I resorted to the internet, which meant unrolling that enormous extension cable from the study all the way downstairs and asking permission to use the phoneline, immediately raising suspicion. I then had to close the study door just enough to achieve some sense of privacy without being conspicuous. I also had to be ready to close the internet window anytime footsteps crept up from the landing and every page seemed to take hours to appear, especially the ones with pictures of the cards and patterned backgrounds. It was at least a *little* bit quicker on the school library computers.

Drichton internet crawled through the phoneline and onto the screen pixel by pixel. Eventually I managed to find a few pages on a site called unlocking-the-tarot.com that told me what The Hermit represented. It felt like discovering some lost holy text.

'*The Hermit signifies that the seeker must look inwards for answers. Allow yourself to be your source of inspiration, rather than relying on the opinions of others.*' Could refer to my mum again, like Iris had mentioned, always going on about exams and university. Maybe the card was telling me to stand up and make my own plans.

'*Think carefully before making any sudden decisions. The Hermit is reflective and never acts on impulse.*' What decisions did I even have to make? Everything was planned out for me. The prospect of some thrilling choice weaving its way towards me buzzed in my chest.

'*If drawn in a 'past' position*' – I didn't know what this meant – '*the individual may be blocking memories from his or her past or refusing to acknowledge important experiences.*'

Of course I was trying to block out memories from the past. As were my parents. Escaping primary school that day and going 'missing'. Telling my teacher I 'wanted to be dead'. And everything else that came after. Including the story.

You'd think I'd have learned that using my imagination could cause trouble. Maybe because it had been near the end of primary school I'd thought I should finish by leaving my teacher with a momentous display of my talent. For the short story homework project, I'd written my own horror piece, full of gore and blood and gruesome descriptions. And a pupil killing his teacher and all of his classmates.

Even at the time I could tell that part of the reason my mum was so angry was because it had been a homework task, so she was in some way to blame because she hadn't even checked it. That summer we moved, of course. New town, new high school in August, new status as a loner.

And there were other 'incidents' I wanted to block out too. Lying about moving to America. The dress-up day.

The cat.

'Nathan, are you doing something important?' My mum pierced the memories.

'Yes! Research… for homework!' I called back. I did have research to do for Modern Studies. But it could wait.

'I need to use the phone. Can you come off the internet?' Her voice grew louder as she climbed the stairs. I didn't respond, but knew I had to disconnect to avoid her coming into the room. Before shutting it down, though, I skimmed over a final sentence.

'*The Hermit represents the most secret part of ourselves.*'

I didn't want to analyse this yet. I closed the page.

On Wednesday after an early and rushed dinner, I lingered around the pavements in the village, walking in circles, lurking in the shop doorways, attracting wary eyes from a couple of dog-walkers. I knew Iris held her spiritual circle on Wednesdays, and I knew from seeing them all leave the time before that it finished around eight o'clock. I didn't know when it started, though, and wanted to find out, as if that would somehow help me become closer to it all. So how long would the session, if that's what it was called, be? I'm sure Iris had said it was an hour. Maybe two? And maybe that other week had been different for some reason; a one-off. Maybe it didn't always finish at 8:00. It had to start after the shop closed at 5:30, though.

After half an hour of wandering around, trying not to attract attention to myself and peeping over at the shop door every minute like a private investigator, the first couple of cars appeared and tucked themselves alongside the kerb outside The Book Cover. I pressed myself back into the alcove of the Post Office entrance, peering out at the arrivals. From one car two middle-aged women bounced out giggling and waving to a woman in the second car. As she opened the door, I realised it was Marcy, the hippy woman who'd spoken to me in the shop weeks ago. The one who already knew who I was. The three of them stepped into The Book Cover and minutes later a third car arrived. This time it was an older woman in a pleated skirt and black blazer. She clutched a handbag as she bustled along the pavement and nipped into the shop. That night I'd seen them all leaving, I'd thought there were only about six of them. But what if there were more who'd left before I'd stumbled across them? Maybe there were ten, twelve, twenty members.

"Scuse me, pal.' A hand touched my shoulder and a grey-haired man I recognised from the village hobbled past me. I had somehow drifted halfway-out onto the pavement, rubber-necking at each of the arrivals. Some private investigator I'd be. As I sidestepped back into my hiding spot, I watched the grey-haired man limp off down the street. And into The Book Cover. He was in the circle too. I hadn't expected that. He was a man. It was like when Miss Paige introduced herself as our Woodwork teacher at the start of Second Year. So far it had all seemed to be women who were involved with Iris though: the three women who'd just arrived with Marcy and yellow cardigan-woman who'd had the reading. And I was sure I'd only seen women leave on that first night I'd discovered the circle.

I crossed the road, walked down the other pavement and past the shop, then hung around for another twenty minutes surveying the street. No more members. So there were five of them. Six including Iris. It meant nothing really – a corner piece of a torn treasure map. But a treasure map all the same. I walked home after that. Slowly.

Stepping back into my room was like returning to a dark

mine after glimpsing daylight for a few minutes. My English homework waited on my desk: a slab of coal to be chipped at. It was due the following day. I always left homework until the night before, although not always with Mr. Young. I pretended it was because I worked better under pressure. In truth, it was just habitual procrastination. For someone living in Drichton with no friends around, my ability to find innumerable things to do when I had other priorities was impressive: working on models, finding chatroom 'friends' when my parents weren't home, reading, talking at length to Freya, rearranging my bedroom furniture and posters, rewatching videos I'd seen a hundred times. Stalking fifty-year-old mediums who owned bookshops.

The homework was to write a clear dissertation outline. I was supposed to have chosen and read my books over the summer. I'd devoured *The Bell Jar* in the first couple of weeks, but my plan to read a second novel over the past month had evaporated. Maybe I could just use a book I'd already read. Or one of the *Mysteries Unsolved* books. I pictured Mr. Young reading *that* proposal through his Clark Kent glasses – he even had a little curl of hair that always fell down, although it was blonde – pretending to take it seriously and thinking of how to tell me my idea was moronic in the most sensitive way possible. I laughed to myself and ended up faking the plan for *The Bell Jar* and a book called *Owls Do Cry* Mr. Young had recommended to me at the start of term. I'd read it soon. And if not, I could always change the plan later. I was sure he would let me. He also wanted us to submit our notebooks so he could read what stories we'd been working on. I made sure to pull out these pages before I handed it in the next day.

That's when Gillian invited me to a Friday night film trip. It felt like a comfort and a trick at the same time. It would be the first time I'd spent with the cinema group since the summer. She even offered me a lift there with her mum. So I agreed. It would be another night out of the house and besides, it felt nice to believe that maybe she and Stacey and Nick had realised how much they missed me and that things hadn't been the same this year. When Gillian and her mum arrived to pick me up, though, Crystofer was sitting cross-legged in the back seat, craning to check his curly hair in the rear view mirror.

'I've asked my mum for hair straighteners for Christmas. Do you think she'd give me them early?' He leaned forward to Gillian and her mum who both laughed with him. 'Or maybe I should just embrace my curls while I still have them. I'll be like Mariah Carey – the early years. What do you think, Nathan?' He turned to me, posing and I shrugged.

After that he didn't even blink in my direction, but continued nattering to Gillian all the way to Perth. I hoped that his presence was just a cameo and that he wasn't going to have a recurring role with us. Gillian's new hazel eyes glanced at me every so often in the little square mirror in her windscreen visor. I tried to smile back but didn't know if all she could see was my eyes.

When we arrived at the cinema, Stacey was waiting for us with some other guy, her cousin I think she said. He didn't go to our school and was wearing a football top. The extent of our conversation was, 'hiya' and I made sure to always keep at least two of the others in between us. Nick wasn't there and I wondered if he either hadn't been invited or had been invited but didn't want to come. I didn't ask Gillian, though, not wanting her to know I still hadn't spoken to Nick myself.

The queue for *The Blair Witch Project* rolled out of the doors and down the street but we still managed to clinch tickets. At least we were legitimately old enough now. It ended up being a shitty atmosphere to watch a horror film in, though. The theatre was filled with idiots my age and some a little younger, probably doing what we used to do when we were never really fifteen, with a constant murmur of chatter and giggles. I made sure to sit at the opposite end of the row from Stacey's lout cousin but it landed me beside Crystofer who still annoyed me for no real reason other than his constant need to be flamboyant. Even in the dark of the cinema every leg-cross or handful of popcorn was overplayed and a big portion of my attention during the film was devoted to being aware of how close his knees were to me. His joke in the car about his Mariah Carey curls was pretty funny, though, I supposed.

Despite the chaos of the cinema, the film still managed to haunt me like the shadow figure from my room. It didn't make me jump or roll out of a bed pulling a lamp with me, and there was nothing gory or graphic about it. But it permeated the crinkling sweet wrappers and whispers and Crystofer's knees. It had all been so believable. No soundtrack. Unscripted dialogue. Handheld cameras. It was easy to imagine yourself in the middle of it; lost in the woods, being followed.

On the way home with Gillian's mum, I huddled against the car door in the back seat and watched streetlamps zoom by making everything orange, dark, orange, dark. I don't know when but at some point Gillian had started talking to Crystofer about me as if I was an invisible Ebenezer Scrooge watching over my own life.

'He works in the book shop in Drichton… we only have History together this year… no we didn't go out, stupid.' The sound of her slapping his leg and giggles.

'How long have you had your job, Nate?'

Hearing Crystofer use Gillian's nickname for me was even more annoying than her using it.

'A few months… Chris.'

'Do you live with your mum and dad?'

'Mhm.'

'Ugh, I hate my dad. So glad we don't live with him anymore. Don't you have a sister or a brother or something, Nate?'

I waited for Gillian to correct him but she'd turned back around in the front seat. When I caught her peering eye in the visor mirror, she blinked away.

'No.' I turned my stare to Crystofer and lowered my voice. 'Just me.'

'… Cool.'

Orange, black, orange, black and the thrum of the car.

'And it's Nathan.'

I had nightmares that night, of course. My dad muddled into my room, half-asleep, to wake me up. I'd been calling out loud enough for them to hear again. The next morning when he asked me what I'd watched at the cinema I lied about some stupid rom-com. I'm sure he didn't believe me but didn't ask any more about it.

☆

When Saturday finally arrived, I galloped towards The Book Cover, keys jingling in my hand. But as I reached up to unlock the door, it budged beneath my hand. It was already open and

Iris was lifting books from a box onto an empty shelf. Maybe she sensed how much I'd wanted to see her and that's why she was there. Maybe someone from spirit was helping me.

Unlike most other conversations, I hadn't planned it out beforehand. Hadn't rehearsed the words I would use or prepared ways to slip it into conversation. It just bubbled up from the purple flames fluttering inside me.

'Can I join your circle, Iris?'

The past few weeks had been spent tumbling deeper into this new tunnel, feeling my eyes and mind being opened wider every time I spoke to Iris about the spirit world. I had been guzzling it down, thriving on each new story and tarot card. Now I was leaping ahead, jumping over a canyon into a new land.

'Well hello to you too,' she said, and laughed.

'If I'm allowed? If I can?'

'I knew you'd ask soon. I've been waitin' until you were ready.' She walked over to me and gripped my shoulder. 'I feel your energy would fit in really well with the group. I want to help you develop your gifts. Of course you can join.'

I don't think I responded in any sensible way. Just nodded and grinned, probably looking more like a child than I ought to.

'You'd have to check with your mum and dad, though.'

'Mm.'

'I've already told the members about you. You can meet them next Wednesday.'

I knelt down and helped her stack the shelves with the dusty books in silence, an electric buzz shimmering through me. She left soon after, telling me she had an appointment at noon. I wondered if it was a reading for someone but didn't ask. I was too busy thinking of the circle, four days away, and how I'd ask my parents' permission.

But that night I didn't ask anything. I told them I was joining a book group. Asking permission to join a spiritual circle was unimaginable. But I'd need *some* alibi to be out of the house every Wednesday night and a book group seemed like the most plausible idea, considering I worked in a book shop and they knew I was a reader.

'And is this going to get in the way of your homework? Sixth year's still important you know. You'll have exams just like last year. And we don't know if you'll be accepted for Uni with last year's grades.'

'Well, it's going to help me with English.' I'd already anticipated Mum's neurosis. 'Iris said *The Bell Jar* might even be one of the books we cover soon. And Mr. Young said joining a book group was a good way to get used to different styles of writing.' I knew she'd never check up on any of this.

'Suppose you could be doing worse things.' Dad shrugged. 'Unless they all light up hash and get high after talking about the books. Does this woman have a tambourine?'

I laughed with my mouth closed and Mum moved on to harassing Dad about her missing catalogues again.

I stayed awake for hours that night, the window ajar as part of my ongoing quest to communicate with the voice. I was clairvoyant after all. But lying there with the breeze flapping past the curtains, something else echoed in my ears. The Hermit card was like a distant beacon blinking on a dark sea in my brain. I'd tried to ignore it since Tuesday but it signalled out to me. '*The Hermit represents the most secret part of ourselves.*'

The words bobbed up and down on waves. Maybe I had some gift, like Iris. Maybe this was the secret part of me. And the circle would help bring it to the surface.

12

I smiled in the school corridors, wearing this new sensation like a new coat I hadn't grown into yet. Watching other people bustle past in their laughing groups, I had my new secret; a one-up on everyone around me.

But the bliss burst as a herd of idiots in my year barged towards me. I thought pupils like them were meant to have been weeded out by Sixth Year. They muttered to one another in put-on deep voices and guffawed in my direction as I winced. Jonnie was amongst them. He shoved my elbow as he jostled past, not even a jot of recognition in his face. The smell of aerosol and cigarettes lingered after them, dampening me back down, cancelling me out.

Stacey sat beside me in English and talked about our cinema visit, laughing at something her oaf cousin had said and gushing over how hilarious Crystofer was.

'Isn't he? Eh? So funny.'

She sounded far off, though, somewhere above or behind me. I half-nodded, enough to both acknowledge her and stop her talking. I didn't want another cinema invite if Crystofer and football-cousin had infiltrated the group permanently. I had a new group to look forward to anyway. The circle would be different. My own secret club.

At the end of the period, I didn't stay to try talking to Mr. Young and I don't know if Stacey left before or after me. Didn't care. I strode out, eager to plunge forward through time and crash-land in Wednesday night.

I was the first to arrive, of course, with my copy of *The Alchemist* that I tucked under the counter, no longer needed. I'd brandished it conspicuously in the kitchen at home; a vital prop in maintaining the book group coverup for my parents. Stepping behind the curtain, I heard Iris call me from upstairs. Permission to cross the barrier of white light. I crept up to find seven chairs had been arranged in an oval shape in the long room. In the middle, a chunk of smoky crystal rested on Iris's little table. Studying the chairs, I picked a seat that gave me a view of the doorway and that was next to the chair I assumed would be Iris's, at the head of the oval. I sat down and rubbed my palms on my cords, obsessing over my posture and the choice of seat. Iris pottered about, rustling through the wardrobe and lifting out a few candles and a box of matches like a chef preparing ingredients.

'You'll be fine, love,' she said.

Invisible glue held my lips shut.

'I felt your nerves as soon as you came in! I can see the red in your aura. Everyone knows you're comin' though; I spoke to them all on the phone. They already knew, really; I'd told them about you weeks ago, seein' and hearin' that spirit in your house! They're impressed.'

I forced a smile and a vague sound of acknowledgement, the mouth-glue melting a little. My smugness at school had evaporated into the fear of meeting new people. Adults. Iris lit an incense stick on her table and the rising tendril of smoke puffed out a musky, pungent smell. It was the aroma I'd noticed the first time I'd been allowed upstairs.

Then the shop door clattered open and voices floated in, nattering to each other, growing louder and clearer. Iris rubbed my shoulder.

'Hellooo!' I remembered the Irish accent as Marcy bounced up the stairs first. She drifted in wearing a long, flowery dress again that floated behind her. She scooped Iris in a wide-armed hug as another two women appeared behind her. It was the pair I'd seen share a car last week. The first was a plump blonde woman with a brightly patterned blouse and white trousers. I could smell her sweet perfume already and it reminded me of someone's mum. The second, a younger, tall woman with straight black hair and a leather jacket. She looked like a cartoon character I'd seen in one of the books downstairs.

'Nat'an! Hello again! Iris said she was going to invite you.' Marcy swayed towards me, opening her arms again for an unexpected hug. I stayed in my seat and bent awkward arms up and around her, giving her a weird pat on the back. It was like meeting up with Aunt Brenda and Uncle Frank when they'd visit from England or being 'comforted' by relatives I didn't know at Granddad's funeral. But despite my pounding heartbeat that I was sure she could hear, especially since I still hadn't spoken, I was glad to have some connection to someone already, besides Iris. Marcy took the seat to my left. At least it felt like I only had four strangers to be introduced to instead of five. The other two women smiled and offered polite waves and 'hiya's, sitting in chairs opposite me. The dark-haired one muttered something about 'sitting over here, then.' I must have been in her usual seat.

Swallowing the glue, I prepared to offer to move when the door downstairs clunked open again and more footsteps trod up the stairs. The older woman – this time wearing smart trousers, jumper, and a purple quilted coat, and still clutching onto the black handbag strapped over her shoulder like last week when I'd spotted her on my reconnaissance mission.

'Sadie, love, have a seat.'

Iris shuffled around the room, lighting the pillar candles on the stands in each corner. The grey-haired lady greeted the others in a near-whisper and scuttled to a chair. I felt like ten glaring spotlights were directed at me, illuminating me as the teenage boy sitting amongst five grown women, out of place and uninvited, especially with Sadie now here. She looked at least ten years older than Iris and I worried how I should speak and what I should or shouldn't say around her.

'Just Patrick we're waitin' on, eh?' Iris stood with her hands on her hips, while the four women chatted. I knew I should try to engage, smile in the right places, nod along, laugh if they made a joke. But my mind had hooked onto Patrick. He must be the man who had passed me in the street last week; the one I'd seen around the town before. Would he recognise me too? Point me out as the lurker who had huddled in the Post Office entrance watching them all arrive? Or worse, tell me he knew my parents. Pretty likely in this place. The possibility hadn't occurred to me until now.

But I didn't have time to linger on the thought, as he limped up the stairs moments later, repeating the routine of hugging Iris and waving a quick hand to everyone, including me. There didn't seem to be any sign of recognition, thank God. Patrick settled into the penultimate seat of the circle, between Marcy and Sadie. Then with a little huff of effort, Iris popped downstairs and I heard the keys jingle as she locked the shop door. A cool wave rippled over my skin, like we'd been sealed into some spacecraft and our atmosphere had been chemically altered. Iris climbed the stairs again and took her place, plonking herself down in the last remaining chair to my right.

'Right folks, let's start with the obvious – that's not a spirit sittin' beside me!'

The others chuckled and I laughed too loudly, alternating between looking at the ridges in my cords and Iris, heat radiating from my face.

'We've got somebody new. And I'm probably old enough to be his granny, but–' She turned to me, tilting her head. 'What age are you again, Nathan?'

'Em, seventeen. Eighteen next summer.'

'God, I'm feelin' old here!' Marcy cried beside me, clamping a hand on my shoulder while the others chortled along. The dark-haired woman across from me whose seat I'd taken didn't smile.

'Go on then, introduce yourselves.' Iris nodded to the blonde mumsy-looking woman to her right who clapped her hands onto her thighs and began.

'Well, Nathan, I'm Katrina. I had a reading from Iris about a year ago, I think a couple of months after my dad died.' She tilted her head towards Iris as if to check. 'And instead of an hour-long reading I ended up staying and chatting about spirit until it was dark outside and past dinner time! Gordon thought I'd run away! I started coming to the circle a couple of months after that, so I'm just enjoying developing my spiritual awareness. Oh, and I like the meditations too! They're fab.'

'Aye, you need a wee bit of de-stressin' sometimes, don't you?' Iris added, grinning. Everyone laughed again at what was obviously some in-joke. I gave a smile back but felt my insides sinking in quicksand. The dark-haired, thin woman spoke next.

'I'm Melissa and I started coming just before Katrina. Been developing my awareness too, I suppose.' She didn't unfold her arms as she spoke.

'More than just your awareness!' Iris cut in. 'Your clairvoyance is really comin' along. You gave me a readin' last week!' The others all murmured in agreement. I felt bad for Katrina, who hadn't been given the same compliment. She just beamed with bright white teeth, though.

'I'm Sadie.' The older woman's small hands were clasped in her lap and she spoke through quiet, thin lips. She reminded me of a terrible Maths teacher we'd had years ago who I felt sorry for after the trouble we'd caused in her class. 'I've known Iris for a couple of years.' She nodded to signal she was finished and that I shouldn't need to know any more than this. I avoided her eyes and joined my hands, mirroring hers.

Patrick took his turn, leaning round a little to look at me. I already knew his name. 'Nice for me not to be the only man in the place anymore, pal.' We all laughed, even as my stomach kneaded itself. 'I've been interested in this for a while and, em, I'm finding it's really helping me.' He smiled and sat back against the chair. I wondered what he meant but couldn't think of much before Marcy piped up.

'Well…' She drew the word out, exaggerating her movements as she turned to face me. 'I'm Marcy, as you know. Pleased to meet you!'

She thrust a hand forward for a pantomime handshake. My hands untangled themselves to return the gesture while I giggled like an idiot.

'I've known Iris for, what, about five, six years? Since right after I moved over from Ireland.'

'Aye, must be about that, eh?' Iris nodded slowly, as if counting the years in her head.

'We met whilst I was in the middle of my divorce and was dealin' wit' a lot of problems I was tryin' to get away from.'

I lowered my gaze feeling I shouldn't be looking at her. Had she forgotten that she had only met me once before? Behind Marcy, Sadie straightened her posture and crossed her legs.

'So, Iris helped me work through it wit' guidance from spirit. And I still just love comin' to the circle and connectin' more and more.'

She grinned with her eyes closed and I examined the wooden bracelets and beads on each of her wrists, tapping together as she rubbed her hands.

I realised then that everyone else was silent, watching me. My cue. I looked to Iris who was already staring at me, grinning.

'Oh.' I gulped sticky air and rubbed my sweaty fingertips on the edges of the chair. 'I'm Nathan and, em, I work downstairs for Iris on Saturdays, so I just... wanted to find out a bit more about this and...' I felt the same exposure as in those dreams I'd had about turning up to school naked.

'And more than that! You've been experiencin' things at home, eh?' I pictured my parents watching me from across the kitchen table, shaking their heads. 'Spirit tryin' to communicate with you.'

I'm sure I made an 'uh' noise when I exhaled. 'Yeah... I heard something in my room, like a moaning sound that was... I think... a person. And then I saw a shape... a silhouette in my bedroom doorway.'

'And you got that smell too, didn't you? That medical smell?'

'Mm. Yeah. But that was a few days later.'

'Aye, I've had that,' Katrina nodded. 'That antiseptic smell you get with spirit a lot, especially if it's somebody who passed over in a hospital.' She echoed what Iris had told me weeks ago when I first mentioned it.

'So, we want to work on your clairvoyance and find out who was tryin' to contact you. Or maybe somebody here'll get a message through for you.'

Iris winked and I wondered if she could still see the red in my aura.

'We've been doin' some dream work for the past couple of weeks.' She spoke to everyone, her voice louder and more pronounced. I could tell the session must be properly beginning. 'We were tryin' some new meditation techniques to get you into a deep, restful sleep, weren't we? So that you could allow your soul to expand and connect with spirit. And I wanted you to tell us about one of your dreams, one that you feel comfortable with, so we could discuss what it is that spirit might have been tryin' to communicate to you.'

I felt the same greed for knowledge I'd had before when I talked to Iris about spirit and clairvoyance and readings and the cards. A giant encyclopaedia of a new language on a new planet in a new universe was being flipped open and I was diving right into the pages, hoping it had answers to all of the questions clogging up my head: the wailing voice, the shape in my room, the nightmares I'd always had... why I lied so much.

'Does anyone want to volunteer first?'

A static silence.

'... I'll go for it.' Katrina slapped her hands together and leaned forward. 'Wait, wait, I've got my dream journal!' She leaned around behind the chair to rustle through a handbag and pull out a little square notepad with one of those plastic 3-D illusion covers on the front. After flicking through to find her notes, she began describing driving somewhere in her car with the back seat packed full of boxes and Iris in the passenger seat. After a long journey through different countries, they arrived at an enormous mansion. Katrina spoke slowly, concentrating on every word as if it was the first dream she'd ever had and couldn't believe what she'd experienced.

'And when we stepped out of the car to take out all of the boxes, they were empty. There was nothing in any of them. I woke up feeling really disappointed.' Finishing, she gazed at Iris with searching eyes.

'Well often in dreams drivin' somewhere in a car represents your life, your journey. I was probably just a symbol in the dream, representin' your spiritual awareness and how you're usin' that to help you move onto your next stage and your new set of lessons.' Lessons for what, I didn't know but no one else questioned this. 'I think the empty boxes are showin' you that there's some area you need to develop first. Somethin' that spirit's tryin' to get through to you that you're missin'.'

'Mm,' Katrina nodded. 'And I'm about to move to the new house, do you think spirit's telling me not to go through with it or that there's something I'm forgetting?'

Iris replied with an explanation I couldn't fully understand – reaching a deeper level of understanding and connection with spirit the more you develop your awareness. Maybe I hadn't 'developed' enough yet.

What she had said about the car being a symbol for life

was familiar though. There had been a dream dictionary on a bookshelf in our old house that I was sure said the same thing. Thinking about it, I was surprised it was even in the house, considering how much my parents freaked out about the Fortune Telling Game I had tried to buy. So whose was it?

Melissa had already started talking about her dream and I'd missed the beginning, lost in my memory. I chewed the inside of my cheek, and peered around the circle, hoping Iris wasn't going to quiz me on any of this. Where I tuned in, Melissa was describing a stranger's house she'd been trapped in. There was no front door and every time she climbed the stairs she appeared in a similar room to the one before, except she could never go back downstairs, only keep ascending on and on in a loop.

As she talked, she looked at the floor, glancing up from time to time at either Sadie, Iris or Katrina. Her ankles were crossed and she held her clasped hands to one side. She said the rooms started off bright but with every level she rose through the wallpaper began peeling and the furniture became more cluttered and the windows shrank. She knew her mum was in the house and that she had to find her. Everyone had become silent and still. She stopped talking and Katrina reached a hand over to rub her knee. I could tell from the quietness and the little gesture that Melissa's mum must have died or was at least ill or maybe missing. I felt like I'd been caught reading someone's diary and knew I should look away again.

Iris thanked her for sharing the dream and offered her interpretation, talking about different 'planes' in the spirit world and how we ascend through them by learning lessons. She said Melissa's dad's soul had learned all of his lessons and had moved

111

on to a new plane. Again, the others nodded and murmured in agreement. Instead of devouring the information, I felt like the dunce at the bottom of the class, struggling to keep up.

At Sadie's turn she said she couldn't remember any of her dreams from that week.

'Nothin' at all? Even if it's just a wee memory or an image or a feelin'?' Iris urged.

'Sorry, no. I've had a bit of trouble sleeping this week. My memory was blank in the mornings.' Iris didn't push any further and looked to Patrick.

He sounded nervous, speaking in short bursts and unfinished sentences. Like Sadie, he said he couldn't remember most of his dreams, but that there was one image he could still recall vividly. It had been just that morning and all he could hold onto when he woke was the image of his childhood dog. He saw the black and white collie clearly, felt her wet nose, smelled her muddy coat, heard her distinctive yapping that he hadn't thought of in years. His voice had changed, describing her – Holly. Holly the collie. The hesitations had smoothed out and his hands reached in front of him, as if the dog was in the room and he was about to pet her. Katrina held a hand to her chest whimpering an 'aw', and Marcy tilted her head towards me making a clownish frown. Patrick gazed at the pink carpet.

Iris explained how pets choose us before they come to earth and that they create very strong links with us, often over many lifetimes. I'd learned about reincarnation in R.E. at school but had never heard anyone I knew talk about it as seriously as this. Even Mr. McCrory had sounded blatantly doubtful when reading aloud from the Religions of the World textbook. And he'd never mentioned pets. Iris continued, telling Patrick that Holly was trying to forge a connection with him and was watching over him. She opened her mouth as if she was about to say something else but stopped and only smiled.

Marcy was next. Like Katrina, she had her dream journal at the ready. This one was much thicker, though, with worn page-edges and extra pieces of frayed paper sticking out at messy angles. She spoke for longer than anyone. In her dream she'd floated out through her bedroom window to a forest where every tree was a different size and type and the leaves were all different colours. There were fairies at one point and they helped her fly above the trees, just grazing the top branches with her toes. Then it moved on to some ceremony in the middle of the woods with different coloured candles and burning herbs and magic incantations she had to recite. I always remembered my dreams in freakishly specific detail – people used to accuse me of making them up for attention, even my mum once – but *this* was like one of my dreams if I'd taken drugs, with descriptions of every hue she saw and every smell of the wood and the herbs and the sounds of the spells she was reading.

'Ooh, that's amazing!' Katrina gasped.

'Aye, the meditations must've worked; you've been really connected to spirit there,' Iris said. 'You might even be comin' close to astral projection. Have I talked to you about that?'

'Yes, yes,' Marcy nodded, while a couple of the others shook their heads. I didn't move.

'We'll maybe talk about that more one week, eh?'

This time Iris didn't offer much of an interpretation of the dream and Marcy didn't ask for one. I wondered how we would analyse it in English if it was in a novel or a scene in a play and what Mr. Young would say about it. Those discussions were my favourite thing about English, but with this I wouldn't have known where to begin.

Then, remembering what had happened fifteen minutes ago during the round of introductions, I realised the inevitable. I was sure Iris would be able to hear the words in my head: 'please don't ask me, please don't ask me, please don't ask me…' repeating like an endless train.

'Right, Nathan. I know you weren't doin' our meditation work, but any dreams you remember havin' recently?'

She might have heard my thoughts and asked anyway. It was what I was here for after all. She was pushing me for my own good. I'm sure I closed my eyes before I spoke.

'I… can't really think of anything.' Lies. The drowned Empire State building gurgled in my lungs. The red-tinted queue of girls facing me at the shop counter flashed at me. And ten other dreams and nightmares I'd had over the past few weeks surged through my mind.

'I'm sure you've mentioned a couple of dreams to me in the shop. What were they again?'

Shit! Which ones had I told her about? What might she reveal? I had no choice but to jump in, owning up to one I hoped was innocuous enough.

'Well, I had a nightmare on Friday. There was a witch outside my room, banging on the door, trying to catch me, but I never actually saw her. Just knew she was there somehow.'

Iris leaned towards me, lowering her head. 'And what do you feel that might mean?'

'… I'd been to the cinema that night to see a horror film so I think it was just that stuck in my head.'

'No.' She smiled and crossed her legs. 'It's more than that, Nathan. It used to happen to me, years ago, before I understood. Scary films and TV programmes can breed negative energy, especially if it's somethin' supernatural. They really influence your thoughts and that creates darkness in your aura and your energy. I don't watch anythin' like that anymore.'

Every horror book and video I owned lined up in my brain and I prayed she wasn't reading my mind this time.

'You're openin' yourself up to dark energies. That's why people have these nightmares. And it's worse if you've developed your mediumship. Or if you're naturally clairvoyant!'

Each stiff movement in my body amplified under the inspecting gazes of the circle. The new boy, showing his inexperience, opening himself up to 'dark energies' without even knowing it. I was no longer the class dunce but the moron.

'I'll teach you how to protect yourself at night, love.'

I imagined her pulling a scythe or a mace out of the cupboard and handing it to me like something from *Buffy the Vampire Slayer*. Instead, she asked us to close our eyes. I always hated when teachers at school asked us to do this, usually for a role-playing exercise or once in Biology for some sort of sensory experiment. But here, without twenty other teenagers and a looming teacher, I exhaled and closed my eyes. Wondering if I'd done it too soon, though, I peeped through tiny slits to check that the others had closed their eyes too. And that no one was spying on me. But in the half-glimpsed candle-gloom, the others all had followed suit, leaning back in chairs as if they'd all fallen asleep simultaneously. Iris started talking once I'd settled. I think she knew what I was doing.

After making us count long breaths to three in and out,

115

helping us relax into the chairs – a feat I had no real chance of achieving yet – Iris asked us to imagine a white flower on top of our heads with every petal opening wide. She called it our 'crown chakra'. I thought it sounded like the name of an Indian restaurant. But I could see it in the darkness of my head; a little daisy unfurling at my will. Iris's voice had changed again, lilting like a breeze through the room.

'Now imagine a bright, bright beam of white light shining down from spirit into your crown, right through the centre of the flower.'

A tickle in my hair.

'The white light fills your head… and passes through your chakras… from your third eye all the way down to your root.'

Warmth spilled through me.

'And now the white light emanates from within you… It fills your aura.'

Pins and needles.

'This white light from spirit protects you and keeps you safe… You are being watched over… Negative energy cannot affect you.'

I basked in the silence and the light. My hands floated in a warm sea. My feet sank beneath the soft carpet. The white in my head glowed like blinding arctic snow.

'Now feel the petals curl over once more… Not completely closed, but tucked up halfway… Wiggle your fingers and toes… And when you're ready, slowly open your eyes.'

It always took me a long time to fall asleep at night. I'd go through my routine of rolling into different positions, flapping and kicking the quilt around, endlessly turning the pillows over, always ending up in the same position on my front anyway before my body exhausts itself into unconsciousness. In the mornings it was the opposite. I couldn't move. Even after my alarm for school rang, I had to battle with my eyelids and bully my concrete legs into shifting.

I had the same feeling after the last words of the meditation. I didn't want to leave the fuzzy numbness. By the time I forced my eyes open, I realised I was the last one in the circle to wake. And I was smiling.

'You look like you enjoyed that, Nathan. I think you were needin' it.'

Katrina chuckled across from me. 'Told you the meditations were fab.'

I felt how far I'd slumped down in the seat and shoved myself upright. How long had we been doing that? What had Iris been saying the whole time? I can still only remember snatches of sentences and drowsy instructions.

'That's what you can do at night before you go to bed. Imagine the white light protectin' you. You know, I was watchin' you all durin' that, and there were little lights from spirit dartin' around the room, weavin' in between you all. I think your energies are workin' together. Spirit's goin' to help us develop as a circle.'

My early seasickness had subsided and I wasn't thinking about who might be looking at me.

'And there was a beautiful big blue light restin' above your head, Nathan.'

Resting in its blue glow, I let the circle blur around me as the others kept talking. Soon, Iris bowed her head and others followed. I joined in, assuming this was how it finished and Iris said a short prayer, different from the Catholic kinds at

Saint Germaine's. She thanked 'divine spirit' and mentioned wisdom and love. I thought we might finish with 'amen' like at the church masses, but it closed with smiling eyes and warm voices chattering.

They began gathering coats and handbags and standing to hug and hold arms for longer than I was used to. Then I noticed each of them hand pieces of paper to Iris from pockets or purses. It was five-pound notes. Fuck. She hadn't said anything about paying her. I suppose it made sense since she charged people for mediumship readings and she had a business to keep afloat, but I'd thought this was just a casual meeting or a hobby like an arts and crafts club or a choir. Or a book group.

Waiting for their final calls goodbye as they descended the stairs, Patrick limping out after the others, I shuffled towards Iris, rubbing my hands.

'I, em, don't have any money with me.'

'Och, that's alright, love. Don't worry about that tonight. Did you enjoy it?'

'Mm.' I nodded, grinning. 'It was great.'

'Oh, fabulous. There was a good energy. I think you'll blend in well with everyone. Marcy loves you.'

I kept nodding, some sort of toy robot with a glitch. Iris blew out the candles in each corner and in my head I chanted my own 'hip hip, hooray!' before leaving the sanctuary behind and walking downstairs.

'And we're goin' to get you,' she said, jabbing me playfully with a pointed finger in the back, 'openin' up that crown chakra and that aura more. You're goin' to be havin' incredible contact from spirit in your dreams tonight.'

'Wow,' was all I could manage as we stepped out of the shop

onto the pavement.

'And no more horror films at the cinema.'

I didn't even need the reminder. Going to the cinema with the others from school might never happen again.

As the cars rumbled off out of Drichton and I waved, not knowing if the circle members were even waving back at me, I floated homeward with Iris's blue light above me, warming me. I was a happy alien gliding around a foreign place, knowing I was different to all the people behind all of the sandstone walls and wooden storm doors around me. Answers were blowing through dark night, still far away, but whistling towards me.

13

Freya had sprung up the stairs and onto my bed. She was my storm-warning. I leaned over the bannister and heard my mum's sighs and tuts from the kitchen. Dad muttered in between. Usually, their arguments kept me hiding in my room with the cat. But nothing touched me that night. I levitated above everything else, immune to my surroundings. Hopping down the stairs, I breezed into the kitchen and weaved around my dad to the fridge.

'It's not my bloody fault, Helen. You're fine at the bank. People'll always need a bank, they're not going anywhere.'

'Yes, we've covered that, Colin. So you need to do something about…' She glanced at me. '…all this. Be proactive.'

My presence never stopped the fights. If anything, I think I made it worse by being there, listening in. I didn't care this time, though, springing between the fridge and breadbin and toaster and back to the fridge. I wanted to linger. Not to eavesdrop anymore or find out what the argument was about. I wanted them to ask. Obviously not about the circle; I couldn't tell them the truth. But the pretend book group. A smile inside was bursting to show on my face. Maybe it was the positive energy Iris talked about or my aura being affected.

Then my mum was looking at me again, and at the same time she pulled a magazine towards her across the kitchen table, covering something up. In her other hand she crunched an envelope.

'How was your reading group anyway, son?'

Maybe I had sent my thoughts to her. Maybe she was just distracting me.

'It was good... really good. It was all older people.'

She smiled with feeble eyes that tried to copy her mouth.

'Helping you with your dissertation then?'

'Yeah... yeah, it is. And they were all dead welcoming. Iris was great at... leading it all and everything.'

'Mm.' Dad shoved his hands in his pockets. 'Would it not be a bit better if there were other folk your age there? Why don't you ask what's-his-face?'

Mum coughed.

'... I don't think anyone else would want to go. Don't think most people in my class could get a lift here even if they did want to.' The soles of my feet planted themselves back to the tiles.

'I take it you're going back next week?' Mum stood up, her back to me, and fidgeted with pieces of paper I couldn't see.

'Yeah. Definitely.'

'Wait a minute, you read a book every week?' Dad asked. 'A bit much, isn't it?'

Shit. I guess book groups don't meet up every week. Sandbags pulled me deeper into the floor.

'Well, we don't read the whole book in a week. We... set deadlines to read certain chapters by and just talk about those together. Then sometimes we're going to do... just... short stories and stuff.'

Dad raised an eyebrow.

'... Right.'

I scurried back to my room, chewing my last bit of toast

until it was soggy mush. My lies were usually more watertight. Should have thought the book group façade through better. Freya padded onto my chest as I lay in bed, my arms behind my head.

Then a tickling in my hair.

I lurched up, frisking my hands through it to shake out the spider or fly or whatever was on me. Freya scampered underneath the bed. Nothing had landed on the covers. And the cat would have spotted a fly well before it managed to land anywhere. I settled down again, staring at the stained coving of the high ceiling. A touch again. Like fingers prodding my head. An electric shudder through my scalp and neck. I reached back, checking the headboard and pillows. Nothing. Then I remembered the flower. The white daisy on our crown chakra opening. I cut the sandbags and floated again. Spirit was contacting me.

Instead of dreading the rigmarole of trying to sleep, I slipped out of my clothes, flinging them in a pile, and jabbed the lamp switch off. I closed my eyes and imagined the flower again, trying to remember exactly how Iris had instructed us. I visualised the petals uncurling and opening to a white light. I couldn't make it as bright as it had been at the circle, though. It only glowed like a yellow flame behind a paper lantern. Maybe because we'd all been there doing it together it had felt brighter, or because Iris had explained it a particular way, or because the candles or the giant crystal on her table did something.

I breathed like she'd told us. The slow breaths in for three, held, then exhaled for three. But I kept drifting from the count.

Mum's furtive hands hiding paper slid behind my eyelids.

Back to counting. In. One. Two. Three. Out. One. Two.

Dad's stare. A book group every single week. What the fuck had I been thinking?

Back to the light, willing it to shine brighter, picturing it flow down through me, reaching out to my fingers and down to my toes. I was a human bulb flickering under the covers, battling the darkness of the room.

And breathing. Slower. Slower. I wanted to talk to spirit. Do what Iris did.

Who was in my room that night? Who is trying to contact me?

I waited for an answer, maybe the voice returning to speak to me. But it was only my own words that bounced around inside my head.

Is the spirit still here?

Nothing yet.

The light didn't grow brighter, and I forgot about counting breaths. As I dissolved into sleep, I imagined new things: the white light changing to other colours; floating around the room in orbs; not being in my bed at all but on the floor upstairs in The Book Cover; staring up through an invisible roof to a navy-clouded sky.

I dreamt about the circle, of course. I sat in the same chair, surrounded by the other members. They were blurred figures like quick brushstrokes in the background of a painting. But I saw Marcy clearly when I focused on her, surveying her features and hearing her Irish accent. Iris searched the room for something: cards or the box of matches or another piece of crystal. No one asked what, though. She rummaged through the wardrobe and her purple hair shimmered as she bent to look under feet and chairs. She even rifled through people's pockets and handbags, sighing and tutting. At some point she disappeared downstairs. I even heard the jangling of the keys in the lock as if she was looking out on the street or in her car.

Then I glanced over my left shoulder, beyond Marcy's hazy figure, and spotted a second door in the wall at the end of the room. It was white and closed, but a thin, glowing border of purple light shone around its edges. I couldn't understand how I'd never noticed it before and wondered why Iris hadn't thought to search in there for whatever it was she'd lost. I didn't say anything, though. I ignored it and faced the centre of the circle again, waiting dumbly.

I woke up on my front feeling the familiar lump of Freya's weight on my legs. Quiet morning glowed through the gap in the curtains and I waited for the shriek of my alarm, wondering why it was that in dreams you always accept the bizarre and illogical things that happen. Why hadn't I seen that new, second door and immediately known I must be dreaming? Why hadn't the smeared silhouettes of everyone in the circle unsettled me?

Iris had said that in dreams we connect to spirit and that opening our crown chakras strengthened the communication. So what had spirit been trying to tell me? And could it be anyone from spirit or the one who'd been crying here and watching me from the doorway? It could be another week before I saw Iris to ask her, and I didn't know if we'd still be talking about dreams next Wednesday.

Then I remembered the dream dictionary we'd had in the old house – the one I'd thought about at the circle. I was sure I'd seen its shiny spine on a bookshelf or in a box somewhere here after we'd moved. I silenced the alarm, before it had time to screech at me, and lurched up sending Freya scooting off. Grabbing the nearest t-shirt to pull on, I clambered downstairs to the living room and scanned the rows of books on the shelves, but the dream dictionary wasn't there. The bookcase was full of sets of old leathery books my mum had bought in antique shops and at markets and that I was sure she hadn't even read. The dining room had a little unit in one corner where she kept her catalogues and magazines. I rifled through it and there were a few other books there too, but I still couldn't find the dictionary. I was sure I could even remember the cover: some fluffy clouds, a moon and stars, and other illustrations of random objects and figures floating about in the sky.

I thought about tiptoeing out to the garage, not caring that I didn't have any socks on, hoping that maybe there were some other books in boxes piled up in a corner in there. First, though, there was the loft. I jogged back upstairs and yanked the folding ladders down, making that noisy springing sound that would probably alert my parents, and scrambled up, whacking my elbows against the edges of the hatch on the way.

I hadn't been up there for at least a year. The wide space had been half-renovated with a long skylight built into the ceiling but my parents had never ended up using it for anything except storage space. It was filled with black bags and boxes and a whole load of other crap. At the back I could see even more books piled up in the corner. Lifting myself through the hatch on unsteady wrists, I manoeuvred through the dust-covered rubbish and kneeled down to sift through the uneven columns, bursting into a sneezing fit. Why did we have so many books in the house that no one was reading? Maybe I should donate some of them to the shop. A wad of old cobweb dropped onto my hand and I pulled back, knocking a pile over. And there it was, peeking out from a heap against the wall.

Dictionary of Dreams.

I'd been right about the cover. Apart from the night sky backdrop there was a treasure chest, a spider, a pig with wings and a girl with her arms stretched out like a plane. I swivelled around, leaning back against the wall and crossing my legs. The hardback cover made a little creak as I opened it, as if it had only been looked at once or twice before. The first few pages had a brief introduction to the book and a little explanation of what dreams were and different theories on why we had them. A small black and white picture I recognised as Freud looked out at me, a cigar in his hand. I flicked through in chunks, looking for the right section. Fire. Back a bunch of pages. Death. Forward a few. Doors. It was one of the longer entries.

'*To dream of a door is an indication that a new opportunity awaits. The dreamer may be in an important phase of life, moving from one stage to another, or perhaps rising from one level of consciousness to another.*'

I smiled, feeling as if I was reading a section from my own notebook that I couldn't remember writing. I skimmed over a couple of paragraphs that didn't seem as relevant – locking a door, opening a door, being trapped behind a door – until I found a section that matched what I'd dreamed.

'*Closed doors can symbolise feelings of restriction. Perhaps the dreamer wants to move on from a situation or needs to change personal circumstances but is being held back, either from forces beyond their control, or often, by themselves.*'

It reminded me of the Hermit tarot card. The book dipped in my limp hands. Maybe I wasn't ready for the circle yet. But then why would Iris have let me join when I'd asked? She'd said that she sensed I'd fit in well. I heard the whoosh of the shower downstairs and I felt the pull of my parents, moving around beneath me, seemingly oblivious to the fact that their son was in the loft at 7:30 in the morning instead of getting ready for school.

I remembered each time I'd told them what I wanted to be when I was older, besides 'dead', and all the ways they had of saying 'No'. I remembered all of the other things they'd found out from school that had caused so many problems. And the things they hadn't found out. *They* were my closed door.

I lifted the book again and flipped forward to L. Lady. Light. Lion. Loss.

'Losing an item or person in a dream is an omen for the dreamer, suggesting they may need to be alert or should focus on something important that may be slipping away or going unnoticed. The lost object itself may be symbolic. For example, a house key may represent security and domesticity or a wedding ring may represent love and connection between husband and wife.'

Something Iris had said at the circle whispered in my ear. She'd talked about getting messages for people. Had this been a message for Iris? Had my silhouette spirit helped me dream about this so that I could tell her? Maybe there was something she should be paying attention to before she lost it.

I grinned, imagining how impressed she'd be with me. Proud even.

'Nathan! What the hell are you doing up there?'

'Nothing.' The standard, pointless answer.

'Get down and have breakfast!'

Even more eager to please Iris I fingered back through the

pages to B. There was no entry for 'blurred faces' but I flicked forward to 'faces' alone. I skimmed past a section about seeing your own face and looking in mirrors. There were paragraphs about faces being ugly and faces that change, all with negative interpretations of mistrust and deception. I supposed the faces in my dream did change; they were blurred and nondescript until I looked right at them, concentrating on their features. But I didn't want to tell Iris about these negative descriptions in the dream dictionary. She might think I was implying everyone at the circle was untrustworthy.

I glanced at one final part in the 'faces' section but didn't even read the whole sentence, just one phrase right at the end – '*being honest with yourself*'. I closed the book and stopped thinking about it. There was enough to tell Iris. I stood, ready to climb back down the ladder. But something pulled me back like I was a fish caught on a line. I still hadn't figured out where the book had come from. I crouched again and opened the front cover. The name was there, pencilled in slanted, tight writing in the top corner.

'*Property of H. Love.*'

The dream dictionary was my mum's.

14

I slouched on one elbow, watching the grey puddles and their tiny splashes on the other side of the glass. We usually kept the shop door open but it was freezing and an open door wasn't going to invite anyone in anyway since Drichton was deserted. Even in the houses across the street, I didn't see anyone walking by the windows or coming in or out of the front doors.

Iris hadn't been in the shop so I hadn't had the chance to talk to her about the dreams I'd been having. When I'd rushed off the bus after school on Thursday and scurried here, the lights were out and the door was locked. Same thing on Friday. I couldn't tell if Iris had closed the shop and gone home or if she'd had more clients in for readings upstairs. No candle flickering out of the skylight, though. I hadn't slowed down too much and kept walking, trying not to look concerned, knowing either Jonnie or Hannah would be behind me. Now that it was Saturday, I thought Iris might appear while I was manning the shop, just to check in on things. Maybe I could meditate to encourage it to happen.

I studied the tiny black digital lines of 10:45 on my watch and urged them to change faster. I'd stopped bringing my *Mysteries Unsolved* books to keep me company. It seemed silly reading them anymore. Why would I want to read about the paranormal when I was living it? It would be like still watching old scratchy videos taped from the TV when you had your own private multiplex. I should have brought something I could be reading for my dissertation, though. Sitting around in the shop during this shitty weather was the perfect opportunity for uninterrupted hours of reading with no distraction. Mr. Young had checked my plan and said it was 'fine'. He hadn't looked at me when he handed it back, though. Just plonked it on my desk and spent time talking to someone else about their homework. Even Stacey had been given a 'well done' as she chewed gum in front of him.

I hadn't brought anything from home, but I was surrounded by shelves of options to work my way through. Most of it was stuff I'd never heard of, but there were the odd copies of some of the classics, tattered and yellow. I didn't go to the shelves, though. Didn't want to read about anything different or new; there was no room in my head. I wanted to stay here in this feeling, wrapping myself in the thick blanket of everything I was learning, pulling it over my head and breathing in close warmth. Wednesday was already only half a week away. I pushed myself from the counter stool and crept behind the curtain to the back area. For a while I stood at the foot of the stairs, chewing the inside of my mouth and pressing one shoe on the bottom step, listening to rain dripping and tires spraying by on wet road.

The wardrobe was up there. I didn't remember seeing a lock on it. That's where Iris kept her tarot cards. And the gemstones. Maybe even a crystal ball. Must be a whole plethora of mystical objects if she needed an entire wardrobe to store them. I could just have a flick through the cards, peer at the pictures, remind myself what The Hermit looked like. Or even shuffle them and see if another card jumped out at me.

I stepped up with one foot.

Or I could divide the cards into three piles like Iris had done, to see which one I was drawn to.

I pushed off with the other and stood on the first stair.

How many cards had Iris drawn from the pile?

Clink. The sound of rain was louder. Clunk. The door shut. Someone was here. Iris. I'd only climbed one step but rushing back through to the shopfront felt like tumbling down a canyon. Making tea, that's all I was doing. Maybe having a look through some of the boxes lying around.

'Hiya.'

Not Iris. My heartbeat changed.

'Emily, hey.'

Shit. Should I be using her name as if I know her? She stood beside the counter, hands shoved in the pockets of her rain-spattered denim jacket. Her hood dripped little sparkles in front of her face and the tips of her blonde hair were wet, making it look darker, almost the same colour as mine. It took a few seconds to notice the others behind her. Another girl from school I didn't know and Hannah.

'Just coming for a look. We're bored and going for a walk didn't last long. So second-hand bookshop it is.'

Hannah and the other girl had slid off to the farthest shelf, whispering.

'... Cool. How come you're in Drichton again? Do you know Hannah?' It was a stupid question. Of course she knew Hannah if she was walking around in the rain with her.

'Yup. We met at a shit weather appreciation club. And Abbie is Hannah's cousin.' Emily obviously thought I'd know who Abbie was, as if I spoke to lots of people at school, and I couldn't help smiling.

We'd stopped speaking. The three sentences I'd already managed were pretty good for me and I still didn't know why Emily had stood at the counter to talk to me. I began to wonder if it was a prank and the warmth inside cooled. I eyed the other two girls.

'So, are you related to that woman who owns this place? Or did your dazzling people skills get you this job?'

I laughed before realising it probably wasn't supposed to be a joke.

'Not related.'

'… Just the people skills then?' I started fidgeting with the shop keys under the counter. 'I'm kidding.' She spun one of the book stands again and grinned. 'Seems like a decent job, though. Every time I've been in, I've been the only customer in this place. Well done on getting paid for not doing very much.' She said the last part with a thumbs up.

'Em, yeah it's… OK. I just bring a book with me and read, really. Kind of passes the time.' Telling her I'd been about to go upstairs and rummage through a magical wardrobe to look at tarot cards and give myself a psychic reading didn't seem like a good plan.

'Cool, what you reading just now?'

'Oh… I didn't bring anything today. Don't know why.' I felt a familiar pain radiating through my head and the urge to maintain eye contact; the feeling of being caught lying, even if you hadn't been.

'We've nearly finished *Gatsby* in class, by the way. You were right, it's actually OK. Apart from, you know, all the dying and stuff. I was rooting for Myrtle. She was cool.'

'Oh my god, it's boring,' Abbie droned, rolling her eyes as she walked over to us.

I didn't know whether to agree with Emily or fake nonchalance to match Abbie, so instead just half-laughed and crossed my arms. What now? Talk about more books? Mr. Young? Try speaking to Hannah or Abbie? Offer tea?

'Right, let's go.' Hannah pulled the door open again, rendering my dilemma unnecessary.

'Well... see you at school or something.' I shrugged. Emily smiled and paused for a couple of seconds before turning to leave.

'Bye, Love.'

The trio crossed the road, skipping over a giant puddle on the other side and jogging off together. I still didn't know why they'd come in. Emily hadn't even looked at any books and Abbie didn't exactly seem enamoured with the idea of reading. Hannah had barely glanced my way. I supposed after never speaking to each other when we waited at the same bus stop every morning, it would have been weird to strike up a conversation here.

All Emily had done was, well, talk to me. She couldn't have just come in for that, though. We had still never spoken at school. She had lots of pals. She was pretty. People knew her. They didn't know me. Or some did for bad reasons. But it didn't feel like a prank. She hadn't done anything to make it a joke. There was no punchline, no grand reveal. Unless Hannah and Abbie had been setting off a stink bomb or drawing penises on books while Emily distracted me. What would be the point though? There was no audience. And wasn't it just boys who did that anyway?

I settled onto the stool behind the counter and leant my cheek back onto one palm. I was still smiling. And I was still warm. Maybe I could even talk to Emily next time I saw her in a corridor or if one of us was in Mr. Young's class after the other.

A figure appeared on the other side of the glass door. Clink. He barged in, shaking off rain and thumping his feet on the mat.

'Bloody miserable out there.'

My smile dissolved. 'What are you doing here?'

I didn't even know if Dad had ever been in the shop before. He'd yet to visit while I was working and I couldn't remember him coming with me before that to buy a book.

'Well nice to see you, too.' He shoved his hands in his pockets. I expected him to go over to the shelves or browse the book stand at the counter. But he just stood there, looking at me, as if he'd asked a question and I hadn't answered.

'Are you looking for a book?'

'Got plenty in the house.' He shrugged, his hands still in his pockets. 'Just came to see how you were getting on.'

I wondered then if something bad was happening. Was he here to give me news? Tell me about one of Mum's family in England?

Or question me?

I scanned over the last five days at school, searching for what I might have done wrong. Had someone's parent phoned to tell them I'd done something weird again? Written any psychopathic short stories? But I knew there had been nothing. The phone calls from school hadn't happened for a couple of years. And I knew he would have been much more direct about it if something *had* happened.

Caught lying then?

The circle.

'Why aren't you at the video shop?'

'Mandy's on today. Jesus, son. Calm down… So, has it been busy in here?'

'Nope. No one's been in at all.' I gulped. 'Well, apart from some girls from school.'

'Oh? Who's that then?' He took his hands out of his pockets and leaned his elbows on the counter forcing me to slouch back against the wall.

'Just Hannah from down the road and a couple of her pals.'

'And do you know them?'

I didn't want to look at him.

'Not really, no. Well, one of them's Emily. She's been in a few times. She's in the year below me.' I felt my chest inflating again as I said it, proud that I could talk about someone I knew.

'Aah.'

His face stretched with a grin and I thought maybe that's why he'd come in; he'd been in Dyrne Street for something else and saw the three of them leaving the shop. He had to know immediately if his son had a real girlfriend.

'Haven't heard you talk about her before. Was she at the cinema with you the other night?'

'No, that was Gillian and Stacey. And Crystofer.' I mumbled the last part.

'All these girls, eh?' He nodded but wasn't smiling anymore. I said nothing back this time.

Routine questions about the shop and what kind of things I had to do clouded the air between us after that. Usually it was Mum questioning and Dad trying to get her to lay off me. Maybe *that* was why he was here. A chance to talk to me without Mum there, interfering. But he could have talked to me in my room any time. He still never did knock before coming in. Or would knock and walk in at the same time whether I'd answered him or not. Although he hadn't done that for a while, I supposed.

'So, what about the woman who owns the place? Where's she?'

'... She doesn't come in on Saturdays. Just me.'

'Putting a lot of trust in you then. What's her name? Ivy? Isabelle?'

'It's, em, Iris.'

'And she runs the book group?'

A burning crept up my neck.

'Mhm. I need to start doing some reading for it actually. Won't have time during the week. Too much homework.'

I grabbed my copy of *The Alchemist* from underneath the counter and pressed it open at a page near the middle.

'I'll leave you to it then. Well... see you at home.'

I didn't even say bye. Just leaned forward and pretended to read until the door clanged behind him and the sound of splashing rain took over again. His blurred shape walked off down Dyrne Street and I stepped around from behind the counter to watch him go. At the corner he stopped, then turned to look back in my direction, as if he'd heard someone calling his name. I swivelled away and pottered around the shelves, pushing a few books back into place. When I lifted my head to peer back down the street, he had vanished.

I decided not to try going back upstairs again. Iris's white light had worked like a security alarm, sending distractions my way to block me. I knew I'd only create problems going up there anyway. Lying to a medium probably wasn't a very good idea.

15

Half-turned away from me, Iris and Katrina spoke in hushed voices beside the door. Patrick, Sadie, and Marcy chatted in the curve of the circle to my left, like last week. I didn't know what they were talking about but each time I turned to them I smiled and nodded, wondering how many weeks it would take for me to join in. Melissa, the woman who'd dreamt of her dead mother, hadn't arrived yet.

I'd been there since the shop closed, helping Iris set the chairs out and light the candles. I asked if the others minded someone so young being in the circle, but she shrugged the idea away, telling me they'd have no reason to, and that my energy had blended in well already. Then she'd asked if my parents had given me permission to come along. I lied with a happy nod.

Every few seconds I glanced over to the corner, listening to Iris and Katrina's mutterings. At one point, Iris had her hand on Katrina's elbow. Katrina shrugged between sentences and jingled chunky gold bracelets and bangles. When their secret discussion ended, they took their seats and the others stopped talking immediately as if a jury was entering a courtroom.

'Well as you can see, Melissa's not here tonight,' Iris started. I looked over to Katrina who looked down with her hands clasped. I realised there was no extra empty chair. Iris must have known. 'She's not comin' back to the circle.'

A creak as someone shifted. Shoes shuffling on the carpet, hands fidgeting, bracelets clinking again. A little 'oh' from

Marcy beside me. Last Wednesday Katrina had been all nods and chuckles and big eyes. Now she looked like a little school pupil sitting on her own at lunch. One who was a bit too chubby or was a selective mute.

'What's happened?' Marcy asked, leaning forward.

'Says she's not got time for it anymore and she feels like she needs to step out.' Iris shrugged. 'I feel like there's more to it, although that's not for me to say. But, you know, these things happen for a reason. There's an energy shift. Nathan's comin' into the circle and Melissa's leavin' at the same time. Meant to be, eh?'

I imagined the others' blaming gazes as I stared at Iris. My house had dropped out of the sky and landed on their sister.

'Is she alright?' Marcy asked Katrina.

'Aye, I think so.'

I remembered last week's feeling that I'd taken Melissa's chair by accident. She hadn't spoken to me much either. Did members of the circle come and go often?

'I think we need to move forward tonight and get started.' Iris stood again and dragged over her small table from beside the wardrobe to the centre of the ring. Looking at the dark wooden top, I realised it wasn't circular at all, but octagonal. I wondered if that meant something. Maybe the number eight had a spiritual significance. There had been a section on numerology in one of the *Mysteries Unsolved* books. Finding it would be the first thing I'd do when I arrived home later.

'Tonight, I want us to connect with our spirit guides again.'

Again?

'And Nathan this will be a first for you, but I'll guide you through it.'

She opened the wardrobe and lifted out a clear plastic bag filled with sand. I had thought everything in there was black velvet and purple silk and sparkling gemstones. This looked like something from a primary school art cupboard. She opened the bag and poured most of the sand onto the table before smoothing it over with the edge of her hand.

'Oh, we used the sand once before, Iris, didn't we?' asked Marcy.

Iris nodded and pulled the last item from the wardrobe. At first, I thought it was a witch's hat like I'd worn once for Halloween when I was about nine. She lay the tall black cone made from card on the carpet beside the table.

'I'm going to guide you through a deep meditation to meet your spirit guide. Nathan, do you know what that is?'

'Sort of,' I lied. I'd once overheard a science teacher saying Oprah Winfrey was her spirit guide and thought it was funny, although I didn't know why.

'Our spirit guides are from our soul group. They're always leadin' us throughout our lives, helpin' us and sendin' us messages. Even if you don't know who your spirit guide is, they're always makin' things happen for you and tryin' to show you the right path to take. And if you can contact them, you can ask them for help and you can see what they're doin' for you so much clearer. It's amazin'.'

I thought it sounded like what people called angels. Iris later told me that these were something else.

'I have two spirit guides. One's a Native American called Dancing Feather.' She pointed to the drawing of the man on the wall. 'I feel him with me a lot, especially durin' these meditations, standin' behind me.' She tapped her shoulder. 'The other's a Russian woman called Veronika. One of them might come through tonight. Make sure that sand is dead smooth and flat, Nathan.'

I felt like a volunteer pulled from the crowd and reached forward to glide my hand over the soft grains. Iris had already done this and I wondered if the others were judging me; if they could tell how psychic I was from the way I levelled it out with my palm.

Iris then placed the cone on top of the table. I waited for the next part of the trick: a puff of smoke or knock on the table. But she sat back in her chair and rested her hands in her lap.

'Last time we did this it was incredible, Nat'an,' Marcy said. 'At the end of the session there was a face in the sand. Somebody's spirit guide.'

I looked to Iris and must have been squinting or screwing up my face because she nodded vigorously.

'That's right. We use the sand to help spirit communicate with us. Sometimes an image or a word or a letter will come through durin' the meditation.'

I waited for one of the others to question it, but they all smiled in anticipation, gazing at the tall cone like it was another person in the room.

I had heard a voice in my garden in the middle of the night; seen a person standing in my doorway; something had been in my room, opening my drawer, breaking my crystal. But now a spirit was going to write in a pile of sand inches from us. This would be immediate; more 'real' than everything else.

'OK everyone, sit back.'

Iris turned the light out. The room sank into faint candle-glow. More goosebumps, shivering up the skin on my neck.

'Close your eyes.'

No hesitation this time. I shut them as if entering the secret door from my dream and closing it behind me, with only the sound of Iris to keep me connected.

She talked to us about our breath again, and conducted us through deep, counted inhalations and exhalations, keeping rhythm and slowing us down. I slid into it like warm water. So much easier here than at home on my own. Everything was lazier: my breathing, the air, sensation in my hands and limbs. Even the solid chair beneath me felt softer.

'Picture gold threads growing out from the soles of your feet, like roots of a tree. They reach down into the ground and plant you here. No matter where your soul takes you in the meditation, you are always connected to your body in this room.'

Iris's voice sounded different when she spoke like this. Mr. Young had used the word 'mellifluous' the other day and I thought that suited it best.

'With your feet rooted to the floor, your awareness rises up to your crown chakra at the top of your head. You feel completely weightless. You start to float up, lifting from the chair.' She paused between every sentence, lilting from one instruction to another. Her tone had changed, almost her entire accent. 'A silver cord begins to expand, stretching between your body's navel and your soul... You rise towards the ceiling, still connected to your body by the cord... Looking back down you can see yourself and everyone in the circle still seated.'

And I could. I watched us from above, dinner guests seated around an invisible banquet table, glowing yellow in the candlelight. The cone rested in front of Iris, like a black plate from up here.

'You rise again, your soul spreading its wings and flying up through the ceiling, outside, beyond the roof, swooping above the streets and into the sky… You float through the clouds and can only see white below you.

'Now you are resting on a soft cloud and can move easily on it, gliding wherever you choose… You hear birdsong and feel warm… In front of you is a bright blue staircase of eleven steps.' Between each sentence the images and sensations formed like smoke unfurling from a campfire. 'At the top is a green door… You float towards it and take the first step.'

She counted out each step one at a time, and with each I felt my head prickle. Every other part of me was already numb.

'At the top, you reach forward to the green door and push it open.'

My door opened to bright white. It was blinding, as if I had really opened my eyes and someone was shining a torch on me.

'You step through the door. A beautiful tree is ahead.'

It sprouted in front of me from nothing and stretched up.

'You walk towards it and are sheltered underneath its long branches fanning out above you. You wait… Your spirit guide will come to meet you here.'

I stood under the tree branches and looked out into the white nothingness. And waited. No one else was there. No Native American or Russian or man in a robe. Iris had been quiet for a while and I wondered if the others were all with their spirit guides having a great bloody time. So even on another spiritual plane I was a loner. Maybe I was doing it wrong. Maybe I didn't have a guide. Although I had seen and felt everything else so strongly. I even heard the rustle of the leaves above me and felt the rough tree bark on my back. I looked up into the branches again.

Shining indigo peeked between the twigs. A shrill call before wings spread and swooped down, landing in front of me. A peacock. Its green and blue tail swept over the white floor behind it like a cloak. I'd seen peacocks at zoos before and a couple of times we'd driven past one in the garden of a big house on one of the winding backroads leading out of Drichton. I'd always liked them. And I knew I was only seeing it behind black eyelids now, but soft pins and needles buzzed in my hands and I knew I was smiling back in my chair. I crouched down to stroke the bird. He didn't flinch and let me touch him. I brushed his soft velvet coat, my fingers melding in.

'Your spirit guide might give you a message.' Iris's sudden words reminded me she was there. How much time had passed? 'The guide may either speak to you or psychically communicate what they want you to acknowledge.'

Even in my hallucinogenic euphoria I didn't expect a peacock to talk, or to send me a psychic message.

'It is time to leave your spirit guide for tonight… You leave the tree and make your way back to the green door.'

I stood and lingered, not wanting to go yet. But as Iris spoke, the bird turned and flapped its wings, floating back up to the branches of the tree, disappearing into the thick green leaves.

'You step through and out onto the top blue step. The green door closes behind you and you move down to the tenth step… And down to the ninth… And eighth… Seventh… Six…'

She guided us down the stairs, back through the clouds. We were inverted scuba divers, the silver cord drawing us down towards our bodies. As we sank, I looked around at different parts of the town. And I saw the others, floating down ahead of me, their eyes closed, smiling.

We glided down through the ceiling of the building and into our chairs. I jumped a little as Iris described the last part, as if I had just been dropped a few inches by a giant hand. My body was heavy again. I felt my shoulders hunch and the back of the chair pressed into my spine. The room was cold.

'You are connected fully with your body again. The silver cord rests inside. The gold threads withdraw from the floor back into the soles of your feet. We thank spirit for their gifts tonight. Breathe in deeply. And sigh.' Loud puffs from everyone around me. 'Begin to wiggle your fingers and toes. And when you are ready, slowly open your eyes.'

I prised my eyelids open just enough to see Katrina across from me in her chair. She was diagonal. The room sloped up towards Sadie. I lifted my head and pushed myself upright in the chair, reaching my legs out, flexing my toes inside my shoes. I looked to Iris who smiled at me, like she was pleased I'd almost fallen asleep. I suppose it must have made her feel she was guiding the meditation well. The others in the circle were quiet. We stretched and rubbed our faces. I turned to Marcy and we both half-yawned, half-smiled.

Then Iris began the next part of the ritual, moving around the circle, asking us one by one what we'd seen and felt. As Katrina began, I leaned forward in the chair, awaiting her description of what had been behind the green door, like I was clutching a lottery ticket, hoping for my numbers to appear. But she hadn't seen a white landscape, or a peacock. She'd entered an opulent room in a mansion, decorated with wall hangings and wooden furniture. Her spirit guide had been a glowing man in a long

145

robe and he'd spoken to her about healing and how she had a natural gift for it.

'It was incredible, Iris. I could really picture him healing me, like he was here.'

Gasps and smiles from the other three.

'He *was* healing you,' Iris said. 'He *was* here.'

Katrina held both hands to her chest and bit her lips.

Sadie, Patrick, and Marcy talked us through their visions next. Sadie had met an old woman she thought she recognised from when she was younger. Patrick met a nun who held his hand and walked in a garden with him. And Marcy had been in a forest again with a Tibetan monk who gave her some message about happiness and contentment. Then they had levitated up into the branches of the tree. I realised as each person spoke that no one else had mentioned any animals and that I must have done it wrongly.

Marcy finished her detailed account and sat back. My turn. At school when I had to speak in front of the class my throat would sometimes seize up and my old stammer hovered at the back of my tongue, waiting to climb out. But the others around the circle rested with hands in laps and smiling eyes. Maybe the dimmed candlelight helped too; I didn't have to worry about my hands or how my lips were pronouncing words.

I described the encompassing whiteness behind my green door and my feelings of warmth and sleepiness, although I was sure that was obvious.

'And I couldn't see a person that was my spirit guide. Mine was… well, in the tree.' I winced. 'There was a peacock.'

'Ooh!'

I turned to Marcy assuming she'd had the impressive

reaction. But it was Sadie. She grinned over at me.

I wanted to tell them about the feeling of the bird's feathers; how I felt a tingling magic when I touched them and how I didn't even want to leave him behind. But I clutched onto these thoughts, tucking them in my pocket.

'It was really beautiful and I felt good around it. Like it was a pet.' That was as close as I could get. I sat back against the chair and crossed my feet.

'You know what that is, Nathan?' Iris asked, although she was talking to all of us. I shook my head. 'That's a spirit animal, that peacock. Spirit animals are incredible.'

I laughed. I hadn't done something wrong. I'd done something 'incredible'.

'Did he have a name?' Marcy asked, beaming at me. 'Your peacock?'

The circle of ten eyes waited.

'... Santiago,' I announced, slapping my hands on my knees.

Chortles and 'ooh's all round and I didn't know if they realised I was kidding, but didn't say anything else; just grinned at my swaying legs.

Iris explained more about spirit animals and how they guide us and live with us through different incarnations and accompany us when we pass over to the other side. I still didn't understand all of it but I devoured the idea, falling deeper into a fantasy novel with myself as the main character.

'Shall we see what message a spirit guide's given us then?'

Iris's eyes glinted around us and she reminded me of Stacey when she'd been cheeky at school – not enough to get into trouble but enough to make the teacher laugh. I didn't know what Iris was talking about – a recurring theme – until she reached forward to touch the tip of the black cone. I'd forgotten about it, even though it was only inches from my knees and I'd been fascinated by it half an hour ago. Or had it been an hour already?

As she lifted it, we all edged forward in our chairs, peering down to see what had been revealed. Faint brushes. A mark swirled in the sand. Katrina leaned back to turn the light switch on. Marcy gasped beside me.

'Oh, look at that.' Even Iris sounded impressed, as if this didn't always happen.

'It's a 'G'!' Katrina whispered.

'I thought it was a horseshoe.' Sadie tilted her head.

'No, I thought it was a 'G' same as Katrina.' Even Patrick was chipping in.

'Nat'an, what d'you see?' Marcy asked.

I had only seen small, curved indentations, the thickness of a finger – inexplicable enough. But as I sat back, squinting, I realised it was more concrete.

'It's an 'e'… I think. A small 'e'.'

They all copied Sadie, tilting their heads, analysing the omen in the sand. I watched them taking my suggestion seriously – a novelty. Iris sat back.

'We're all seein' it differently dependin' on what it means for each of us. Our spirit guides have made us see it that way.'

I pictured my peacock prodding about in the sand with its little feet and wondered what the 'E' might mean. English? I still hadn't done my homework. I doubted that was important enough for my spirit animal to leave me a message in sand.

End? The circle was over for Melissa. But why would that be a message for me?

Escape?

'Maybe it's 'G' for Gordon! Wait until I get home and tell him that!' Katrina and the others laughed. I assumed Gordon was her husband. Maybe a son.

'Aye, my downstairs neighbour's called Grant. Maybe it's to do with him,' Patrick suggested.

They were all picking up on people's names. Maybe that was the most obvious thing that I'd missed. One name jumped into my head.

Iris closed the circle with another short prayer. The others bowed along in silence and, again, I joined them. Afterward, everyone stood and gathered coats, saying bye to one another and giving Iris a hug as they left. I waited behind, pretending to tie my shoelaces and fidgeting in my coat pockets looking for things that weren't there. As Marcy finally descended the stairs, I spoke.

'I think I might know what the letter in the sand meant. For me, anyway.'

'Oh?'

'It might have been an 'E' for Emily. She's a girl at my school and she's been in the shop a few times.'

'That's right, she was the girl who came in with her mum on your first day.'

I smiled. Just Iris saying this seemed like confirmation.

'Do you think she's important? Should I try to talk to her at school?'

'Do you fancy her?'

My smile drooped. Heartbeats were suddenly audible. Iris stood with her hands on her hips, looking back at me as if she'd asked an utterly ordinary question like whether I took sugar in my tea.

'I… eh… no…. well…'

She laughed. 'I was only askin'! There must be somethin' drawin' you two together.'

'But… maybe that's not what the 'E' really meant. Maybe–'

'–But it's the first name you thought of. Spirit's helped you make that connection. Must mean somethin'. There's no such thing as coincidence. Spirit are makin' paths for us. Leavin' signs. You've seen that girl in here, what, twice?'

'Three times.'

'Aye, well, there you go. Three times. And now you get the 'E' in the sand. Spirit's tryin' to tell you somethin'.'

'Mm.'

Iris began tidying: tipping the sand back into the plastic bag, shoving the table into the corner, putting the cone back in the cupboard. I hated that word, 'fancy'. Or at least I hated it in questions. I heard my friends: 'Do you fancy her?' 'Do you still fancy Gillian?' 'Which one of them do you fancy most?' It always made me squirm, and the questions were never asked in private or in a whisper. Always in front of a group or the girl in question.

It reminded me of my mum and dad too. Not so much recently, but a couple of years ago. 'Fancy anyone at school then?' 'You talk about her a lot. Think you might fancy her?'.

'Nathan!' I looked up to see Iris lifting a chair. She must have called me already whilst I'd been glued in my daydream. 'Move some chairs for me, will you?'

I lined three or four up against the wall and wondered why she bothered clearing them away like this. She'd only be rearranging them in a circle again next week.

'Need to clear the space a bit – got a private reading tomorrow,' she said. I smiled, noticing how often she did this, responding to something I'd been thinking, picking up on my brainwaves.

What other thoughts could she hear?

'I had a dream about you the other night.' Might as well tell her. She might have thought I was hiding it from her if she read my mind on her own.

'Oh aye?'

'We were all here, in the circle, and you were looking for something, searching about everywhere, even downstairs. But you couldn't find it at all.'

'Ha! Sounds like me! Always losin' stuff. You know what I'm like.'

'… Do you think it was about Melissa? Deciding not to come back?'

Iris put down the last chair and turned to look at me, tilting her head from side to side as if weighing up the likeliness.

'Could be. Aye, definitely could be.' She tilted her head the other way. I wondered if she was listening to spirit. 'You're really developin', Nathan. Maybe you get messages most strongly through your dreams.'

I nodded enthusiastically, as if I knew this was true. And then I spotted the pile of money. A little bundle of five pound notes on a chair by the door. I stopped nodding like an idiot jack-in-the-box and felt the pink rush to my face. I thrust my hands in my pockets, searching like a pearl-diver.

'It's OK if you don't have it, love.'

Iris knew what I was doing. Of course.

'Oh.' The heat in my cheeks faded.

‘I could just take it off your pay for the shop each week. That would maybe be easier, wouldn’t it?’

I didn’t dream anything that night. Or anything that I could remember. I woke up disappointed. Even Freya hadn’t slept in my room.

I shuffled downstairs to the sounds of clattering and sighing below me. My mum’s kneeling legs stuck out from the cupboard underneath the stairs. A box of ornaments sat behind her in the hallway and she heaved out a couple of huge picture frames. I assumed she was taking them to some market or car boot sale at the weekend. She lay the pictures against the wall as I squeezed past, heading for the kitchen, and the painting on top of the pile glinted up at me. I stopped, hand on the door handle. Frenetic, vibrant brushstrokes filled the canvas. Green, blue, yellow, purple. A peacock.

16

Mr. Young's was the first aura I saw at school. He was perched on the edge of his desk, talking to us about our dissertations… or something. I leaned my chin on my palm and stared in his direction. I'd been looking at his hair and then felt like my eyes weren't working properly, as if it was still summer and I'd walked inside after being out in the sun for too long. Colours were beginning to bleed into each other. The wall behind him was a stained, cream colour but the outline of his blonde hair blurred into it and became a vibrating dark green. Even after he stood and moved around to sit at his desk, I could still see it follow behind him like a buzzing, fluid shadow.

The rest of that day I tried it in other classes, staring at teachers whenever they stood against a blank wall or screen. That's how we'd practised it at the circle: standing one by one against the wall while the rest of us sat in a row, looking on and using our third eye to sense the colour of their aura. We did it for a few weeks but I hadn't been very good at it, despite Iris insisting I was clairvoyant. I'd only seen grey outlines and wasn't sure that was any more than just their shadows. Last week, when it was my turn to stand, the others gasped. Most of them said I had a purple aura and Iris could see orange too. I clasped my hands behind my back and chewed my lips, wondering what the colours meant and what else they might be able to see. After they'd all clapped, for me or for themselves, I wasn't sure, it was Iris's turn to be the aura model. She planted her feet with purpose, thrust her shoulders back and closed her eyes, as if she was meditating while standing up. I looked at her earrings first, wondering what the violet jewels dangling from them were. I thought I glimpsed a yellow glow by her shoulders but couldn't tell if it was just candle flicker. The others said they saw oranges and yellows though, and I nodded along eagerly.

Now what I was seeing and doing in the circle wasn't just contained in the four walls of The Book Cover on a Wednesday night. It was expanding, rippling out through my life at home and school.

When the Accounts teacher was droning at me at the end of class about my recent lack of homework, I was too busy watching the edges of her head to absorb anything she was nagging about. I was sure I could see a brown shimmer.

Iris was right. I was developing my gifts. She had struck a match and lit a candle inside me, illuminating hidden parts. I felt it a couple of days when ago I was leaving one of the Art rooms. The period had been a bit of a waste. I'd spent most of it sketching my peacock on scrap paper instead of working on the design project I still hadn't made any progress with. As I walked out into the corridor when the bell rang, Crystofer came into my mind, almost like I could feel him beside me, or smell his stupid aftershave. I don't know why; I hadn't been around him in days. I stopped in the corridor and waited, standing on the spot whilst others shoved past me and muttered. A moment later, he flounced around the corner, beaming a ridiculous over-the-top grin in my direction when he spotted me. I didn't even speak to him. Just flashed a hurried smile then kept walking. It didn't mean anything important, but I had sensed him… and then there he was.

I couldn't command it yet, though. Not like Iris. If I could, I'd use it all the time: sense when my parents were about to knock on my door so I could hide my notebook quicker; anticipate Mr. Young's questions in English so I wouldn't look like I'd been caught out; find Nick or Gillian or Stacey in school during lunch and break times.

Or maybe I wouldn't. Not anymore.

I don't think they'd been trying that hard to find me and whenever I'd spotted one of them on MSN messenger they'd vanish offline moments later. My last message from Nick was four months old.

I'd started dropping by The Book Cover on my walk home from the bus stop. I didn't bother to wait until Jonnie was out of sight anymore. Some afternoons I'd just give a quick wave if Iris was with a customer or on the phone. Other days I'd hang around for half an hour talking about the circle or telling her about dreams and nightmares I'd had the night before. I told her about the painting of the peacock in my house too. She said it was a message – my spirit animal was protecting me. It had always been around me and the people in my soul group – something else I'd learned about. That was why my mum must have bought the picture in the first place. I smiled at the explanation behind it, but also realised that my mum must be in my soul group permanently, not just this life. I hadn't expected that.

During the last week before the school holidays, I stepped in from the slushy pavement to give Iris a Christmas card. I'd picked one with a wintery scene and a full moon. I thought it suited her since her star sign was Cancer, like me, ruled by the moon, and hoped she'd notice I'd paid attention. Two women browsed some books by the window. Normally I'd have said a quick hello and left her to deal with the customers, but since the circle was going to be on hiatus for the next three weeks, I wanted to take every opportunity I could to spend time with her. I lingered behind the counter, rubbing the card between my fingers, telling her about the colours in Mr. Young's aura that day. I kept my voice lowered, glancing over at the women to check they couldn't hear, but they soon left under tartan umbrellas.

'I got you a card.' I thrust it forward.

'Oh thanks, love!' She ripped the red envelope open and pulled the card out, rubbing the glittery front. 'I love the moon. I'm a true Cancerian.' I grinned. 'Here, I have somethin' for you too.'

She squatted, looking back and forth underneath the counter like she'd forgotten where she'd put something.

'Ah, here it is!'

Bending over, she yanked a notepad out of a plastic bag on the floor and handed it to me.

'Thanks,' I said. 'I could do with a new notebook. Old one's nearly full.'

I rubbed my hand over the cover – a swirling blue and white whirlpool image, a little frayed at the corner.

'Not just a notebook, love. It's a dream journal. Every mornin' you write about what spirit's shown you. You can use it for meditations too.'

'Perfect. Thanks!' I said again.

'Aye, I love Christmas,' she went on, 'even though it has odd memories for me. Have I ever told you about what happened to me when I was wee?'

I shook my head. The purple flames sparked to life inside me again.

'It's when I first really knew that I was connected to spirit. More than other people. I was eleven and it was Christmas day. Me and my big brother and wee sister had opened all our presents – well, back then we didn't have that much, nothin' like what you folk get today!' She elbowed me and I grinned, anticipating the rest of the story. 'Anyway, it really was a white Christmas, and we'd spent all day in the house, playin' with our toys and havin' my granny and granddad over for a visit. A perfect Christmas, really. Then we sat at the table for our dinner.'

Iris popped up onto the stool and leaned back against the wall.

'You don't remember all the cookin' that your mum must have done, the food all just appeared in front of you in big heaps.' She smiled. 'Everyone was tuckin' in, but I couldn't start. Not straight away. I just sat starin' across the table at my Dad and my brother – he was sixteen – watchin' their faces, takin' in every little detail. It didn't make any sense at the time but I just had an overwhelmin' feelin' that I should memorise their faces and take a photo in my mind of that exact moment. I must have watched them for about five minutes before I touched a bit of turkey. I don't think they noticed. Then in the January Daddy died.' The flames inside dissipated. 'My brother died later that year too. Car accident.'

I bit my thumbnail and stared. She was fidgeting with coins beside the till, though. Not sad or looking like she might cry. She'd said it in the same tone as the rest of the story, recalling an ordinary memory like any other. She must have been used to telling it.

'Aye,' she continued, 'so I knew. My soul knew that they were goin' back to our soul group, that I should memorise exactly what they looked like so that I'd have a vivid picture of them in my head on a perfect day. I still didn't know what mediumship was, but I think that was the startin' point. That was when I knew that nobody else was like me. I was different. And you're goin' through the same thing.'

I swallowed so loudly she had to have heard.

'That's why I knew you weren't too young to be in the circle, even if some of the others weren't so sure at first.'

They weren't?

When I'd asked before she told me no one minded. Protecting me I suppose.

'This is an amazin' time in your life. You're openin' up to spirit and you're realisin' what your lessons are.' I squinted a little, enough for Iris to notice, I think. 'We're all here to learn a set of lessons for this lifetime. Some of my lessons have been about grief and dealin' with members of my family dyin' when I was young. And anytime I get upset about it, I get a bit of comfort too because I know I'm learnin' and my soul's developin'.'

My breath was heavy and my fingers felt cold clutching the journal.

Don't ask me.

'And you're goin' to start figurin' out what some of your lessons are soon, Nathan.'

No questions. Good.

Freya trotted towards me when I opened the front door, yowling, as if in warning. I peered ahead, spotting my parents in the kitchen – Mum at the table, Dad pacing around. But this wasn't our usual time for dinner. Far too early. There was something else alerting me too. Maybe I was picking up on their auras from here, sensing the change in energy. The sharp atmosphere felt familiar.

I squeezed the door closed behind me and crouched to slide my shoes off without untying the laces. Their voices drifted out to me.

'… Need to talk to him… this just isn't on…'

Dad.

'… Knew this job wasn't a good idea… think he's going in there most days after school.'

My mum.

The shoes were off but I waited, head bent onto my knee.

'… want him to quit…'

Dad's words boxed my ears.

'… seems happy though… talks about his books… different.'

Eh? She didn't sound right. The wrong words from her mouth.

Freya butted her head against my knee and I toppled like a skittle back against the door.

'Nathan?' The scraping of a kitchen chair.

Freya abandoned me, escaping upstairs. I pushed myself up and crossed the parapet into the kitchen, tucking the dream journal in the waistband at the back of my jeans and covering it with my jumper.

'Any idea what we want to talk to you about?'

The nostalgia was sickening. Primary school sucked me back through time. Every idea of what they might have found out rushed through my head. The circle. My time with Iris. Had

159

they finally realised there wasn't a single poster advertising a book club anywhere in the village?

'No,' I muttered, sounding more defiant than I'd meant.

I glanced to my dad and noticed the sheets of paper wedged under his leaning hand.

'Your report from school,' he said.

My fingers unclenched. The circle was still safe.

'Nathan, almost every one of your teachers has written about your lack of effort or no homework. What the hell are you playing at?'

That was it? A bad report on homework? I should have cared. A few months ago I would have panicked, spilling excuses and wringing my hands. Instead, I shrugged.

'Eh? Is that an answer?' Dad was never usually as angry about this stuff as my mum was.

'I don't know. I mean, I already have my Highers from last year. Sixth year's not as big a deal.'

It was like dropping a match in petrol. The next five minutes were filled with my mum's rantings about the importance of work ethic and Uni applications and extra qualifications, practically thumping the table with her fist, all whilst my dad shook his head and rubbed his eyes with one hand, crunching the report in the other.

I had found a spot on the counter behind my mum to stare at, seeing what shapes I could make out in the woodgrain. Two little knots were looking back at me, swirling into place above flared nostrils and a crooked mouth-line that ran over the edge and into a cupboard.

'Nathan? Are you even listening to your mother?'

My daze must have been more obvious than usual. I looked

back to him and nodded slowly. My mum sat back with her arms folded.

'I thought we were past this?' she sighed.

We?

'We're not going back to the way things used to be, Nathan. No more letters or phone calls from the school about...' She waved a hand in the air, batting the words off before looking away. 'We thought you were... changing. Getting more...' Even if she'd have finished the sentence I wouldn't have heard.

I turned and walked upstairs to my room then closed the door behind me and pulled out the dream journal, dropping it on the bed before sitting to look out of the window. The sleet had turned to rain and I watched it slither down the pane. Then I knelt on the floor and budged closer, pressing my nose right up to the cold glass. I stared out at the blue-grey sky and imagined a different room at my back. Not a bedroom anymore, but a living room – my own living room, with no one else in it, in my own flat somewhere far from here. The walls had exposed bricks like in an American sitcom and I'd have couches with throws on them and a coffee table with my crystals and books. There might even be an open-plan kitchen farther behind. And if I tilted my head down I wouldn't see a tree-lined back garden with a shitty old swing set and patchy grass. I'd see a dense city block and rows of other little windows with all sorts of people in them living incredible lives.

I'd pictured my imaginary life like this before, usually when I was lying awake in bed after midnight. It had been a while though. Being in the circle had given me different places to escape to. And the confrontation with my parents – if it can even be called that, considering I barely said anything – hadn't

161

even made me storm upstairs with thumping steps and a slammed door. It wasn't that it didn't affect me. I didn't want to stand around and listen to their usual shit about University again. But I'd just floated away from them, like in the meditations Iris guided us through. I'd left their version of Nathan behind and drifted off. I knew what mattered now. Not earning millions of pounds and keeping my parents happy and secure. Not even keeping teachers at school satisfied enough to write charming reports home about me. The only lessons that matter are the ones we've chosen this life for, before we're born, to help our souls grow. Staying stuck in Drichton forever, chained to my parents' commands, wasn't going to achieve that.

I spent ten minutes scribbling down quick answers to an Accounts task that was due a week ago. Then I flipped through the blank pages of the dream journal Iris had given me. The last one had its top corner folded over and I spotted 'Iris' in pencil with a six-digit number underneath. This wasn't the shop's number – I knew that by heart. This must be her home phone number.

She was my friend. Real friend.

For the next couple of hours, I read from the Dream Dictionary, sure that the more I uncovered the more likely it would be that I'd dream that night. I didn't leave my room and my mum and dad didn't bother coming to speak to me. I climbed under the covers earlier than I had done in months and meditated like Iris had taught me. My empty stomach growled at me and it still wasn't as easy without her voice, but I imagined floating into the clouds and levitating up the blue steps to find the tree with Santiago the peacock. This time my surroundings glowed with curling, kaleidoscopic patterns and colours. As I felt myself falling asleep, I left my spirit animal and descended back down through the sky into a new city in a new house in a new bed. And imagined someone lying beside me.

17

On Christmas morning I sat beside the tree with two little hills in front of me. One was made of presents I'd asked for and the other of things my parents guessed I would like: more socks, a generic compilation CD, a jumper that was too big for me and some action videos that I'm sure were ex-rentals from Dad's shop. Maybe this was my punishment for the pathetic school report I'd had, the next stage after Mum going on about it every night over dinner – dinner that I hadn't been allowed to scuttle off to my room with. Mum and Dad had both been glancing over at me between unwrapping their own gifts. They hadn't said much. The choirs and church organ from *Songs of Praise* droned out of the TV, filling the space.

I opened each present with stiff hands, displaying my prepared smile before arranging every item in its neat place. The whole process was part of the routine that had to be followed like basting the turkey. I always wondered if they each just bought their own presents and wrapped them themselves, opening them in front of me with feigned surprise. They looked too smug with what they had and it didn't make sense that they knew exactly what one another would like yet neither of them could figure out what their son might be interested in.

Even the presents from Aunt Brenda were more personalised than this. Every year she and Uncle Frank sent a package for us, along with a nativity scene Christmas card – one of the few religious ones on the mantelpiece. My present this year was a book voucher and a new edition of Scrabble. I already had the regular version but at least they knew I liked it.

'Nathan you'd better send Brenda and Frank a thank you card.'

Merry Christmas to you too, Mum.

Upstairs in my room I unrolled one of the asked-for presents – a *Titanic* film poster. I'd seen it with Stacey and Gillian three times at the cinema. Once had been enough for Nick. Like the videos, I think Dad had just taken the poster from the shop, although it was in pretty good condition. The other gifts I had dumped at the end of my bed. I stuck the poster to my door and stood back to look at it. Kate Winslet had been my answer when Stacey had asked me months ago who I fancied. In the poster she was pretty and her skin looked so soft. Leonardo DiCaprio's skin was spotless too and his hair was perfect, the way I wanted mine to look but could never manage. My skin wasn't exactly smooth either. His hands looked so big on her waist as well. I looked down at my own skinny fingers.

'You getting ready, Nathan?'

My dad had peered in around the edge of the door and I jumped back.

'Em, yeah.'

He craned his neck even further to look at the back of the door, obviously wondering what I'd been staring at. He saw the poster and stayed where he was for a few seconds before glancing back at me. Then he left.

St. Germaine's was cold. You'd think on Christmas Day they might have turned the radiators up or that the people packed in might have heated the place a little. But I could almost see my breath in the freezing air. Mum had made me take off my scarf but my coat was still buttoned all the way up. The modest tree on the altar with its multi-coloured lights and handmade decorations was an attempt at a festive atmosphere, but it didn't match the grey walls and the simple, wooden pews. I was sure we only came so that my mum could claim with some sense of honesty that we were still church attenders when she spoke to the family in England.

The priest murmured somewhere in the distance. I could guess what the sermon was about: Jesus; the nativity; celebration; new life; giving is better than receiving; we're all sinners for talking about Santa and reindeers but if we apologise to God we'll be fine. I gazed down at the cover of the hymnbook – a cheery picture of the crucifixion with angels floating in the clouds above, looking down pityingly at blood-covered Jesus. So I couldn't watch *The X-Files* but this was fine? The angels reminded me of our guided meditations at the circle. I wondered if Iris believed in Jesus. Was he some kind of healer? Or a medium? I didn't think she believed in a God like my parents did, but she always mentioned 'divine spirit' in her meditation prayers and she said we were all learning lessons so our souls could grow and become part of a 'greater energy'. Was this God?

The buzz of the organ drilled me out of my daze. I copied everyone around me and stood for the hymn, mumbling along to the few words I could remember. At the other end of my row, parishioners paraded down the aisle towards the altar. The priest handed out wafers as they blessed themselves. My parents and I didn't move. I suppose we didn't attend often enough to deserve the papery treat. The procession moved along the front of the altar where some of them paused to sip from the silver wine cup. Then they trooped back down the aisle on my left and filed back into their seats. I watched them with their hands joined and heads down and tried to figure out if they were enjoying this part of their Christmas morning or if, like me, they were here against their will, mindlessly drifting through a ritual.

A woman walked towards me, pulling her son by the hand behind her. He had half a tinfoil snowman in his hand and chocolate smothered all over his mouth. An older woman followed behind, stopping for the wine, then bowed her head and clasped her hands like the others. She was wearing a navy pillbox hat with a little bit of a lace veil underneath. I watched her as she chewed the bread and wondered if she was related to the younger women with the kid in front. She walked nearer. Then she lifted her head.

Sadie looked at me.

And dipped her head again. I pressed myself back against the hard bench. I'm sure the thud made my mum turn to me, but I stared straight ahead. Sadie had never mentioned coming to church when we were at the circle. I didn't even think she lived in Drichton. There was a bigger church in Ballahan. And why hadn't she smiled at me?

I started doubting she'd seen me. Maybe she'd just glanced in my direction without settling her eyes on anything. She was probably too busy thinking about the rest of her day and where she was going for Christmas dinner. Or praying, I supposed. But I knew. She *had* seen me. She had looked right at me. I saw the recognition, even in that split second.

As the final carol finished at the end of the mass, I turned to scan the rows, looking for her again. All I could see were the backs of heads huddling together and swarming out the door. Outside I lagged behind my parents and searched through the faces gathered on the pebbled path. People were hugging one another and swapping Christmas cards. Some chatted to the priest. But Sadie wasn't anywhere. She must have hurried away. To avoid me? Not that I could have spoken to her in front of my parents anyway. They'd wonder how I knew this stranger in her 60s, or maybe 70s – I didn't actually know. Christmas morning outside the Catholic church probably wasn't the most ideal setting to reveal the secret spiritual circle I'd been attending and lying about. Maybe I could say she was a customer I knew from the shop.

Giving up, I moved along, my slow feet crunching stones underfoot, the laughs fading behind me, my parents marching off in front of me. Walking down Dyrne Street, we passed The Book Cover, locked and dark. I wished I was stepping inside. Instead, I treaded back to my house to watch special Christmas episodes of TV programmes I didn't like and swallow dry turkey like sand.

After my parents had sunk into the couches to gulp wine, I crept upstairs, pulling the telephone from their room to my own, the wire tightrope taut in mid-air. I closed my door as far as it would go, the wire stopping it from shutting over fully, and flipped open the back page of my dream journal to the six-digit invitation. Iris must have wanted me to have it. And she'd said Christmas could be a difficult time for her. Maybe she'd understand how I felt.

I clutched the phone in both hands, preparing what I should say.

And then I jumped as it buzzed, sending its digital ring drilling up my arms.

Was *she* phoning *me*? Did she know?

Grabbing the receiver, I thrust it against my cheek.

'Hello?'

Nothing.

'… Hello?'

And then a breath. Clipped. As if a hand had been clamped over a mouth. A noise in the distance – someone talking? A TV? Another inhale and the guttural crack of a voice about to speak.

'… Iris?' I asked.

Another sharp inhale. Fuzzy nothingness. A beep, and then the dial tone. I jabbed at the big flat button a few times as if this would bring them back. Then I dialled 1471 to check who had called, wondering if the number might match the digits scribbled in front of me. The robot phone lady spoke to me.

'The caller withheld their number.'

I glanced to the window, remembering the spirit I'd heard out there months ago. Was this its new way of getting my attention? If it was, it was working.

'Nathan!' my mum shouted from downstairs. 'Who was on the phone?'

'No one.'

'What?'

'I mean… it was for me! Nick.'

She muttered something and I heard the living room door close.

I couldn't phone Iris now. The line had to be kept free. Spirit was trying to communicate. Or maybe spirit just didn't want me to phone her. Either way, I kept it in my room for the rest of the night, staring at it, ready to pounce whenever it should drill into life again.

Spirit had come and gone, though. The phone sat mute on the carpet, plastic and useless; a toy that had run out of batteries. When my parents came upstairs to bed, I shoved it back to them without speaking and stayed awake drawing patterns shaped like crystals around Iris's number.

18

Iris told me she wouldn't be reopening The Book Cover until January. Every day I slipped out into the frostbitten street and wandered past, peering in the windows like the shop was a museum exhibit behind glass. On Hogmanay I'd wanted to make my daily pass at noon but my mum cornered me with a list of chores that we could do together, as if it was supposed to be fun. She had a routine of cleaning the entire house like this every year. Some sort of tradition about starting the New Year the way you want it to carry on. I don't know why she was still doing it – hadn't worked any other year. I managed to sneak out a couple of hours after I'd wanted to when she'd vanished into the shed to reorganise her junk.

I suppose things were meant to align that way in the end, since I spotted Iris just as she parked her car outside the shop door. If I'd come earlier, I wouldn't have met her at all. I told her this as we hugged then stepped inside the shop.

'So, what are you doin' for Hogmanay, love?'

'Nothing really, well… no, nothing. Just staying in with my parents.'

I never 'did' anything at New Year. I always thought it was a night for adults or teenagers who thought they were cool. I'd either stay up with my parents watching bland TV parties or sit in my room, pretending I'd missed midnight altogether or that I'd gone to sleep early.

'Are *you* doing anything fun? Going to a party?'

'I'm doin' a firewalk with a couple of the girls.'

The girls?

'Girls' from the circle? Or some other never-before-mentioned friends? Iris had climbed upstairs while I trailed behind. She moved some things around in the cupboard before pulling out a set of cards I'd never seen before and shoving them in her handbag.

'What's a firewalk?'

'Oh, I've always wanted to do one! It's this ceremony they do outside – ours is up North somewhere, headin' off in a couple of hours – where you chant in the woods and meditate. Then at midnight we'll be doin' a barefoot walk through fire! Or coals, maybe…'

I pictured Iris gliding across glowing coal, smiling with her eyes closed.

'It's all about embracin' your fears, doin' somethin' new that scares you but lifts your whole energy up. And the soles of the feet have chakra points. So the heat of the fire opens you right and up and completely rejuvenates you. That's why I want to do the Hogmanay one. What a great way to start a new year, eh?'

'Yeah.' I'd thought sitting in a circle in a room above a bookshop and talking about auras was esoteric, but a firewalk was part of some other life; some fantastical world I'd thought was only printed in faded ink on yellowing book pages.

'Jimmy thinks I'm daft, right enough. He's goin' out with his brother-in-law.'

Iris had only mentioned her husband a few times and it was usually to Katrina or Marcy, but never with much detail. Maybe this was why – he wasn't spiritual; didn't understand what we did. How did she end up marrying someone like that?

'Right, got what I need, let's get out of here.'

Already?

'Iris…'

'Aye, love?'

'Did… did you call me?'

'Call you?'

'Phone me. On Christmas Day?'

She stood with hands on hips, one eyebrow raised.

'No, I didn't. I don't know your phone number.' Hearing her confirm it both sank and lifted me. She hadn't wanted to contact me. But something else had. 'Why did you think that?'

'Someone did. Right when I was holding the phone, about to…' Telling her I'd been ready to call her home on Christmas Day seemed ridiculous now. '… to phone one of my friends.' Not a lie. 'When I answered there was just breathing on the other end. And the sound of a faraway voice. Then it hung up. Number withheld.'

Iris nodded vacantly, and I couldn't tell if she was figuring things out or just trying to look interested.

'Do you think it was spirit?' I asked. 'The same spirit who contacted me before?'

'Could be, love. Could be.'

With that, she turned to descend the stairs, leaving me to follow behind, empty of answers. We stepped back outside onto the icy pavement and as Iris plodded into her car seat she called out to me, 'Well who knows if I'll ever see you again. We might all be doomed!'

'What do you mean?'

'That Millennium Bug thing – Y2K!' She laughed. 'Might be the end of the world!'

173

She slammed the door and started the engine as I scuffed some leaves with my shoe.

'And when we're back at the circle we'll find out who it was.' I looked up to see she'd rolled down the window. 'Get some answers about that phone call. And everything else that's been happening to you.'

The window slid back up and she drove off, beeping the horn as the car rumbled away. I jogged home, kicking puddles on my way and grinning like I'd run away from school again.

☆

Sitting on a couch in silence watching a ceilidh band was like going on holiday to Barbados and staying in the hotel room. My mum sipped a glass of wine and Dad lounged back with his feet up on the coffee table, tapping along to the music. I slid away, unnoticed, I think. Even in my room the fiddles and accordions chanted up to me and I pushed the door closed, nearly squashing Freya as she wriggled in, escaping with me.

I pulled the pillows and cushions from my bed onto the floor, arranging them in a little cocoon, before yanking the bottom of the quilt across to my desk, suspending it between the chair and the headboard like a tent. Then I crawled underneath. I knew my parents wouldn't catch me; I'd memorised the sound of each stair creak and could tell when someone was on the way here and how many seconds I had to dismantle anything I wanted to stay hidden.

Sitting in my den, I remembered the adventure mazes I used to make in the loft of the old house with my friends. I'd push cardboard boxes and old chairs together and drape them with blankets and sheets to build passages and 'rooms' you had to squeeze through on hands and knees. A couple of boys from my class used to come over and I'd build the dens in the old house for them. But that stopped soon after the story I wrote at school about the boy killing everyone and we moved soon after.

I tried it here once with a new friend too, but it didn't last long.

I pulled the box of matchsticks from my desk then opened my bedside drawer for the photographs. One was a school picture from last year. My forehead was shiny, my hair greasy, one shirt collar was tucked in and another out, and I had cracked, red skin on my nose where there must have been a spot before. The photographer hadn't told me when he was going to take the picture either, so I wasn't even smiling, just looking beyond the camera with empty eyes, like I was waiting for bad news.

I struck the first match, holding it up to the photo's corner and watched myself curl away into black ash. This was my firewalk. I wanted to do what Iris had described – rejuvenate myself for a new year and open my energy for new experiences. A box of matches was the closest thing I had to hot coals. After the grey crumbs floated down into a bowl I'd kept from the kitchen, I lifted another few pictures from the drawer. I didn't look at these, just held them to the next match, gazing at the printed words on the back side of them. Then they vanished too. The smell of the burning paper was a cleansing incense.

A creak. Stair one.

Then nothing. One of them must have changed their mind about coming up. I realised the scent of the smoke might be noticeable if they came back, though, and crawled back out from the quilt-tent to open the window. I prized it upward then leapt back at the whistle of a firework. It boomed into gold somewhere across the river, followed by a few more screeches and bangs and sparkles. Must be a party at someone's house. Who knew Drichton had such people? I thought about who might be there and, for some reason, pictured Emily. She'd be one of the 'cool' teenagers, having a drink with her friends or older family members who were liberal enough to treat her like an adult and let her have a glass of champagne. Or maybe she'd be too cool even for that and was watching the fireworks from indoors, pitying everyone else and their boring traditions.

After the last explosion had fizzled out, I glanced at my clock. 12.02.

Y2K.

I leapt out of the room and along the hallway to the computer in the study. As I switched it on and waited for it to come to life, if it even would, I imagined what kind of apocalypse might await us. I could end up like the boy in *Empty World* – the book I'd told Iris about when she'd first interviewed me – fending for myself, raiding supermarkets for food and travelling through the country alone. Or maybe I'd stay here, protecting myself in my quilted den in Drichton like Ann in *Z for Zachariah*.

The desktop blinked to life. The clock: 00.03. *Auld Lang Syne* moaned downstairs. No Millennium Bug. No dystopia. Stair one creaked again. Then stair two. I abandoned the computer and scurried back to my room, shoving the door closed. Stair three. Four…

176

I threw the quilt and pillows back on the bed and waited for the knock. But it was the door to *their* room I heard brushing open. Then closed. The click of a light switch.

Happy New Year, Mum and Dad.

19

I was the first to arrive, marching through the shop door and striding up the stairs.

'Nathan, love! You're eager!'

I jerked to a stop. Iris stood in the kitchenette behind me. I'd walked right past her.

'Hi, Iris. Yeah, a bit early. Sorry.' I slid back down the steps, shoving my hands in my pockets.

'No need to apologise! Lovely to see you.'

'You too. How was your fire walk?'

'Well-remembered! Oh, it was incredible. Totally rejuvenatin'. Really cleansed my energy and made everythin' so much clearer. I want to do it every year. Hey, you should come next time!'

'… Yeah.'

Did she mean that? Had she asked anyone else to come? I bounced on the carpet, heat in my cheeks from the smile that had returned.

'… So you didn't burn yourself then?'

'Ha! No! You don't feel a thing. Mind over matter! The mind's incredible, Nathan. Power of positive thought. If you believe you can walk over the flames without gettin' hurt, then you won't get hurt. You'd have loved it.'

I opened my mouth to tell her about my own fire ceremony, then stopped in case she asked about what pictures I'd burned.

'In fact, I brought something back with me,' she went on.

'Funny you arrived early, love. You must have known I needed someone to help me. Here, give us a hand with this, will you?'

I hadn't known she needed help. I just wanted the answers about the phone call like she'd promised.

Iris tapped the top of a cardboard box on the tiny counter-top beside her. I assumed it was more books at first, but lifting it, I heard muffled clinks and felt different edges and bumps through the cardboard underside. No flat book covers.

'They're goin' upstairs.'

Padding my way up with the box blocking my view, I listened to its contents jingling and tinkling together. I reached the top and plonked it down as gently as I could on a chair near the wardrobe. It had been three weeks since the circle met but on my last Saturday shift before the Christmas holiday I'd snuck up, in the gaps between customers, just to sit on the floor, rubbing my fingers through the pink carpet, picturing where everyone sat, wondering what Iris had planned for us in the new year. The white light hadn't felt like a barrier to me anymore. I'd been invited in; an integral member of the circle; part of its circumference. Maybe Iris could sense that I'd been up here, feel the traces of my energy. I hadn't gone anywhere near the wardrobe, though.

'What's in it?'

'I'm wantin' to sell them in the shop. Should've done it before Christmas but I got these discounted. I want everyone in the circle to have their pick first. Open it.' She grinned and I kneeled to pull back the lid.

It looked like I had cracked open a giant kaleidoscope. Glints of light twinkled out. Tiny triangles and jagged lines of purples and greens and whites glittered.

'Crystals!'

'Aye. Amazin, eh?'

I recognised some of the stones from the gemstone magazine my mum used to buy me, and others I knew because Iris has showed me them on her pendants: quartz, malachite, fluorite. Others were new treasures still to be discovered, all with their own healing abilities and vibrations that worked in different ways.

'Have a wee look through. See what you like.' She winked at me and turned to finish setting up the chairs and candles.

I delved into the treasure chest, lifting out the crystals, most of them heavy and as big as my hand. I arranged them around me; mini-standing stones circling a giant. In the corner of the box was my favourite – an amethyst, like Iris sometimes wore in her pendant and like the miniature piece I had on the shelf in my room. I held it and brushed the violet points and edges like a careful archaeologist. Arriving first had happened for a reason. I felt the stone's cool but strong energy vibrating and knew it was meant for me to have.

'You like the amethyst?' Iris knew, smiling down at me. I nodded and the shop door clanged open downstairs.

Patrick arrived, followed by Katrina and Marcy. They all gave Iris and I Happy New Year hugs and kisses before each taking their turn of sifting through the stones, lifting each one as I had, examining them for the one that felt right. As the box finished its circuit around us, Iris nestled it between our chairs and I had another look in it. All sorts of crystals were piled in – glinting soft colours and shining prisms. At the bottom, though, was one much smaller stone. It was smooth and black, about the size of a fifty pence piece and I wondered if this little shiny pebble was just a normal stone that had ended up in there by accident.

I wanted to ask Iris about it, but everyone was busy chatting about Christmas, the presents they'd been given and what relatives and friends they'd seen. I thought of my Christmas afternoon, upstairs in my room, tidying away my gifts and sitting cross-legged on the bed with a book I hadn't asked for. What would my parents say about my new 'ornament'? They already knew I liked rocks and stones, but this ostentatious addition might be difficult to explain. I'd have to tell them Gillian or Stacey had bought it for me. My mum would wonder what it'd sell for at a car boot sale. Dad would crack a joke with a punchline about girls or old grannies.

Everyone around me had filed into the usual seats, each of us with a gemstone cradled in our hands or resting between our feet now. No one had picked out the little black stone. Only then did I realise Sadie was missing. And at the same time the door rattled downstairs. I laughed to myself, knowing I must have sensed she was about to appear. Iris had said that would happen, that we'd all become familiar with everyone else's energies.

Appearing in the doorframe, Sadie hugged Iris before giving a generic wave around the circle. I was sure she glossed over me before taking her seat further along to my left. I hadn't told Iris I'd seen Sadie at Christmas Day mass.

'It feels nice to be back, doesn't it?' Everyone murmured in agreement as Iris flicked the switch on the wall and the familiar soft candlelight I'd been waiting for bloomed. She exhaled into her seat. 'I've missed feelin' everyone's energy.'

'Aye, I've noticed that too,' Katrina added in. 'We've become so connected it feels strange not being around one another.'

'Mhm!' Marcy piped up.

My turn. 'Yeah, I've missed being here.'

And I want to know what was on the other end of the phone.

I wondered if Iris would start with this or if it would come later.

'Since it's January and we're startin' a new cycle,' Iris continued, 'I want us to look forward tonight. We're goin' to do New Year readin's.'

Later then.

I brushed my heels back and forth on the carpet. I didn't even know what New Year readings were but assumed it involved the tarot cards again.

'It's been a wee while since I've had a reading from you, Iris. This is just what I need!' Katrina nudged her chair forward a few inches.

'I didn't say *I* was doin' it! I said 'we'!'

I stopped swaying my feet and shoved my hands underneath my thighs. Marcy gripped my arm.

'Oh, I don't know if I'll be any good,' she said. But her lip-biting and excited glances around each of the others betrayed her modesty. She was looking forward to displaying her mediumship. I didn't know if I had any mediumship *to* display. Iris had kept telling me that I did, since I'd met my spirit animal and had seen and heard the presence in my room that night all those months ago. But I hadn't seen anything sense, and the breathing voice on the phone call hadn't even spoken to me. How could I do a reading for someone else? How could I do anything like Iris did, on command? I felt my crown chakra and third eye shrivelling closed at the thought.

182

I looked to Patrick. He seemed smaller, shrinking back in his chair, fidgeting with his hands in his lap. I glanced at Sadie and caught her eye.

'OK, Marcy. You've done this before. I want you to read for Katrina.'

Iris stood and swapped seats with Marcy who hopped across, giving Katrina's hand a quick rub as she sat. She turned the chair to face Katrina, tuning into her energy. Katrina mirrored Marcy, straightening her posture and resting her hands flat on her thighs.

Iris's voice melted into its liquid tone, guiding Marcy to open her crown chakra to spirit; to clear her mind and attune her attention to Katrina's aura. Patrick, Sadie, and I looked on at the candlelit ritual, worshippers at an altar. I tried to let my eyes blur, gazing around Marcy's outline, hoping to catch a change in her aura. A shimmer of colour or a flicker of energy. But I couldn't. My heartbeat banged in my ears.

Me next. Me next. Me next.

What the hell was I supposed to say? How could I do it?

But Iris would talk me through it. She'd help me. Maybe it would just come to me and I did have a gift. I might really connect with someone from spirit. Hear their words. Even see someone.

'Oh, Katrina, there's a man.' Marcy sliced through my haze.

Could I act my way out of it? Pretend? Lie? I was good at that.

'I see his hands on your shoulders. Someone from spirit is healin' you.'

Katrina nodded, smiling. Static fuzzed over my scalp.

'I'm gettin' the most incredible feelin's of love and care. And there's a dog here too. He's runnin' about your feet.'

'That might be Sandy! What does he look like?'

'I think it's…'

'*Feel*,' Iris cut in.

Katrina and Marcy turned to face her.

'You don't *think* in a readin'. It's about what you *feel*. Say 'I feel'.'

The women faced each other again.

'I *feel* it's a golden colour. A golden retriever, or a Labrador.'

Katrina covered her mouth with a hand, her eyes smiling. Iris's elbow nudged me.

'He was a pet you had for a long time,' Marcy went on. I couldn't tell whether this was a question or not but Katrina was nodding enthusiastically. 'He's so content and happy. I thi-feel he's runnin' around you to protect you. Keepin' you safe.'

Katrina was cupping her cheeks with both hands, her eyes glistening. 'Aye, that's him!'

'Amazin'!' Iris called, bringing it to an end. The two women hugged, Marcy shaking her head in disbelief at her own abilities. Now it was worse; so much easier to look like a failure. She was a concert pianist and I would be a kid banging on a toy keyboard.

At some point I realised that it hadn't exactly been a 'New Year' reading, but that was a concern that no one else seemed to care about and I brushed it away like dust. Next Katrina returned a reading to Marcy, following the same relaxing routine as before, Iris guiding her through breathing and cleansing her thoughts, casting the spell. At least I had been practising meditations. I might be able to manage some level of clarity. I forced myself to stop breathing so noisily.

Katrina's reading for Marcy was different. She picked up on an older female spirit and could hear words being given to her – the name of a town in Ireland Marcy had visited when she was younger, and two names of women who Marcy knew. She transitioned between wide-eyed awe, more lip-biting and hands held to her chest in a gesture of appreciation. Another hug at the end. The rest of us clapped for them. And then the spotlight swung in my direction.

'Hmm, let's see... Patrick and Nathan!'

My stomach filled with heavy marbles as Iris stood, urging me to take her place in the chair beside Patrick. Standing, I felt my knees shiver under me and I thought of ways to say I didn't know what I was doing. But looking to Patrick, he still fidgeted with his hands, rubbing them over one another, hunching. I was looking in one of those circus mirrors that reflected a warped version of yourself back at you. I sat in front of him and avoided looking over to Sadie. At least I hadn't been paired with her. Seeing her at church didn't seem so odd anymore, but there was still a fuzzy friction between us.

Patrick was the member of the circle I'd spoken to least but he was always pleasant and had the calmest energy of all of us. He was even quieter than me, though, and he reminded me of other older men in Drichton my parents would always say hello to, and of old male relatives who would grip me on the shoulder and call me 'young man', clearly having no idea of my name or age. He turned in his chair to face me and smiled without looking me in the eye.

'Patrick, you're goin' to start.'

The spotlight shifted to him, allowing me a temporary escape from its hot glare.

'Here, hold this.' Iris reached down and picked up the big stone that had been under Patrick's chair. It was a rough, blue and white layered stone, not shiny like my amethyst.

'Your kyanite will help you channel spirit.' She passed him the stone and he clasped it like a wand with both hands. I wondered if she'd given it to him to stop his fidgeting, as well as for its abilities.

The ritual began again. Patrick closed his eyes, probably to avoid our gazes as well as to focus and open his crown chakra. As Iris counted him through slow breaths, I followed, inhaling and exhaling more and more slowly. The marbles in my stomach softened to berries. I tried to forget Marcy and Katrina at my back and Sadie over to my right. I wanted Patrick to be able to read for me. I wanted my energy to be open and to help him.

'Open your eyes, Patrick.' Iris's voice was soft and slow. 'Who do you sense is here to give Nathan a message?'

Patrick looked me in the eyes for the first time and I stared back through the flickering yellow gloom. I'd never noticed how dark his eyes were behind his thick-framed glasses. He breathed through his nose in long, noisy lungfuls. And said nothing.

'Don't think about it. Just say what's there. Feel what's there. Focus on your solar plexus.'

Seconds stretched out. Someone shuffled in their chair behind me.

'Can you sense someone there, Patrick?'

'… Aye.'

I bit the inside of my cheek.

'Right, is it a male or female presence?'

More long seconds.

'It's…'

'Say what's there. Don't think!'

'Male.'

Soft pins and needles shivered up my arms. I imagined the sound of the telephone ringing again. Remembered the wailing voice from all those months ago. And the watching figure. A man.

'Good. What else? Can you sense what they look like? Can you hear a name? Do you feel an emotion?'

'I feel… happiness, I think.'

I was sure I heard a clipped sigh from Iris. She knew who was there. She was sensing the spirit and wanted Patrick to feel it too.

'And what else?'

'And he has brown hair. He's got a shirt on. And braces.'

'Good!'

The pins and needles coursed down my legs, into my toes, up my back. My guts hardened again.

'And do you know who it is? Or what he's saying?'

I held my breath and couldn't let go. Iris was leaning in to Patrick. He was somewhere else, on some other plane, reaching for the next part.

Marcy coughed.

'I… I don't know.' He blinked a few times and sunk back. Iris didn't wait. She pulled her chair forward and tapped my forearm, taking over from Patrick.

'Right, Nathan. There's an older man here. Neil.'

Neil. My granddad's name.

'Is this grandpa?' she asked.

The berries inside me all burst at once, pinging through me, pushing my mouth open in a grin.

'Yeah. Yeah, it is.'

The three other women gasped. Patrick slipped his chair backwards towards Sadie. Iris sat back in the chair and closed her eyes.

'He's showing me a cat. Your cat.'

Freya. I nodded.

'You know animals are much more attuned to spirit than us?' She chortled. 'Your cat's been seein' him in the house for ages. Every time you see him actin' funny or starin' at an empty wall or a doorway, he's seein' him there.'

'She.'

'Eh?'

'The cat's a she.'

'Oh, aye.'

I knew Freya had some sort of intuition. She was usually around me when weird stuff happened in the house. 'Neil's watchin' over you and your mum. Is this your mum's dad?'

'Yeah.' Hearing Iris say his name sparked something in my brain. I squinted, trying to remember.

'It's been him, Nathan. Grandpa was in your room. He made the phone ring. That breathin' you heard, it was him.'

Electricity sizzled through me and over me.

'Aye, there's such strong feelin's of protection he's bringin' with him. That's what Patrick was pickin' up on. And there's somethin' else about this side of the family. Somethin' important comin' soon.' She paused. 'What are you sayin' to me, Neil?'

Hearing his name again in Iris's voice snapped the memory into place.

'Neil!' I yelped. 'That's what you called me when I came into the shop for my first shift! You called me the wrong name!'

Iris tilted her head. 'I must have been sensin' his presence even then. His spirit was around you. Amazin'.'

A shadow flickered to my left. I turned to the empty wall but saw nothing there. I looked back to Iris and her eyes smiled, as if she knew what I'd sensed.

'Grandpa has another message for your mum, Nathan. It's money. Somethin' about money.' I puffed an almost-laugh. A message for Mum about money – what a surprise. 'She needs to be careful, pay attention to somethin'.'

'What? … Me?'

'Some money's goin' to go missin', or she's goin' to forget to pay somethin'. I feel this is one of her lessons.'

I bit my lip, nodding. Behind Iris, Patrick placed the kyanite back on the floor. I stopped moving, realising we'd hijacked his reading. Surely he was glad of it, though.

'Well done, Patrick,' said Iris, reading my mind again. 'You sensed Neil's presence there. I think it just wiped you out, didn't it?' Patrick smiled back at her and shuffled in the chair. 'We don't have as much time left as I'd thought, so, Nathan, you're goin' to do a readin' another night.' I was floating too high to care about any relief this might have brought ten minutes ago. 'Patrick is that OK? If we give Sadie a wee bit of time just now?'

I don't know what Patrick answered, and I didn't listen to any of Iris's reading for Sadie. Or maybe Sadie did a reading for Iris. It played out on the other side of a blurry cloud, while I nestled in my own cocooned corner of the room, saying my message from spirit over and over in my head. My message from Granddad. It had been weeks since I'd last thought about him and I wondered why he'd want to give *me* a message. He had other family in England he lived around whereas we only saw him once or twice a year. But maybe that made sense: they knew enough about him when he was alive. He might not have had the chance to say everything he wanted to me and my mum. I pictured him, remembering how his brown hair had hardly greyed by the time he died. Patrick was right. And I'm sure he used to wear braces clipped to his trousers.

Iris closed the circle with another prayer to divine spirit and this time, as I bowed my head with the others, I said my own thank you. I left without asking Sadie about seeing her at church. But by then I didn't care. Another crack in my old life had been splintered open and white light was gleaming through.

When I arrived home the living room door was ajar and white and blue TV glow lit up the corner of the room I could see. I knew Mum was in there and that Dad would be upstairs either in bed or doing something on the computer. I waited and thought about pushing the door open, stepping in, sitting down on the couch. And what next? Tell her I had a message from her dad? How the hell could I bring that up? I barely spoke to her about school or friends or my job, never mind communication with the dead.

But didn't I have an obligation to tell her if my granddad had come through from spirit with that message? And she did buy that Dream Dictionary at some point. Or at least someone gave it to her. Either way, she must have had some interest or belief in spirituality, or the supernatural, or whatever she would call it. Maybe that meant she would listen.

Or more likely it would be another one of my 'incidents' she'd freak out about. A sign that I still wasn't 'OK' or 'normal'. And more realisation settled in like cold water. Telling her meant exposing the circle. I couldn't explain what had happened without explaining what I had really been doing every Wednesday night for the past three months.

A creak from the couch and a click to another channel. My dad calling from above – 'Is Nathan home?'. My mum didn't hear, or ignored him. I crept upstairs, avoiding the noisiest steps, with Freya padding up behind me. Sneaking into my room, I closed the door behind me. Writing Granddad's message down in the dream journal – I stopped using Mr. Young's notebook a while ago – was as close as I could come to telling my mum. For now. Maybe spirit would lead her to find it one day, like an undiscovered last will and testament.

Drifting away on my silver cord of sleep, Granddad stood outside our front door, waiting for someone to open it. I ignored his frosted silhouette through the glass and it looked like he was talking to us but there was no sound coming from him. Then he started pushing lots of the shiny black stones I'd seen in the box of crystals through the letter box. Hundreds of them pouring in, spilling out across the carpet. Mum and Dad walked past me but didn't see anything.

20

'So, when is your dissertation actually due?'
'Haven't you read all the books you need to by this point?'

'Still hanging out with the oldies at the book group?'

Their questions weren't sirens drilling me into conformity anymore. They were distant church bells, pealing behind me as I drifted off. I mumbled vague answers, shrugged shoulders, muttered half-explained excuses. In some part of my brain I knew I'd have to think up an eventual replacement for the book group alibi, but that could wait until the next week, and the next. Like my schoolwork, and my studying, and my dissertation. Even Granddad's message.

My brief reunion with the cinema group had disintegrated too. I'd gone with them once in the last couple of months. Gillian had asked me after I sat beside her and Crystofer at a blood donor assembly and heard them talking about it. We saw some crappy comedy – rich kids in an American high school with a five-minute-long scene about a condom. Instead, I was spending more time with Iris in the shop, even working extra shifts on Sundays and long weekends off from school. The energies of everyone at the circle had become knitted wool in a scarf and my one hour on a Wednesday night was the pair of needles holding us all together. I couldn't be unravelled from it.

In March, Iris introduced 'energy work'. Most of our chairs were moved against the wall with two left in the middle of the room. These were placed back-to-back, like a penultimate round of musical chairs. We each took our turn in the chair facing the wardrobe. Someone else would randomly come and sit in silence in the second chair while we closed our eyes and tried to feel whose aura was at our backs. I had managed to avoid ever giving Patrick the reading I owed him but this time I was first to volunteer. Sitting in the chair, staring at the wardrobe doors, my chest fluttered like a little bird was trapped inside, but it flew free after a minute or two. When Iris asked, I filled myself with white light and smiled.

'Imagine your aura expandin' with every breath, growin' and reachin' out.'

I'd already begun focusing on my aura before she guided me.

The first steps shuffled across the carpet behind me. The other chair at my back creaked under sudden weight and pushed against me. I inhaled through my nose and centred all of my awareness on the vibrations emanating from my shoulder blades. Warmth. Shorter than me. Giddiness.

'Is that Katrina?'

Her gasp and squeak confirmed it, followed by claps from the others. Iris congratulated me with a touch on the arm and I rubbed my palms together, as if warming them up to perform. Silence returned and the next steps tapped towards me, resting into the seat. The aura was gentler this time. Smaller. Colourless. Cool. In my third eye I saw the navy pillbox hat from church.

'Sadie?'

'Oh my goodness,' she replied and stood. Katrina started the round of clapping again. I grinned ahead and felt my energy beaming out, almost through the giant wooden wardrobe and even the wall behind it. I was used to hearing people whispering behind me at school, but now the murmurs at my back were different.

'He's good, isn't he?'

'It's amazing how he's sensing us so quickly.'

'Maybe he's clairsentient, too.'

'Final one,' announced Iris.

The chair jostled a little. I hadn't even heard footsteps this time. The aura behind me was different again. There was heat and it was more static. Patrick or Marcy? But Marcy was always so frenetic and excitable. This didn't feel like her.

'... Patrick?' I asked squinting.

No applause.

'Turn around.' Iris spoke from a different place. I swung my legs around to the side and looked over my shoulder. She smiled back at me from the chair.

'Oh.' The others laughed. 'I didn't think you were part of it. I hadn't thought you'd–'

'–But you need to feel. Not think. It's not about logic or figurin' anythin' out. Just feel it. You obviously can. You felt Katrina and Sadie's energies.' I c if she was angry with me. Had I disappointed her?

I took my place with the others in the row against the wall and watched each of them take their turn. Marcy guessed one correctly, as did Sadie. It made sense that we'd sometimes get one another confused, Iris told us, since we were all so linked now. During Katrina's turn, Iris pointed to me – my signal to take my spot in the vacant chair. About twenty seconds of concentrated silence passed. I closed my eyes to help Katrina.

'Is it Marcy?' she finally asked and craned over her shoulder to find me. 'Oh no!' She clasped her hands over her eyes and giggled.

The same happened with Patrick during his turn to sense us. 'Marcy?' He shuffled around to check and saw me. I watched his cheeks flush red and felt my own doing the same.

After we'd each had a turn, Iris sat in the 'guessing' chair herself. Or the 'feeling' chair. With nods of the head and nudges we made silent decisions amongst ourselves about who should sit behind her. First was Patrick. She sensed him right away. Next was Sadie. Iris waited longer this time but soon enough called out her name. After Sadie sat back down at the end of the row, Katrina gave me a pat on the back, pushing me forward. I took the chair and rested my palms on my cords, closing my eyes. I sensed the inevitable.

'Marcy,' Iris announced.

'Nope!' Marcy laughed from her chair. 'Again!'

I kept my eyes closed for a few seconds longer before opening them to find Iris out of her seat, standing beside me. She planted both hands on my shoulders this time. 'God love you!' she chuckled. 'You have a soft energy, that's all. Feels more female.'

I felt the red blush pierce my face. Jonnie and the others from school flashed in my head. Calling me their names. But the members of the circle didn't join in. I forced myself to look at each of them, but they smiled back before talking to one another. No staring. No jeering. Even Iris had moved off. She stood with hands on hips, talking to Patrick through the fuzzing noise in my ears.

Like always, Iris closed the circle with a prayer to divine spirit, although I didn't hear the words that night. Everyone filtered out one at a time, leaving me behind like something too big caught in a sieve.

'Need to get home sharp tonight, love.' I wasn't sure if Iris meant her or me. I put my coat on, though, and shoved my hands into my gloves. She dashed around from corner to corner, blowing the candles out in a flush of darkness. I stood dumbly in the doorway to the stairs.

'Iris?'

'Aye, love?'

'You know… tonight… what you said about my energy?'

'Aye?'

She wrapped herself in a thick scarf and was buttoning up her coat in the dull moonlight. My loud gulp filled the room.

'It reminded me… with everyone guessing I was Marcy… it just reminded me of when I was wee…'

'Right let's head out.' She came towards me, ushering me to turn around and shift downstairs. 'I'm still listenin'.'

'Well… it might make sense, in a way,' My voice quashed itself at the end of each phrase, but the words couldn't stop themselves from being dragged forward on a tug-of-war rope. 'I dressed up as a girl once when I went to school.'

She thumped into my back. I had stopped at the bottom step.

'Flippin' hell! Come on, love!' I stumbled down the final stair and forward. 'Well, I suppose, aye, that was maybe somethin' to do with it.'

For once, Iris sounded unsure, unable to make a connection. I didn't even know why I'd said it. And the tug-of-war reeled me further still.

'It was a dress-up day – can't remember what the theme was

or why we were doing it. And I dressed like a girl. Took some of my mum's clothes without asking her and got changed in the school toilets. I just thought it would be funny. I think. Primary Seven. The other kids didn't laugh. Teacher spoke to my mum when she picked me up.' I'd stopped again at the counter.

'Out we go.'

Iris's keys jingled and the locks clunked shut behind us. I didn't know if she was even listening anymore and maybe it didn't matter. I was having a conversation with myself – the confessor and the priest at the same time.

I don't remember us saying goodbye. Iris probably did and I didn't answer. I shuffled back along the cold street, hands buried deep in my pockets, watching my reflection stretch down into every silver puddle in the pavement I crossed. I hadn't planned on telling Iris that story. It had just simmered to the surface on its own. But now that it had revealed itself, I felt bigger and smaller. Bigger because I'd spoken about it aloud for the first time in years. I hadn't told anyone at high school the story – none of them had been at my primary. But smaller because Iris hadn't taken notice. I'd released the memory like a bubble, but watched it drift to the floor and pop silently in a corner.

Without remembering the rest of the walk home, I'd appeared at my house. Freya sprang from somewhere and stood at the edge of the door, meowing and staring at me, desperate for me to push the handle. Sighing and stepping in, I saw my mum on the phone in the hallway. She clutched the handset to her cheek and bit a thumbnail, caught in a daze that made me shiver.

Granddad?

She broke her blank gaze to look at me and I heard the distant murmur on the other end.

'Who is it?' I asked, but she held a finger to her lips.

This could make telling her easier. I could give her the message now, somehow.

But then she spoke and I knew I was wrong.

'OK… OK… we'll see you soon, then… take care.'

She placed the receiver back in its cradle and held it there for a few seconds before glancing at me. I turned to dart up the stairs.

'Nathan.'

Her fish-hook voice yanked me back on a sharp wire. Freya escaped, skittering away to my room. I looked around, feet still poised on the stairs heading in the other direction.

'That was your Aunt Brenda on the phone.'

I turned.

'You'll have to help tidy the house. She's coming to visit in a fortnight with Uncle Frank. They're staying for Easter.'

Her words prodded at me.

'And Jack. He'll need to stay in your room. OK?'

My guts squirmed. Looking at her, I saw my own awkwardness reflected. She folded one arm across her chest and chewed her nail on the other hand again. Her question was rhetorical, of course. She stared at me, or in my direction, stuck in some viscous thought. I opened my mouth, hoping sensible words would come out, even just an 'OK'. But before I could speak, she snapped out of her haze and wandered into the living room.

When people at school or my friends in the circle talked about family coming to stay, it was always with smiles and happy eyes; something to look forward to. And our visits to

Brenda and Frank were usually… fine. But now the thought was a grey cloud rumbling in over a hill, powering its way towards our house and I didn't know why. I wondered if my mum sensed the rain coming too.

21

She told me I couldn't go to my book group that week. Aunt Brenda and Uncle Frank were due to arrive on a Wednesday. When I first joined the circle, Iris had told me how important it was to commit and make sure we were there every week so that we could build up a unity of consistent energy together. If someone wasn't there, we'd be like a machine with a part missing. Katrina had missed one or two weeks at the end of last year and Iris had complained about it to the rest of us.

The day after the phone call I stopped in at the shop on my way home from school to tell her. She just smiled, though, saying I shouldn't worry. At first, I thought it meant that my presence didn't matter. Maybe I was the least important part of the machine and they could work on without me. But Iris must have seen the panic in my aura because she gripped my shoulder.

'I could sense you were anxious when you walked in, love. You can't change a family event, can you? Have fun with them.'

I half-smiled back.

I'd left cleaning my room until I came home from school on the night of their arrival. I didn't think it needed much, and I was pretty sure my cousin Jack wouldn't care what it looked like.

'Here.' The door opened as my mum threw an old sleeping bag in. 'You have that. Let Jack have the bed.' She marched off and I heard the hoover thrumming downstairs a minute later. I kicked the Aztec-patterned sleeping bag over to the side of the bed, sure it was the same one Jack had slept in last time he'd visited about five years ago when he was ten. Only one other person had used it since, but that had been in First Year. No one from school had stayed over since. Not even Nick. And I doubted he ever would now.

I looked around the room at my gemstones and the crystal ball on its stand in the bookshelf. My *Mysteries Unsolved* books were lined up in order with a new Tarot book tucked in at the edge. My still-unfinished Empire State model sat uselessly on the desk in the corner. I hadn't touched it since I'd joined the circle.

I gathered the crystals and the books and stashed them in the giant plastic chest at the end of my bed, covering it with a blanket.

I heard them arrive. Muffled coos and aaahs and laughs down in the hallway while I perched on the edge of my bed with the door ajar. I pictured them hugging and lugging in suitcases for the weeklong stay and wondered how long I could linger up here before being forced to join in and make uncomfortable small talk.

'Nathan!'

Not long.

I sighed and pushed myself onto my feet, waiting another few seconds.

'Nathan!' An irritated edge to my dad's voice this time.

I crept downstairs rubbing my hands on my trousers, preparing my smile.

'Ah, there he is! Come here!' Brenda squeezed through the others towards me, pulling me in against her chest and furry coat collar that almost suffocated me. She released me eventually, leaving bits of fluff in my mouth and the taste of sweet perfume in my throat. Frank was next, towering in on me for a thick handshake that nearly cracked my fingers.

'How're you doing, laddie?' He laughed at his own version of a Scottish accent and I chuckled along without answering, which I don't think he wanted anyway. My mum and dad ushered them into the living room, pointing towards the abandoned luggage.

'Nathan, put that away upstairs, son.'

And as they filtered in, a stranger was left behind in the hallway. He was taller than me, even with slouched shoulders, and had messy brown hair down to his thick eyebrows. He gave me a nod and a bland 'hiya'. Although he was only fifteen, Jack looked older than me, or at least the same age. In my head, he was a ten-year-old, chubby kid who didn't say much and clung to Brenda most of the time. He'd been replaced with an unknown lanky teenager. Maybe the not-saying-much part was still the same.

I took the cases to the spare bedroom for Brenda and Frank and then slumped back downstairs. In the living room, I leant on the edge of a couch beside my dad. They talked about holidays they'd been on, work, the rest of the family in England and a load of other shit I was no part of. Brenda squawked on and on, flapping her hands about, while Mum nodded along putting on her best interested face and adding in little noises of agreement or surprise here and there. Every few minutes Frank would interrupt either to correct her or to make some crappy and obvious joke that everyone seemed forced into laughing at, my dad guffawing loudly beside me.

My daze was cracked at one point with Brenda's mention of 'Dad'. Her and Mum's dad: Neil. And I thought about Iris's reading – his message for my mum about money. It floated around in my head like an unstamped envelope lost in the post.

Jack was on the other couch, wedged in at the end beside Brenda with his parka still on. He'd said as little as I had, but didn't even glance anywhere near me once, thankfully. He looked like he could be any one of the pricks at school who I'd do everything I could to avoid. And here he was: this mini-Gallagher brother sitting in my house making me want to vanish.

After what felt like hours, yawns and stretches passed around us and the adults finally stood.

'Take Jack upstairs then, Nathan,' Dad urged, giving me a nudge in the back. 'You must be shattered, Jack.'

Jack didn't answer. He only had a backpack with him and kept it on his shoulders even after we'd walked in silence to my room.

'Pretty much the same as when I was here last time.' He looked at me for the first time but his expression was so nonchalant I couldn't tell if his comment was a compliment or a criticism.

'Yeah…'

I neatened and fidgeted with the bedcovers. Jack turned towards the window, noticing the pictures I had pinned to a corkboard on the wall; a collage of photos from last year of me with Stacey and Gillian and a couple of other girls in my year.

'Is this your girlfriend and her mates or something?'

I considered lying. He'd never meet them to find out. Or

maybe I could mention Emily. I hadn't seen her in the shop or at school for a while, but she'd be ideal for an imaginary girlfriend. Jack might mention it in front of my parents, though.

'No, just friends from school.'

He looked back at me for a few seconds before giving a vague nod. Freya slid out from under the bed and rubbed against his leg. He ignored her.

'Do *you* have a girlfriend?' The words sounded stupid as they tripped out of my mouth.

He glanced at me again, giving a 'Nah, not just now,' and a raised heavy eyebrow. I felt like he was speaking a foreign language.

Still moving the pillows around, my hand bristled, sending a whistle into my brain like a metal detector. The moonstone in the pillowcase. Marcy had given it to me a couple of months ago and I'd tucked it in there to help me sleep after my mum had told me about the visit. Jack was still surveying the room, looking everywhere but me. I thrust my arm in to grab the smooth stone and clenched it behind my back for the time being. I didn't want to put it in one of the drawers and pull his attention to what was in there.

'So, is it expensive living here?' He'd scuffed his way to my side of the room, dumping the backpack on the floor and looking at me again, with his arms folded.

'Not really, I don't think.'

''Cause the house isn't *that* big. So, what did all your parents' money go on?'

'What do you mean?' I sounded more alarmed than I'd meant to.

He shrugged and averted his eyes again, this time catching

the *Titanic* poster on the back of the door. His gaze lingered there before he looked back at me. It reminded me of my dad doing the same thing on Christmas Day. I expected a smirk or even a joke at my expense, but his expression only changed a fraction, the edge of a glower intruding on his blankness.

'I'll just sleep downstairs on the couch,' I muttered. 'You sleeping on the floor is stupid. Have my bed.'

I gathered the lumpy sleeping bag and used it to hide my burning face before thudding off downstairs. It wasn't until later, in the dark of the living room, that I connected Jack's questions to Granddad's message. Problems with money. And if Jack knew something then my parents already knew too. Maybe they didn't need granddad's message now. I was too late.

I imagined hearing Iris in my head, guiding me through a meditation to help me sleep, but she sounded distorted in my mind and my own voice kept taking over no matter how much I didn't want to hear it. After a while I gave up on the meditation and stayed awake for hours, staring through the blinds at the half-moon that dimmed every time I blinked.

22

The following week was a swinging pendulum. Sometimes it swayed away and I would be grateful for Brenda and Frank's presence – a distraction for my parents that averted their attention away from me. Then the pendulum would zoom back towards me and my aunt and uncle harried me with questions about school and friends and girlfriends and my job at The Book Cover.

And then there were other moments. Frozen spots where I would catch the pendulum stopped dead. I'd walk past the closed door of the living room and hear the chill of mumbles on the other side knowing I wasn't supposed to hear. One night I'd stumbled into the study to find Dad and Frank at the computer, quickly pressing the mouse to change the screen. Frank diverted me with questions while Dad coughed and pretended he was looking up football results. Dad had erased the browsing history when I checked later, too.

Jack had successfully moved into my room, which, after the initial frostburn, ended up relieving me of having to talk to him before bed every night. I did want to ask him questions soon, though, like what he meant about my parents' money 'going' on the house. When Crystofer asked me about a cinema group visit – he'd passed me in the Art corridor again on Thursday and talked to me – I'd thought it could be the perfect chance, away from my parents. I didn't even have to invite Jack, knowing my parents would do it for me.

'Take Jack with you, Nathan,' Mum had said. 'He'll be bored out of his mind here.'

'Go on,' said Dad, 'show him around Perth.' Yes, the great city of Perth. Can't possibly let Jack visit Scotland without *that* tour. 'Introduce him to your pals.'

Pals. The cinema group's faces weren't the ones that appeared in my head.

'Here, take this and get yourselves some popcorn and a hotdog.'

A fiver. My dad must have seen my expression.

'Well, you're earning big bucks at the shop, aren't you?'

He dropped us off outside the cinema after talking to Jack about English football for most of the car journey. The others were waiting for us in the foyer. Crystofer hadn't even turned up in the end.

But Nick was there.

He was too busy watching the trailers on the giant TV screens to notice I'd arrived. He'd developed some new mullet hairdo and had an ear pierced. He eventually turned around and gave me a nod, arms folded. The girls usurped the small-talk duties with Jack and I sat beside Nick in the theatre. But the space that used to be occupied by computer games catch-up and what books we were reading was filled with popcorn-crunching and pretend itches.

During the adverts I listened to Gillian jabber on with Jack. As I looked at them, I thought I could see his aura, a neon blue. I supposed blue was the colour of the throat chakra: communication. He spoke, or at least mumbled, more to her in those fifteen minutes than he had done with me since he'd arrived three days ago. Fine with me. If I could, I'd have brought her home with us and handcuffed her to him. She might have even been flirting, I couldn't tell. Sort of ironic seeing as this was the setting for my pathetic attempt at asking her out two years ago, although nothing sentimental was attached to that memory anymore. Even sitting beside Nick with nothing to say made me realise how much had shifted. My 'cinema group' was a remnant from a past life; a childhood holiday spot you re-visit years later, finding it's exactly the same but that you've outgrown it.

After the film, Nick leaned against a wall outside the cinema to smoke a cigarette; a new habit he shared with a couple of the guys I'd seen him hanging around with after school last month. I waited with him in more cold silence. Besides computer games and books, we could always at least complain about teachers and idiots at school. But now we were studying different subjects – when he actually turned up. And the start of every sentence I wanted to say was connected to Iris and the circle. Nick wouldn't understand. He was a drifting fleck, light years away from all of that.

After the girls had walked off to catch a bus and Nick bundled himself into the back seat of an older friends' car, Jack and I were left alone.

'Jack…' I forced myself to sound deeper than usual. 'What did you mean the other night? About my parents' money?'

'Huh?'

'You asked about it being expensive living here and about… about my mum and dad's money being… gone, or something.'

Jack's hands were buried in his pockets and he scuffed stones around the car park tarmac. He shrugged, without looking at me.

'Dunno. Just stuff I heard my parents saying… money problems and stuff.'

'Like what kind of money problems? How bad is it?'

'I dunno.'

A stone flicked towards me and I jumped back, smacking the bumper of a parked car.

'Sorry,' he said, finally looking at me. 'Look, I shouldn't have said anything. Probably got it wrong. They might have been talking about someone else in the family. Aunt Kirsty maybe. She's a riot.'

He turned away, maybe looking for the next stone he could launch at me.

'Gillian was in one of those photos, wasn't she?' he grunted.

'Eh?'

'Those photos in your bedroom. Gillian's in 'em.'

'Yeah,' I answered.

And then nothing else. Another code I couldn't be bothered breaking.

This time it was my mum who arrived to collect us, pulling the car up before I could figure out any other way to pull answers out of Jack. On the black roads that winded home I stared out of the passenger window at empty fields. I think my mum made a stupid comment and she and Jack both snickered.

✩

I knew not to question it when my mum told me to get ready for church on Sunday morning. The taut look on her face showed me she was as uncomfortable as I was about putting on our costumes and playing along with Brenda and Frank. Until now, the adults had been jovial and familiar with one another, even conspiratorial when I caught them whispering until I'd enter a room. But the charade must have been becoming apparent. I don't know why visiting church was such an important façade to keep up. The only mention of religion from Brenda and Frank since they'd been here had been our swapping of Easter eggs, and Jack certainly wasn't emanating Christian devotion. I guessed their churchgoing was just a habit, like continuing to write your old address after you'd moved house. Jack even gave me his egg saying he didn't like chocolate. And I'm the weirdo?

We walked to St. Germaine's in a ridiculous silence. I didn't know if the pretence was so obvious to Brenda and Frank that they couldn't speak, or if we were taking part in some silent, Jesus-induced reverie. Dad made me sit beside Jack during the never-ending mass and it reminded me of sitting beside Crystofer in the cinema, only instead of me worrying about his leg rubbing up against me, it felt like Jack was recoiling from *me*.

During Communion, I watched the procession of the rows in front of us, like on Christmas Day, and prepared to pull my legs back and let others past. But to my right, my dad stood, following my mum up to the altar. This was an added, desperate touch; joining in with everyone else, playing our parts, acting like we were here every week. For what? I wondered if the priest would notice us, refuse us our bread, call us out as imposters and end the mass. Instead, he blindly handed out the little white circles, glancing at me like I was a cardboard cut-out when it was my turn.

'Body of Christ'.

'Amen,' I mumbled, wondering if that was what I was

supposed to reply with. Maybe the response had changed since I'd last done this. Maybe on Easter you said something different, gave the priest a special crucifixion-themed handshake. I gulped the dry wafer down and felt it lodge in the middle of my chest like a paracetamol I'd swallowed without water. I thought my body might be rejecting it.

Walking back to the pew, I watched Brenda and Frank, wondering if I could gauge the success of our family act by checking their expressions. How would they look? Proud? Righteous? Fulfilled?

Blank. Frank stared ahead like he was thinking about something else. Maybe the football scores or what we'd be having for our happy Easter lunch. Brenda mouthed along with the hymn, kneeling on the padded bench on the floor, hands clasped loosely.

As we left the church, I scanned the parishioners mingling outside. Kids ran around and grabbed little eggs from the priest's wicker basket he held out to them with a grin. I knew they were probably imposters like us, never there any other week. Amongst the adults, though, there was no sign of Sadie's pillbox hat or wisps of white hair. Walking home behind Jack I imagined a whole scenario in her secret life – having to find a new church, checking that no one else from the circle attended mass there, hiding in the back row with a black-lace veil like Meryl Streep and Goldie Hawn in the final scene of *Death Becomes Her*, hoping no one would question her or why she fled from her last parish.

'That where you work?' Jack nodded towards The Book Cover as we passed it on the opposite side of the street.

'Mhm.' I felt the wafer in my chest dissolve away. When I

glanced at Jack, he had one eyebrow raised above his little black eyes. I don't think he understood why I was smiling so much.

'Did you have to get that job to help your mum and dad?'

There it was again. Why would I have to help my parents? And why was Jack bringing it up again? I shook my head as my smile slid away and dripped onto the pavement.

My parents, Brenda, and Frank reached the end of the street up ahead and turned the corner. But coming back in the other direction were giggling, racing voices, bending around the corner towards us: Emily, Hannah and Crystofer, stamping in unison like a pop group. I didn't even know the girls were friends with him. Emily's hair was down today, all loose and wavy so that you could see all the different shades of blonde and sandy brown in it.

'Hey, bookworm.' She spoke first, sticking her boot out to give me a pretend tap on the shin.

'Hey.'

Hannah pouted, her hands shoved in her jacket pockets and Crystofer looked Jack up and down.

'What are you all doing?'

'Just checking out the wonders of Drichton.' Emily gestured around, smiling.

'Yeah, absolutely stunning,' added Crystofer.

Jack yanked his hood up over his head like it was a space helmet and he might have breathed in some alien toxins.

'This is Jack, by the way. He's my cousin. Visiting. From England.'

'Cool,' said Emily. 'Special occasion?'

'And why weren't we invited?' added Crystofer.

I stifled a laugh.

'Just Easter, really. How come you aren't all with your families?'

They all looked like they'd just caught a sudden smell of something weird. I suppose not everyone cared as much about Easter as my family. I doubt anyone else in my school even came to Mass like this, never mind have a compulsory dinner with their parents.

'Well, I don't know about these guys but after I got my egg we were kind of done with it all,' said Emily.

'Actually,' Crystofer piped up, 'we didn't do eggs this year. My mum gave me gift vouchers and a little chocolate box thing.'

Jack's hooded head had turned to face out across the road, allergic to the conversation.

'So…' I focused on Emily. 'I haven't seen you in The Book Cover for a while. Your mum not want you to get anything else for school?'

From the corner of my eye, I saw Jack's furry hood turn back.

'I'm all good on ancient books for the moment. Thanks for asking, though.'

'Cool…'

'But, you know, now that I'm a massive Fitzgerald fan, if any of his other books come in, let me know.'

'Yeah. I'll keep them aside for you.' We laughed a little even though we both knew it was kind of stupid. 'I suppose we should go. Having an Easter dinner thing…'

'See you at school when we're back.'

'Can't wait.' I gave a sarcastic thumbs-up. 'Bye.'

Emily waved and we all drifted off from one another.

'Cheerio!'

I didn't turn around but gave a hurried wave over my

213

shoulder to Crystofer's call.

'That girl. She wasn't in any of those photos, was she?' The deepness of Jack's voice made me realise how annoying my own airy pitch was and I cleared my throat.

'No. That's Emily. Only just started talking to her this year.'

No response.

'She's been in the book shop a few times. In the year below me at school.'

We reached the house and pushed open the creaking black gate. Jack spoke again right as I reached for the front door.

'My last girlfriend was in the year below me too.'

My hand rested on the door handle for a couple of seconds before I pushed down on it. I even thought I felt Jack's hand giving me a pat on the shoulder. Opening the door, heat and the smell of toast wafted out. My smile came back.

23

I felt cocooned between the magic of the circle room and the reality of Drichton. The landing on the stairs of The Book Cover had become my spot to sit in and sift through new boxes of donations. The weather was becoming bright enough that the skylight even created a bit of warmth. I'd spent most days of the Easter holidays hanging around, 'helping' Iris, even when she hadn't asked. But she never asked me to leave either.

Crouching on my knees and pulling out another pile of old books – a mix of ancient school textbooks and children's fantasy stories – I heard the shop door clang open followed by a chirpy voice. Katrina. After a minute of muffled chat, she called up. 'Hi, Nathan!' I shouted a hello back, leaned against the wall, and took my shoes off, stretching my legs out. I didn't even say hello to my parents anytime I walked into my own house.

Flicking through the pages of a familiar-looking Enid Blyton book, my focus drifted again to Katrina and Iris on the other side of the flimsy curtain. I'm not sure whether I was listening for a while before they mentioned her or if it was her name that made me tune in in the first place, but at some point Katrina said it: 'Melissa'. Her name was like a lost postcard arriving years after the holiday was over. I hadn't thought about her much since she left the circle months ago. I'd only met her once on that first night, but I remembered she was Katrina's friend. I edged down a couple of stairs to listen.

'… in Glasgow living with the new man.' I pictured Katrina

leaning on the counter enjoying the chance to trade gossip.

'That was quick.'

'You're telling *me*. I never even met the guy! Anyway, she's doing readings now.'

'Oh?'

I wondered for a second if a third person was there before realising it was just Iris speaking again. Her voice had changed.

'Aye, and charging for healings too,' Katrina said.

'Healin's? She never did any healin' here.' She still sounded different, like a ventriloquist was operating her.

'Mm. Apparently she's working out of some kind of centre in the West End.'

They stopped talking. I backed up the stairs, thinking they knew I was listening in – years of conditioning from eavesdropping on my parents. But then Katrina and Iris wouldn't care if I heard them. I was their friend.

Iris spoke again, quieter, in abrupt mumbles. I trod down the stairs and through the curtain. Katrina beamed at me but Iris didn't smile. Wasn't even looking at me. She gathered papers and pens and spare change behind the counter into piles. I spoke to Katrina for a few minutes as she told me about a presence she'd been sensing in her house. Iris didn't offer any suggestions and continued tidying things away pointlessly with her back turned to us most of the time.

When Katrina left, I watched Iris. Her aura had become darker, her energy colder. I slipped through the back to finish rifling through the books I'd been looking at and decided to leave after that box was finished.

'Most of those are too damaged to resell I think, Iris,' I said, pushing the curtain aside and slipping my jacket on. 'But there are a few kids' ones you could put in the bargain box.'

'Mm. Thanks, love.'

I crouched down to tie my laces in front of a new table Iris had set up by the counter: an old mahogany piece with flower carvings on the legs. She'd picked it up from the antiques shop around the corner. I was surprised my mum hadn't beaten her to it first. On top, Iris had set up a display of the new crystals she was selling, and had made little labels for each one, describing their healing abilities. That's when I spotted a collection of the little shiny black stones I'd seen before – in the box, the first time Iris had given us all one. Not just pebbles after all, then. 'Onyx,' read the label. 'Promotes steadfastness and strength. A secretive stone that upholds willpower.'

I suddenly wondered what my dad would think if he ever reappeared in the shop and saw all these crystals on display.

'You alright down there, love?' Iris sighed.

'Yeah.' I switched to the other shoe, taking more time so I could talk without looking at her. 'I heard Katrina mention… Melissa.'

'Aye,' she sighed. 'Why?'

'Just wondering. I thought maybe you still spoke to her.' Finally, I stood.

'Nope. After she left the circle she just sort of vanished. Tried phonin' her a couple of times but…' She shrugged and leaned both palms on the counter. I was ready to say goodbye when she continued, looking at me again. 'You know you could do what I do one day, Nathan – be a medium. I see that for you.' She had a new intensity in her eyes: a mix between smiling and concentration.

'I don't think I could.'

'You could.' She nodded. 'Some folk think they can come to a circle for a few months and they're Nostradamus. But you're clairvoyant, we know that.' I thought again about the moanings I'd heard outside my house that night months ago, when I'd had no idea that it was Granddad. And his silhouette, standing in my door, waiting to connect with me. Then the Christmas Day phone call.

'Maybe even clairsentient too,' Iris said.

I squinted. Someone had used that word before at the circle. 'You can feel spirit, right here.' She put both palms just above her stomach. 'In your solar plexus.'

'Is that why I feel sick at home so often?' I laughed. But Iris only had a quick curl at the edge of her mouth.

'Aye. I think you're goin' to be doin' what I'm doin'. You're a medium. Maybe that's why spirit brought you here in the first place. Or brought me to you!'

She picked up one of the piles of papers and scuffed off behind the curtain. A helium balloon grew inside my chest. I was sure I was on my tiptoes, filling with warmth, my energy expanding. It reminded me of the feeling I'd had when Emily had come into the shop to speak to me months ago. Everything had aligned to bring me here. A medium working in my favourite shop. The job. My parents' uninterested acceptance of my 'book group'. This was why I'd always been drawn to the gemstones, had such vivid dreams, read the *Mysteries Unsolved* books. Maybe even why I'd heard my granddad's voice that night.

Clang. The shop door catapulted into my heel. I tripped forward, gripping the counter and turning. Jonnie. He looked as confused as I felt, staring at me with a furrowed brow, one foot in the shop, one back out on the street. Like Jack, he wore an over-sized parka, the ridiculous furry hood collar hiding half of his face.

'Do you…' he started. Then he backed out, letting the door slam. A cold fist had squeezed my heart.

'Who was that, love? Thought someone came in there.' Iris had popped her head back through the curtain.

'Em… no one.'

'Mm. Thought it might be one of your pals.'

I shook my head and watched Jonnie scurry down the street without looking back. Iris pottered off again and my magnet hand reached down to the table of crystals. I grazed the black onyx. The secret stones. And put one in my pocket before I left.

24

On our houseguests' last night, we all squeezed in around the kitchen table for dinner, elbows and knees bumping. Steam clung to the windows and Dad clattered around, slamming cupboard and oven doors and dishing out plates, while Brenda and Frank kept saying that my parents had 'gone to too much trouble'. I don't know if it was the euphoria of knowing he was leaving the next day or if he genuinely thought we'd connected but Jack spoke to me a few times during the meal, once Dad was settled in a chair. 'That film was alright, wasn't it?', 'When'll you be going to the cinema again?', 'Do Nick an' that live close by?', 'Are you in classes with them at school?'

I answered without asking much back in return, sending thoughts out to spirit that he wouldn't ask me any more about The Book Cover – a topic I could sense him verging on. I wouldn't mind him asking about Emily though. I tried not to mutter too much in front of Brenda, Frank, and my mum, who was always complaining about my mumbling. But glancing at my parents, expecting confusion or disapproval, they looked different than I think I had ever seen them. Their smiling teeth glistened with spit and bits of food and the crease lines at the side of my mum's mouth looked unnatural. She even glanced at me right in the eye without tutting or shaking her head or looking away with a sigh.

Brenda was talking about other members of the family down

South again. I imagined asking her and my mum about my granddad, their father. Maybe things had aligned this way on purpose. Maybe spirit had sent Brenda and Frank and Jack here to encourage me to pass the message from spirit on. And it *had* been about money – just what Jack had talked about. I thought about how I could start the conversation. Maybe one of them would mention Gran or Granddad or the house where they both grew up and I could jump in. Pretend I'd had a dream about it? I reached into my pocket and rubbed the polished black of the onyx.

'Nathan?' Mum nudged my elbow. 'Brenda's asking you a question.'

I'd been staring at a spot on the tablecloth, a forkful of soggy potato in my mouth.

'I was just asking,' said Brenda, 'what about the boy you made friends with right after you moved here?' I gripped the fork between my teeth. 'He was over here nearly every night last time we visited.'

My mum tapped my hand. 'Don't bite your cutlery like that.' I dropped the fork onto the plate with a crack. 'Just sort of stopped coming round, didn't he?' Mum answered for me.

I grunted in agreement, unable to even form a 'yeah'.

'Oh, that's a shame,' Brenda chirped on. 'You were a nice little pair, the two of you.'

I sighed, too loudly, and turned it into a cough.

'I remember him,' Jack butted in. I clenched my back teeth. 'He was cool.'

Of course you would think that.

'Still lives in the village,' Dad said. He was looking at Jack as he spoke, as if encouraging him to go off on a search.

'Jonnie. That was his name, wasn't it?' Brenda spat crumbs towards me.

'Mm,' said my mum, looking down at her plate. I couldn't see her stupid grinning teeth anymore.

'Yes, Jonnie. What a nice boy.'

The secret stone burned in my fingers.

My teeth chattered as I watched Jack through the gap between my mum and dad. He jogged to the car through the rain, bundled himself into the back seat and blanched out Drichton with his headphones. Brenda and Frank hauled their cases down the doorstep before turning back for final hugs and handshakes. Brenda had already squeezed me before she'd put her coat on and pulled up her hood. Frank gave me a nod from outside on the doorstep as rain dripped into his hair.

'Bye, darling.' Brenda blew a kiss and waved.

And I'd thought that was it. The goodbyes done. More waves as their car would splash off. We'd forget them until another few years passed. I shifted my socks around so that my big toe wasn't sticking out of the new hole I'd made. That's what I remember looking at when I heard Frank.

'I've given him your number. He'll be in touch.'

I looked up to see Frank patting Dad on the shoulder. It could have meant anything. The words themselves weren't particularly ominous or sinister. But it was Dad who let me know. Something was wrong. He'd shoved his hands in his jean pockets and was nodding, but not really at Frank. He was nodding and looking down at his feet. I did it all the time. I'd *just been* doing it. Avoiding what was happening.

Whatever number Frank was referring to wasn't about football or a mutual friend. It was something else that made Dad shrink.

'See you soon,' said Brenda.

And her voice struck me like one of those tuning forks a science teacher had shown us. I hadn't heard this voice the whole time they'd been here. It was small and deep and her eyes were creased, pretending to smile.

Brenda and Frank piled into their car and my parents didn't speak. Jack didn't look up and I rubbed my arms folded across my chest. The door closed and I didn't move.

They passed by me on either side staring straight ahead. Did they know I knew things weren't right and couldn't look at me? Were they even aware of me? They drifted off to separate rooms and I watched Brenda and Frank's blurry car fade off behind the frosted glass of the front door.

When I walked up and into my room, I realised I'd travelled back in time. Jack had left me without my stones and my crystal ball and my tarot book and my dream journal. They were all still stashed away, and the bed covers were ruffled into a lumpy mess at the end of the mattress. I even felt shorter, tapping the back of my head against the doorframe, standing where Granddad's spirit had been that night months ago. I closed my eyes, asking him to make the phone ring again and tell me the answers.

25

'The mist begins to clear. You can see through the branches in front of you. You feel leaves crunch underfoot. White light flows through your crown chakra. Spirit wants to communicate with you.'

I saw Jack's back, still wearing the parka and backpack. Coins fell from his hand without making a noise on the ground. The mist wasn't clearing like Iris had described. It just clumped around me, stubborn and thick. A black cat lay on the ground at my feet.

'Explore the landscape. White light pours into your crown chakra. You are connected fully to spirit.'

I couldn't move and no one except Jack's spectral figure appeared. Not even my peacock. We hadn't talked much more about that since the spirit guide meditation months ago.

I hadn't spoken to my parents nor them to me since Brenda and Frank's departure. We'd pass each other on the stairs or in the kitchen and I'd feel them wincing away from me, just praying I wouldn't ask them to explain Frank's comment or answer Jack's money questions. It wasn't an elephant in the room; it was a rotten, black, stinking jelly-fish in *every* room.

I don't remember how Iris guided the meditation to end. I just opened my eyes when I'd had enough. Time for sharing and the others around the circle detailed their experiences. At least I assume they did. I only heard muffled tones like I was submerged underwater. I watched their shadows flickering on the blank walls, morphing into new shapes. Coins. Jack. Brenda. Frank. A backpack. A cat.

Granddad.

When heads turned towards me and Marcy touched my forearm, I blinked the silhouettes away then described my meditation as if reading from an instruction manual. No elaborations or real details. No theories or communications from spirit.

'Maybe this is a message for Jack. Are you close to him?' Marcy asked.

'No.' I didn't even turn to her. 'Before this visit I hadn't seen him since he was ten. And we weren't close then.'

No one else asked anything and after Iris watched me for a few moments she leaned forward, probably about to move things on. But I started talking again.

'I hadn't been in Drichton for long when Jack was here last time. Had just started at high school. I'd been at a different primary from everyone else so I didn't have any pals for a while. We moved because of me. I took a cat into primary school one day.'

'You saw a cat in your meditation. Maybe there's a connection there.' Sadie wasn't usually this vocal but looked like she was trying to help me.

'Oh, I saw a cat too!' Katrina piped up. 'It was walking around everywhere, in between all the trees. It might have been the same one you saw.'

'Mine was dead.'

Katrina withered back into her chair like a popped balloon. A muffled cough and the creak of a chair.

'That might represent somethin' important.' Iris said in a faraway voice.

I shook my head slowly.

'The cat I took to school was dead.'

Everyone's shadows juddered in the candlelight and sickness flooded me.

'Found it on the road behind our house one night when I was playing and I put it in my schoolbag. I wanted to show people. Someone told a teacher. Someone else went home and told their mum too.'

A car zoomed by outside.

'Did stuff like that all the time. Told lies. Said weird things to my teachers. Snuck out of primary school one day and walked away. They had to call the police. Told my teacher I wanted to die. That's why we moved here.'

I blinked a few times, realising I'd been staring at the framed drawing of Dancing Feather for minutes and my eyes had blurred over. The room fuzzed around me with static waiting for someone to fill it with words. I chewed the inside of my cheek, breathed heavily through my nose, and chose a shoeprint on the carpet to focus on instead.

I knew the others would either be looking at me, analysing or gawping in horror, or staring at Iris, waiting for her to take charge. She tried to explain why I was bringing all this up. Something about working off karma from a past life or my soul realising what lessons I was here to learn. I don't remember. I know what Patrick said to me as we were packing up to leave, though.

'I think sometimes the meditations are just for you, not for spirit.' His voice was lowered and he was saying it just to me as he fumbled to put his coat on. 'When you're a bit worried, you need to just, sort of… process it. Your mind needs to work it out. Takes a wee bit of time to get over some stuff.' He even touched my shoulder as he limped past me to leave.

Normally, I'd hang on until the end, waiting to savour Iris for myself. Tonight, I just wanted to get back to my dark bedroom. Sleep was good at rinsing out unwanted memories. And since Brenda, Frank and Jack were gone the house felt a little bigger. I weaved through the others, after Patrick, but Iris hooked me back, calling on me.

'Hang on a minute, love.'

Everyone else filtered out around me and I shoved my hands in my coat pockets, finding the stolen onyx. Iris tidied up around me.

'Your relatives are away now, you said?'

'Mm.' I nodded.

'What were they visiting for?'

I hadn't been given a 'for'. Mum told me they were coming and two weeks later they appeared. Then left with a crooked goodbye. I lowered my head a little and felt an itchy point between my eyebrows. The coins from the meditation rolled in front of my third eye.

'Just here for Easter, I suppose.'

'What about your friend – that girl, Emily? Seen her back in the shop?'

'Nope. Saw her at school the other day, though.'

'Oh aye? Were you talkin' to her?'

'A bit. She just asked about Jack mostly.' I rubbed one foot in a little slow circle on the carpet. 'Maybe likes him or something. Think my friend Gillian did too.'

When I glanced up again, Iris was standing in front of the wardrobe watching me.

'Why did you tell us the story about the cat, Nathan?'

She spoke softly as if she was starting another meditation with just me. I tried reading her face, decoding her tone. Why did she call it a 'story'?

'I'm… not sure. Because I saw the cat in my meditation I suppose.'

She looked at me before answering and exhaled. A smile in her eyes. Of course she didn't think I was lying. 'It was a message from spirit, love.'

The purple flames of magic sparked inside, just a little. And then the smiling eyes changed. Iris reached forward and put a hand on my shoulder.

'Somethin's goin' to happen soon, Nathan. Your parents have somethin' to tell you.'

Light glowed from the open kitchen door at the end of the dark hallway. My parents muttered and seethed. I marched forward then stopped, pushing the door open and watching them, as if I was busting in on some illegal activity. Their conspiratorial voices shut off.

'Why were Brenda and Frank visiting?' I spoke as if someone had jabbed me between the shoulder blades, pushing me on.

My mum, seated at the table, frowned before rubbing her forehead and leaning forward on her elbows. Dad stood at the counter, one hand on his hip, sighing. Neither bothered faking shock or outrage or defence.

'Well, it was Easter, son. And Mum invited them up to talk

about a few things. Get a bit of advice.'

'About money?'

Mum looked up at me between her fingers. Her face was deep pink. 'Did Jack say something to you about it?' she asked, before turning to Dad. 'Brenda told me they hadn't said a thing to him.' She looked back to me. 'Well?'

'Yeah. He asked about your money and where it had all 'gone'.' Granddad's message teetered inside its envelope, waiting to be yanked out.

'So you actually *spoke* to Jack?' asked Dad. 'You didn't seem to be making much of an effort as far as I could see.'

'*Me*? He didn't want to be around me! I slept in the living room because he was being so... weird.'

'Nathan!'

'What? He spoke more to my pals on one cinema trip than he did to me the whole time he was here!' Too loud. My heart throbbed and punched at my ribs.

'Yeah, the girls...' Dad turned around to look out of the window. The pain in my chest sank into my stomach. I'd heard this before. 'We thought having Jack here might have been good for you.'

I looked to my mum again. She looked different: her hands rubbing together, almost shaking. She hesitated before speaking. Not her usual curt orders.

'... Be good to have a... new pal around. Your own age... A boy.'

They'd discussed this. Planned. Connived.

'And enough of that book group,' Dad spat. 'Hanging around with old women...'

I pressed my eyes shut and shook the words away. 'It's not

229

all women. And what does that have to do with money? Are you bankrupt or something? Are Brenda and Frank giving you money?'

'For God's sake, no.' Mum waved the idea off with a hand before standing and gathering mugs and plates from the table so she wouldn't have to look at me anymore.

I stood limp and useless.

'Away you go, son,' said my dad with a vague glance in my direction. 'We'll talk about this later.'

But I knew we wouldn't.

As I turned and drifted towards the stairs, I caught the whisper of my mum's words behind me.

'We need to tell him.'

26

I sat under the bridge and watched the rumples and foam of the river for half an hour after I left the house. I even heard the minibus trundle above my head as it arrived to pick up Hannah and Jonnie. Then it droned off and I stayed behind in this new universe – Drichton during a weekday with pensioners venturing outside and posh people in farmer's coats walking dogs. The secret stone had become my talisman, familiar and protective in my pocket. I took it out and looked at it in front of the river, checking it as if its smooth surface might have rubbed off.

When I crept back home, the driveway was empty and Freya sat by the front door, as if she'd known I wasn't going to school and was just waiting for my early return. I snuck back to my room and flopped into the bed, enveloping myself in the covers with my uniform still on, sucking in hot breath and not moving. I couldn't move my feet much under the quilt with my shoes on, but after a while it became easier to just surrender and not bother trying to wriggle to a more comfortable position. I sank deeper into the mattress and squinted at the tiny threads right in front of me.

Light slithered away and the threads turned into snow. Everyone I knew stood in the back garden and giant flakes fell on them. They were waiting for me to get out of bed and come to the window. No one spoke and everything was muted and blank, the way it really does sound when it's snowing and you're in an empty street just listening to muffled crinkles all around you.

When I felt sweat seep through the back of my shirt, I shoved the quilt away and waited for a while before hauling myself up and kicking off my shoes without untying them. The hole in my sock, the same pair I'd been wearing for days, was bigger and had a twin on the other foot. My big toes stuck out like they were trying to escape the smell.

I gazed around at every familiar object in its place and every mark on the wallpaper and every stain on the carpet taking photographs in my mind so that it would be mapped forever. Then I lifted the cork board and all its pinned photographs of Stacey and Gillian and Nick from the wall and shoved it under the bed. I ripped the *Titanic* poster from the door, knelt down, and crushed it into the little wire bin in the corner. The Aztec sleeping bag was still there beside it. As I stood back up fuzzy blackness closed in around my eyes and I tipped over, steadying myself against the bookshelf, nudging my amethyst towards the edge. When I felt like I was standing on the carpet again instead of the moon, I picked up my dream journal then grabbed the sleeping bag and dragged it into the hall behind me. Then I pulled the ladders down from the loft and climbed up.

The whole room smelled like the damp fustiness of the sleeping bag and the skylight was coated in so much dust and cobweb that it looked more like dusk than the middle of the day. Once I'd crawled up, I tried hauling the ladders back up behind me to lock myself in, but they wouldn't budge from here. There was a sliding door from one of my parents' old fitted wardrobes propped against the wall and I used it as a barrier, laying it across the opening in the floor so that I could peek back down through a little sliver. I plugged in the over-head lightbulb and slid into the cocoon of the sleeping bag, laying on my front like I'd done in bed downstairs. The piles of books I'd rifled through months ago when I was looking for the Dream Dictionary still lay strewn around. I breathed in dust, feeling my shirt buttons press into my chest but not moving anyway, and hoped I could drift back into my snow dream. Maybe without everyone else in it.

I'm not sure how long I slept or how quickly I'd fallen into it and I didn't dream anything I could remember. At some point, though, I'd opened my eyes and my head was facing the other way, different from how I normally sleep. A stiff pain nestled in my neck like a piece of folded card was wedged under my collar. That's when I saw the Game Boy box, squashed between an old board game and one of my mum's jigsaws and I knew it was empty. I'd loaned it to Jonnie when we first moved here. But after he'd stopped coming over I couldn't ask for it back. I couldn't talk to him at all at school. Not after what had happened.

And he still had it. My fucking Game Boy. I bet he still used it. Showed it to his pals and pretended it was his old thing. No, probably told them the truth, that it was mine and that he'd nicked it. Told them why he didn't hang around with me anymore and they would all make sick faces and spit names they'd made for me.

Names that I still can't write down.

I bet he had the Game Boy in his bag at school. Played it up the back of the bus while I was sitting there at the front like a fucking idiot staring out of the window on my own while they would laugh at me and chuck little bits of paper at me and kick me as they shoved past and smack me on the head with their stupid bags that all looked the same like they wanted to match. Fucking pricks.

I wasn't lying down anymore. I was crossing the opening in the floor back and forth, lunging across the wardrobe door barrier and swearing out loud.

I could go to the bus stop. Wait for Jonnie on the way back from school.

Every time I crossed to the wall I'd turn and kick my foot off it, pushing myself back across the wardrobe door.

Could ask for the Game Boy back. Follow him home. Make him give me it. Tell his parents he'd stolen it.

Kick off the wall.

He wouldn't be with his pals. Just him and Hannah getting off the bus and she wouldn't care – she wouldn't even speak to me when Emily was with her so she sure as shit wasn't going to talk on her own. Jonnie wouldn't call me anything without an audience. He'd have to listen to me. Look at me again.

The wardrobe door slipped under my foot. The hatch frame flew up at my chin and the ladder stubbed against one heel. My forearms smacked into the edge of the opening, just catching me. I heaved myself back up, scraping skin off my wrist. I must have screamed or at least yelped but I don't remember. Just the sound of panting breath afterwards as I stared up at the light bulb. That's when I started crying and I know it took longer to fall asleep that time.

27

At school, teachers seemed to use the words 'revise' or 'study' in every sentence. Made sense given that the exams were beginning in a month or two, but to me they were just dates to be crossed off on a calendar. I'd even stopped listening in English. Shakespeare didn't compare to messages from spirit. My creative writing pieces were finished, sealed away in some mysterious filing cabinet Mr. Young kept referring to. I'd written a story about one of my dreams – Mr. Young said it was 'messy' – and a last-minute poem I'd scribbled during a Saturday shift at The Book Cover.

All we did now was write essays on *King Lear*, which I hadn't finished reading, and pore over old exam papers. At least, the others pored over them. I used them as meditation prompts, letting my eyes blur over the tiny printed text as I filled my crown chakra with white light and held the secret stone in my blazer pocket. It worked. I could visualise it on my own, without Iris guiding me.

Sitting at my desk, a dull pain creaked in my shoulder blades from sleeping on the floor of the loft the night before. My dad had only shouted up once to ask about dinner. I waited for them to call me back down later to go to bed but it never happened. I heard them muttering as they walked to their room, edging around the ladders. Any more than a day wouldn't have worked, though. They'd have *had* to speak to me then. So I clambered back down in the morning for a shower.

Jonnie was at the bus stop, of course, but I didn't even look at his face, let alone demand a toy back from six years ago that he wouldn't remember.

I ended up being the last one left in the English classroom. Not because I'd stayed behind to talk to Mr. Young like I used to, but because I'd barely heard the bell ring. I packed my things away, still floating in my self-induced torpor, before looking at him, tucking his shirt in at the front of the room. He wasn't wearing his Clark Kent glasses. This was a Superman day. For him and me. Invisible hands pushed me towards him and squeezed my heart, pumping it like a machine gun.

'Sir, I can see your aura.'

He looked up under his blonde curl. He'd been growing his hair longer.

'What?'

'Your aura. It's yellow and blue. I can see it.'

I waited for his impressed response as my heart carried on thrumming proudly. Maybe he'd ask more questions about what the colours meant or how I'd learned to do this. But he'd stopped moving and stared back.

'Eh… OK. Come on, let's move. Next class.'

I should have left then. But the hands were touching the back of my head. I felt a feminine energy. She pushed me right up to his desk.

'There's a spirit here, sir. A woman.'

He still hadn't moved, but his stare had slipped from confusion to a glower.

'Nathan, I don't have time for this. Get a move on.'

And I persisted.

'She has a message for you. I can hear words coming

through.' Iris would tell me to focus on my third eye, shift my awareness, feel the words from spirit. 'She's saying… 'Mum'.'

Mr. Young's book slammed closed on the desk. I jerked and stepped back, suddenly aware how close I'd been standing to him.

'In fact, don't go to your next class at all.' I'd never heard his voice so low and grim before. 'You're coming with me.'

★

I looked at the shining trophy cabinet behind Mr. Hunter the whole time. Little gold men kicking footballs, marble squares topped with metal wreaths, a silver rugby ball on a miniature plinth. I remembered it from the last time I'd been in his office. It had been years ago, after I'd started at the school on my own with no friends. I suppose, being my Guidance teacher, he had a duty to check on the loner kid. Didn't quite offer me any guidance that I can remember being of use. I knew even then that I'd never lay my hands on any of those shiny prizes behind him. I doubt he even remembered who I was when Mr. Young marched me down there.

'Like to repeat to Mr. Hunter what you've just said to me in class?'

I looked between the two men towering over me before I answered. 'No. It wasn't a message for him.'

Mr. Young's eyes widened and his mouth even opened a little. I'd never spoken to him, or any teacher, like this before. I'd also never announced a spirit was in the room and trying to contact him, so I don't know why *this* was particularly shocking. He told Mr. Hunter what I'd said.

I was at least given the luxury of waiting outside when he

phoned my parents. Even through a telephone across a desk I'd have been able to hear the horror in my mum's voice.

Familiarity wrapped its cold arms around my ribs. This even looked like the dim corridor outside the headteacher's office at primary. Instead of felt pen scrawlings and crudely painted animal shapes, though, this place was adorned with tattered posters for teenagers.

'*Need to know more about sexual health?*'

'*Being bullied? Here's what you can do.*'

'*Why an apprenticeship might be for you!*'

As hard as I looked, I couldn't spot the 'Are the parents who think you're a creep anyway about to murder you for joining a secret spiritual circle that you've lied about for six months?' poster.

'Hey, bookworm.' The sudden words shattered the tension in my forehead.

'Emily. Hi. What you doing here?'

'Interview about what subjects I'm choosing next year. The options aren't great. I'm thinking of requesting some new ones. Maybe martial arts. Or sorcery. What about you? Sexual health emergency?'

She nodded towards the poster of the boy and girl with their arms around each other before perching on the chair beside me, resting her bag on her lap.

'Just… well…' What was the point in lying? 'I'm in trouble.'

She giggled. I didn't.

'Sorry. Just didn't think you were the trouble-making sort. Thought you were pretty… normal.'

Then I laughed.

'What the hell did you get in trouble for?'

238

'Just said something stupid to Mr. Young. He wasn't impressed.'

'Maybe hanging around your cousin's been a bad influence on you. I wasn't getting the academic vibe from him when I met you in Drichton.'

'Mm… what vibe *were* you getting from him?'

She shrugged and tilted her head. 'I dunno… an I-don't-want-to-be-here vibe?'

I snorted. 'Spot on.'

Beside us, the office door opened. Mr. Hunter stepped out, looking down at us both.

'Right, Mr. Love…'

He looked to Emily, prompting her to leap up and head on her way further down the corridor. She twirled around behind his back, though, giving me a quick thumps-up.

'Your parents are coming in to see me tomorrow morning. We'll talk about it together. Just go to your next class. And I don't know what you're smiling about.'

I expected a night of barked lectures and shaking heads. In my room, when I heard my mum's keys in the front door, I gripped the bedcover, anticipating the first screech within seconds. But nothing. Only her slow footsteps across the hall, up the stairs, into her own room. The door was pulled shut behind her. She never nursed her anger or disappointment for long, though. I spent the next hour clutching my smooth piece of blue lace agate. I'd bought this one, not stolen it. A crystal book Iris had given me said it was useful for cleansing anxiety. It hadn't kicked in yet.

Front door again. Dad this time. But straight to the kitchen. No thudding footsteps charging in my direction. No yell of my name. Maybe I *could* have stayed in the loft another night without protest.

A gentle knocking on the door.

'Nathan? Can I come in?' Dad's voice was steady, quiet.

I waited, knowing he'd walk in anyway as he always did. But he only knocked again without pushing the handle.

'...Yeah?'

He slid in, peering round the room. His gaze stopped on the open drawer beside me. Then he looked at me. It was his habit – this detective-spotting-the-final-clue-and-figuring-it-all-out moment. He'd done it with the *Titanic* poster, even though he'd given me the fucking thing. And what he thought he was figuring out I didn't know. Or didn't want to think about.

He sat on the bed beside me next. Another new move.

'Mr. Hunter spoke to me.' He sighed. I stared at the bedcover, tracing a finger over the pattern. 'It's a bit... odd, Nathan. Been a few years since anything like this has happened. Thought we were past this.'

My lips clamped together. His first shout was due any minute.

'Look, I know why you were talking about... ghosts or whatever.'

A stinging in my solar plexus. The circle.

'We both do.'

How?

He lifted something from his side I hadn't seen him bring in.

'I know you love your reading but you know this is a load of rubbish, eh?'

The dream dictionary flailed about in his hand. Only that. The circle was safe.

'Found this beside your bed. You know someone just gave Mum this as a silly present? She's hardly looked twice at it.'

Why'd she write her name inside it then?

'Why were you in here?' What I meant as a defiant stand whimpered out a pathetic whine. 'Don't come into my room when I'm not here.'

Or even when I'm here.

'Well, when you get a phone call from the school telling you your son's been talking to a teacher about his bloody *aura* you tend to want to find out what the hell's going on!'

The shouting – at last. I hadn't heard Dad like this in a while. Not quite bellowing but boiling hot. He'd grimaced at the word 'aura' like it tasted disgusting in his mouth.

'I'd donate this to the bookshop but I'm sure you'd just take it right back off the shelf so it'll just be the bin! And what's with all these crystals and–'

He broke off, wanting to swear, I think. I'd pulled my legs up to a hug without noticing. I was shrinking. De-ageing back to eleven. It wasn't as if he'd found a stash of heroin in here.

'Anyway... your mum will be in school tomorrow to talk about this. I can't get away from the shop.'

That was worse. With both of them, one would always act as the buffer. Usually Dad, although maybe that had changed too. But just one on their own? Lethal.

'I don't think there's much point in trying to talk to you about it tonight. Is there?' The boiling voice had reduced to a simmer.

I made a pathetic attempt at a shrug, willing him to leave.

And then he shifted closer towards me. His hand touched my other shoulder. Then his arm was across my back. He made the beginnings of words, a series of hesitant noises that never finished themselves. He rubbed my upper arm.

I shook my head and mumbled a pitiful noise of objection before pushing away from him. Whatever he wanted to tell me was banished. He heaved himself up, wrung his hands as if washing them and left, closing the door with a soft click behind him.

I lay in bed on my back, palms upturned, swallowing heavy gulps of air and wondering if it was clairsentience and my solar plexus making everything inside me churn and gurgle. He hadn't hugged me since we'd moved to Drichton six years ago. I knew for certain now that my intuition had been right when Frank and Brenda left. Iris had been right. Things were changing. My parents were different.

I threw up in a bin beside my bed and waited until after midnight to creep out and clean it.

28

The trophies taunted me again, shining smugly behind their glass. But staring at them was still preferable to watching Mr. Hunter as he retold the whole thing. Couldn't bear to hear my mum either. I wasn't sure if she'd be compliant, nodding along and agreeing with every suggestion about how to deal with me, or tight-mouthed and rigid, neurosis breeding inside her waiting to erupt at home.

Or maybe a third kind. Maybe my mum would understand. The icons from the dream dictionary's purple cover danced in front of my third eye: the treasure chest, the spider, the flying pig. She must have kept the book for a reason. She *had* written her name inside the front cover. Maybe she knew what auras were and would feel we finally had something in common. She'd be calm and not say much, giving me a little smile. Maybe even defend me.

'Where were you?'

Two pairs of eyes were on me. My mum's angry lips twitched, waiting for a response.

'Where was I?... when?'

'Nathan,' Mr. Hunter responded, 'you weren't in school last Thursday and your mum—'

'—And I didn't know anything about this!' she squawked. 'If you weren't here, where were you?'

Crying over a Game Boy in a sleeping bag in the loft.

'I felt sick. Went for the bus but then came back home. You

and Dad had gone to work.'

'Why didn't you tell us you were sick? Or at least phone the school yourself.' She turned back to Mr. Hunter, resting her forearms on his desk, patting it with her palms. 'We didn't realise he'd been at home all day.'

Mr. Hunter nodded and scribbled a quick note. I don't think he saw my mum's hands clench into fists.

I shrunk back even farther into the chair and escaped into the blurry daydream of the trophy cabinet again. My mind flicked through imaginary pages in a newspaper showing different iterations of my sitcom apartment for rent. I could live nearby so that I'd still be close to the circle, maybe in my own flat in Ballahan or even Perth. Or I could go to Glasgow or Edinburgh and start my readings. Maybe even do medium demonstrations. I wondered if Iris thought I was ready for that.

Or London?

'Nathan!'

I jumped and turned to Mum's glaring eyes.

'You didn't submit your UCAS form?'

Oh shit.

No point in denying it or even trying to explain it.

'You told me it wasn't due until next month!' she seethed. Mr. Hunter coughed and readjusted his tie. Mum turned back to him. 'Can we still submit? Pay some sort of late fee? I'll take the form right to the UCAS offices. Where are they? Glasgow? Edinburgh?'

I thought she was going to pass out – both of her hands gripped onto the edge of his desk, pulling herself forward. Mr. Hunter shook his head.

'I'm afraid it's too late. Nathan would need to write a

personal statement, choose the University courses, compile teacher references…'

She stared at me again. 'What the hell are you going to do now?'

'Nathan suggested in his Guidance form that he was thinking of employment after school. That's why we never followed up on the UCAS application…'

Maybe Mr. Hunter was trying to save me, seeing me curled into my chair like some stick insect failing to merge into its surroundings. Maybe he was so used to shrieking parents that he was oblivious to her meltdown. Or maybe he was trying to cover his own back in case my mum turned on him next.

I don't know if she had become catatonic or just decided Mr. Hunter didn't need to hear any of this, but she stopped speaking after that. While he finished the meeting, she nodded curtly without looking at him and gave a quick handshake as if closing a disastrous business deal. She didn't say bye to me as she fled.

The next class was English. Of course. I pushed the creaky door open and bumbled my way to my chair, focusing on the stained navy carpet underfoot, rather than explaining to Mr. Young where I'd been. I assumed he'd either already know, or at least wouldn't fancy another interaction with me just yet.

Sitting down and looking around, none of the others even glanced in my direction, too busy with the tin of muffins being passed around for 'Cake Day', a tradition I hadn't been invited to take part in. Even Stacey, sitting at the desk in front of me, didn't deign me with a 'hello.' I slid down the stiff plastic chair.

In the hundred paces from Mr. Hunter's office to here, I'd transitioned from my mother's hysteria to utter nonchalance.

Mr. Young continued talking to the group at the front as if he hadn't noticed me. He had though. I could still see his aura. It was red. Probably shouldn't tell him this time, though.

29

I thought murder would block everything out. But I only managed to read about eight pages of *And Then There Were None* in between the bus-fuls of old ladies and annoying families piling in and out of the shop. Some stayed for thirty seconds, having a shifty skim over the shelves before wafting back out like they'd wandered in by accident; maybe they'd been looking for the entrance to the Bridge Hotel. Others scoured every book in the place. The older they were, the longer they stayed, dawdling between the shelves and stopping every few minutes for a chat with one another. I'd wedged the door open but everyone who plodded in dragged a cloud of baked summer air with them from the street and the sickly smells of ice cream and pick and mix. One little boy managed to clamber into the window display, stickering the glass with candy floss fingerprints.

Most people glossed over the little display table with the crystals. Maybe a nod and an 'Oh, that's nice,' but only one or two picked any of them up and no one asked about buying one. I even rearranged them, putting all the big pieces of amethyst and quartz at the back with all the smaller tumbled stones scattered out in front of them like a miniature alien planet landscape I was modelling, but none of the old ladies seemed to care.

The bargain box by the door was empty by two o'clock, though, so I chose another few books to fill it back up – mostly dusty, warped ones that had been on the shelves since I'd started working in the shop. I filled the new gaps left behind with some *Mysteries Unsolved* I still had tucked under the counter and had already read at least twice. Someone else could try to solve them now.

Amongst all of that I'd been trying to skim through the *Perthshire Observer*. I'd started by hiding in the kitchenette between customers coming and going but after realising how busy it was going to be, I'd snuck the paper through to the front, keeping it tucked underneath the counter. Just buying it in the newsagents had felt like an illegal exchange. I'd checked over my shoulder expecting to see my mum or dad watching me, knowing what I was looking for. Then after shoving the fifty pence into the woman's hand I'd rushed to The Book Cover with it tucked inside my coat.

After the last whiny kid had left with his mother, I unfolded the crisp sheets and rifled through the ads. But each flip of the rustling pages offered nothing: a treasure map with no X. Most of the listings were for houses and flats to buy. The rentals section only took up half a page and almost all were giant holiday homes 'ideal for big family getaways'. I needed a getaway *from* my family. Two rentals were flats in Perth. £250 a month. My few pounds an hour for a Saturday job wouldn't quite stretch that far. Maybe if I had a flatmate… or a second job… or maybe there was another paper I should've bought. Was this kind of thing being done on the internet? Checking anything in the house was risky, though. The school library could be an option.

The door clunked open. I threw the Observer down at my feet, squishing it under my shoes, imagining my mum or dad pointing an interrogative finger at me.

'Hey, bookworm.'

'Emily!'

She leaned on the counter, practically headbutting me, and I lurched back.

'Are the press onto your bad behaviour?'

The newspaper crinkled underfoot as I shifted. 'Yeah... I suppose me chucking it on the floor wasn't really that subtle?'

I bent over to lift the crumpled sheets, holding them out for us both to laugh at.

'Are you not supposed to be reading the paper while you're on shift?'

'Sort of.' I tried folding it back into shape, pushing it underneath the counter a bit more carefully this time. 'Think this is the first time today the place has been empty.'

'Empty? I'm not a ghost, you know.'

'Apart from you, I mean.' I fumbled with the secret stone in my pocket while Emily grinned.

'So, I'm guessing you haven't been expelled yet?'

'Just the belt this time.'

She laughed and I was impressed with how quickly I'd thought of my quip. It also gave me a few seconds to think up stories I could tell her about why I'd been in trouble, expecting that to be her next question. But she had already leaned back from the counter and lifted a little piece of tourmaline from the crystal table, holding it up to the light. It matched the green ring she had in a piercing at the top of her ear. I'd never noticed it before.

'Are you here visiting Hannah again?' I asked.

'I was. But she had to go to some hideous-sounding family

249

thing with her parents so I was turfed out early.'

'Ah.'

'... So thought I'd come and see how you were doing after your meeting with Mr. Hunter. Plus, you know, I wanted a proper tour of the book shop. Behind the scenes and all that.'

Iris's white barrier of light blazed against my back. 'Oh, I can't really. I mean, there's money and stuff back there in the safe and all that so... I'm not really supposed to let anyone through.'

'That curtain's not going to keep anyone away from a safe is it?' she snickered and I forced myself to join in.

'Yeah, I know. Stupid.'

'I was kidding anyway.'

Clink.

The door jingled open again behind Emily.

'Oh, hello you two.'

Iris stepped in, beaming at both of us. A man with dark grey hair, wearing jeans and a checked shirt followed her. He was at least a foot taller than her. She unbuttoned her cardigan and held up a plastic bag. 'I have a readin' tomorrow at somebody's house and I've left my bloody cards upstairs.'

I burst into a cough, as if it would stop Emily from hearing or understanding what Iris was talking about.

'Brought some books from my sister while I'm here, too.' She dumped the bag on the floor beside me. 'I'll never read them so just goin' to put them out on the shelves.'

'Iris, this is Emily. Remember?'

'Aye, of course I do. How you doin', love?'

'She was just visiting,' I cut in. 'Maybe going to buy a crystal.' I was desperate to stop her from mentioning readings again, not realising I was only leading her down another undesirable path.

'Oh fantastic. Tourmaline, eh?' She nodded down at the green and pink jewel still in Emily's hand. 'It's a really powerful healin' stone. Shamans used to use that.'

I was used to concealing any notion of the circle. Even the crystal ball and the amethyst in my room were a risk. But Iris spoke about her cards and healing and crystals to anyone, as if she was mentioning the weather or the price of a book. My face tingled and I clenched the onyx, suddenly wondering if Iris had ever noticed one had gone missing from the table. I looked to Emily. She was still gazing at the tourmaline, rolling it between her fingers. The man beside Iris folded his arms.

'Well, Nathan, this is Jimmy.' She nodded towards him. 'Jimmy – Nathan.'

I'd still never met her husband. This man didn't seem anything like what I'd expected. Although what did I expect? Some old sage with long hair, psychedelic robes, wooden beads, and sandals? Jimmy nodded towards me with a 'Hiya, pal,' while I smiled back, not knowing what to say or if I was supposed to shake his hand. He hadn't offered so I kept mine clamped around my stolen stone.

'Here, Jimmy, that tourmaline's meant to be a bit of an aphrodisiac too, ha!'

Emily raised her eyebrows and looked at me, hiding a laugh. My face prickled with more heat.

'Christ, here we go again. If you're talkin' about all that mumbo jumbo then I'm nippin' into the wee shop for a packet of fags.'

Iris rolled her eyes and batted him off. 'Aye, away.'

Jimmy swaggered back out of the door without a goodbye. Seconds later, another two men stepped in, chuckling to one another. They both wore similar coats and matching scarves like a living catalogue picture. Must have been visiting the town for the day like everyone else seemed to be.

'Right, I'm goin' to make a cuppa while I'm here. Can you look at these books, love?' Iris handed me the plastic bag. 'Do you want some tea, honey?' she asked Emily.

'It's OK, thanks. I'll leave Nathan to it and get going.'

Iris vanished behind the curtain and Emily turned back to me.

'I'll head back to the bus stop. Have fun with your new books,' she nodded to Iris's carrier bag, '…bookworm.' On her way out of the door she swivelled back. 'And the tourmaline!'

I laughed with her this time and even after she'd walked off past the window I must have still been smiling; one of the men who'd come in mirrored my grin back at me. I shuffled behind the counter, trying to uncrumple the *Perthshire Observer* again, but spying over its edges at the pair. They both looked about the same age as Mr. Young, early thirties I'd always guessed, and wandered between the shelves together. One kept whispering to the other, giggling. When the second man caught my eye I snapped away, diving into Iris's carrier bag.

'Look quite new, don't they?' She re-emerged from behind the curtain.

'Em, yeah. Not my kind of thing, though.' I pulled one out and held the cover towards Iris. A topless, tanned man with long hair held a woman in a pink dress to his broad, shiny chest. The title swirled below them – something about 'Desire'.

'No, I suppose not, eh?' Iris chortled.

"No," I said, sneering hard enough for her to notice.

A new trio of old ladies had bumbled into the shop and the two men walked towards us at the counter. One of them placed a short story anthology in front of me, handing over the two-pound coin. I think Iris said something to them before they left but I didn't hear. I'd been focusing on the counter. She waited until they'd wandered out before she spoke to me again. I remember still staring at the woodgrain, analysing the lines and grooves while she talked.

'Past lives make that happen.'

'Mm?' At first I thought she was talking about the wood or trees.

'You can live so many lives as just the one gender, then in the next reincarnation you change.'

The laughing, the closeness; I suppose it was obvious that they'd been a couple. I'd never seen two men like that. Only on *Eastenders* once before my mum had changed the channel with a tut. Iris took the plastic bag of romance books to the shelves, still talking to me.

'Imagine living hundreds of years as a woman, then your soul chooses life as a man for your next cycle of lessons. That's why people are gay.'

She was doing that thing again – talking about whatever she felt like, no matter who was listening. One of the old women had given Iris a stubborn look. Iris either didn't notice or didn't care.

'Their soul has lived so long as one sex, it stays with them. They can't change when they come back. Must come with a whole new set of lessons to learn, a life like that. Don't you think that makes sense, love?'

'Mm.'

253

The three old women left without buying anything and I saw Jimmy walking back down the high street towards us, stopping to stub out a glowing cigarette on the pavement. I chewed my lip, watching him.

'Can I go outside for a minute?'

'Eh? Oh aye, love. If you're quick—'

I didn't even wait for her to finish before I jogged out into the street, escaping the stiff, hot air of the shop. I bustled past the old women, who hadn't made it far, and raced to the bus stop at the far end of the bridge, calling out Emily's name and waving.

She looked up, squinting, and pulled headphones back from her ears to hang them round her neck.

'Hey. Don't tell me, you've just been fired and—'

'—Do you want to go to the cinema with me?' My throat squeezed the words out like a jack-in-the-box. Too quick. I stared at Emily's chin, shoulders, the glinting metal of the headphones, waiting for the burst of laughter or revolted rejection.

'Yeah. OK.'

'OK…. Cool… OK.'

She chuckled again, shoving me on the shoulder. 'So unlike in films you have to do the boring part and arrange a time and day.'

'Oh. Tonight?' I squeaked.

'Wow, steady on. I'm kind of busy tonight; we have family friends coming over.'

I must have screwed my face up or raised an eyebrow.

'Yeah, believe it or not, sometimes I, you know, hang out with my parents. But one night next week? If you're not working?'

'Yeah. I don't usually work during the week. Except Wednesdays.'

I'd lowered my voice, as if Iris could hear me lying from here. 'We can figure it out at school.'

'Sure. See you then.'

I turned and floated back down the street towards The Book Cover.

'Sorry,' I murmured, stepping back inside the shop. Jimmy was leaning against the empty doorframe in the back wall, reading my wrinkled newspaper. Iris popped a final book into a shelf and watched me with smiling eyes.

'Off to chat to Emily, eh?'

'Yeah. I just had to… ask her something. About school.'

'That 'E' in the sand might have been for her, remember?'

'Mm,' I nodded, but the memory didn't spark a coloured flame inside me like before.

'Aye. You and that girl were meant to cross paths. You just might not realise why yet, love.'

☆

I dreamt and woke and dreamt and woke. The same visions waited for me every time.

I had killed the black cat from primary school myself and hid it in the drawers beside my bed. And everyone knew what I'd done. People were coming to my house to find me and hurt me. Police and my parents and Iris and Emily, Stacey, Gillian, Nick, Crystofer, Jack. The thought of them all pressing towards my house to round on me and attack was crushing. So I set the house on fire to hide what I'd done; flicked a match and threw it down on the carpet in my bedroom, watching it curl around the furniture and blacken everything in seconds. I woke up when I felt the flames cooking my skin.

30

My parents sat on separate couches in the living room; two figurines from a dollhouse who'd been shoved in the wrong room together.

'I'm going to the cinema. Getting a bus into Perth. Meeting Emily.'

Dad looked up.

'That girl from school.' I said the last part louder.

He nodded with his mouth open a little then looked back to the TV. A soap was on, but the volume was turned down so low they couldn't really have been listening to it. Mum didn't look in my direction. She still hadn't spoken to me since the meeting with Mr. Hunter, not even to yell at me about the University applications. Dad had avoided the subject too. I'm sure by then they'd given up hope of me being the normal son they'd hoped would emerge at some point. Maybe they'd been discussing how best to move me on from their lives, like a pet they'd bought that had been much more hassle than they'd expected. I closed the door as I stepped out backwards, creeping off.

Emily was already waiting for me inside the cinema foyer. She'd put little bits of glitter through her hair and the giant TV screens on the wall display made it sparkle different tiny colours. She had a new piercing in her ear tonight: a purple one.

My throat tightened with thick syrup breaths. I'd practised our conversations in my head all the way on the bus. I'm sure I'd even been whispering phrases, drawing screwed eyes from the old woman across from me. But now all my ideas felt stupid, like lines from a film that no one ever said in real life. Instead of being relaxed and making her laugh with every sentence, we shuffled towards the queue with quick 'Hi's and 'How are you?'s. We'd already talked about my run in with Mr. Young at The Book Cover. Maybe there was nothing else. Emily hadn't even called me 'bookworm'.

I looked at the blonde hair of the woman in front of me, searching the curls for something else to talk about. Then the woman spoke to the huge man in a denim jacket beside her. Her voice rang like a phone I knew I should answer.

'...Katrina?'

Turning around, she looked at me for a few seconds before speaking.

'Nathan... Hello.' Seeing her here didn't make sense. She was in the wrong place. She only existed in our room for the circle. In the middle of a cinema it felt like another dream. And she hadn't smiled like every other time I'd been with her.

'Hi... This is Emily, my friend from school.' I felt heat in my cheeks even saying this. Was she my 'friend'? Was I allowed to call her that yet? Or maybe I should have called her my 'date'? It felt like another movie-phrase. I avoided looking at Emily.

'What are you two going to see?' Katrina asked.

'Um, *The Virgin Suicides*.'

She screwed up her nose like she'd just smelled something awful.

'It's based on a book I read,' I added, as if this would fix her expression.

'Oh, sounds a bit too serious for us. We're going to see that new comedy with the girl from *Friends*, aren't we?' She looked up at the man I assumed was Gordon, her husband, who she'd talked about at the circle. He nodded without smiling.

'And who's this?' he muttered.

'This is Nathan from… my wee group I go to sometimes. You know, all our daft nonsense.' She looked between Gordon and Emily, adding a jittery laugh. 'Oh, our turn.' She pulled Gordon by the elbow to the box office counter. 'Bye, pal.'

It was Sadie in the church again – seeing me and vanishing.

'So…?' Emily nudged me.

'That was Katrina.'

'And that was weird.'

I smiled, liking that she'd sensed that.

'Weird? How?'

'It just felt… I dunno, strange. You must know her but her husband was acting like a big freak.' Laughter surged out and we both giggled our way to the ticket desk. I paid for both of us, assuming that was what was expected.

'I'll get the popcorn,' said Emily. 'So what's this group then?'

The book group alibi rose in my throat like a hiccup. But I forced it back down. Emily was intuitive – she'd felt the odd energy with Katrina. And she hadn't flinched when Iris had mentioned her cards and readings. I remembered her joke at school about sorcery, too.

'It's a sort of spiritual-type group thing.' Needles pricked my face as I spoke and the words felt foreign coming out of my mouth. Emily was the first person outside of the circle I'd talked to about this. I darted looks around, checking to see if anyone else I knew was milling around the foyer.

'Spiritual?' Emily raised an eyebrow.

'Not religious or anything. Just, like, meditations and analysing dreams and stuff.' No point in telling her that at the last meeting I'd mostly stared at the floor and then talked about a dead cat. 'Iris at The Book Cover organises it. Remember she was talking about the crystal you were holding in the shop?'

'Cool. No self-flagellation then?'

I laughed out the stiffness in every muscle. She didn't laugh at me. Didn't call me a name.

'You know who else is into all that supernatural stuff? Crystofer!'

I watched her face, trying to decipher signs of a conspiracy. First this guy had become Gillian's new best friend then Emily was hanging around with him in Drichton. And here she was, mentioning him again.

'… Really?'

'Yeah, his mum had a psychic reading a while ago. Loads of the stuff was so accurate. And he talks about spirits and the afterlife all the time. I don't know that much about it but I'd love to have my fortune told.'

'That's… cool.' We joined the long queue that was filing up to the food counter couple by couple. 'I think my mum might be interested in fortune-telling and stuff too.' I casually echoed Emily's words as if I was as naïve about mediumship as she was. 'Or she used to at least. She has a dream dictionary in the house.'

'Haven't you asked her about it?'

I nearly laughed in her face but just shrugged and shook my head.

'This is why I was in trouble at school, by the way. I told Mr. Young what colour his aura was.'

'What!'

Shit. Too much.

I looked to her, at least grateful I hadn't mentioned that I'd told Mr. Young about his dead mother being in the room. But Emily was grinning.

'That's hilarious. Not only is Nathan Love the new school rebel but you're also a part-time mystic! Nice going, bookworm.'

The queue shifted forward and we brushed arms as we stepped ahead.

'So what colour's my aura then?' She stood aside and posed with her hands clasped in front of her.

'Em, not sure. Suppose I'm not that good yet.'

Inside the cinema screen we whispered through the trailers and a giddiness hopped around inside me. Maybe in a couple of weeks I could tell her what colour her aura really was. Pretend I'd read up on it. Maybe she'd even want to come back to the shop and ask more about the crystals. But when the film started and Emily stopped talking, I ended up looking down in front of us at the couples peppered around, holding hands, resting heads on shoulders, knees crossed in towards one another. I glanced at Emily, realising we must look like two bookends holding up the giant popcorn bag she'd propped between us. Then, creeping in after five minutes, Nick appeared, holding hands with a girl I didn't recognise. His hair had grown even longer and he looked taller and skinnier. They snuck into a pair of seats in the front row and he pulled her in with his arm, morphing into another one of the random couples around us. I'm not sure he'd have recognised me even if I'd waved.

I don't remember much about the film except that I thought the sisters in it looked a bit like Emily and the sapped colours in some of the scenes made me feel sick. I focused more on the popcorn, reaching into the bag after she had taken a handful, wondering if she cared as much as I did about accidentally touching her hand.

Afterwards, we waited outside as it drizzled.

'My dad'll be here any minute if you want to head off for your bus?'

'Don't mind,' I shrugged.

I hadn't thought of Emily as being someone who'd be picked up by a dad. Even though she was younger than me she seemed too mature for that – leather jacket, lipstick, ear piercings. A lift home from a dad made her a regular teenager.

'Did you like the film? You've read the book, haven't you?'

'Yeah.'

'Of course you have.' She nudged me and I watched her rippling smile in the reflection of a puddle.

A few seconds later, a wheel pulled up, spraying my shoes. Emily yanked me back by the elbow.

'Woah. Wake up, bookworm. Don't want to ruin those cords.'

Looking up, a man in the driver's seat nodded at me with a tight smile. Emily leaned forward and opened the passenger door.

'My dad can probably give you a lift home, by the way.' Her eyes flitted up to the rain.

'Mm-mm.' I shook my head. 'I like getting the bus.' Possibly my weirdest lie yet.

'Ookaay then… See you at school next week probably. Or maybe even your book shop if the urge to read takes over again.'

She'd let go of my arms and brushed my hand as she stepped forward and into the car. Her skin was soft and much warmer than mine. Her dad was still looking at me, and I smiled, giving a quick wave and stepping backwards. They both waved in return through the glass and drove off, the rain spitting at me from the wheels again. I shoved my hands in my coat pockets and took the long route back to the bus stop, hoping I wouldn't see Nick and his new girlfriend around. My shoes were soaked through and I felt each squelch seeping into my feet but didn't care.

The blue lantern lights of the TV still flickered from the living room. I'd left my sodden shoes and socks at the door and tiptoed towards the stairs, hearing Dad muttering as I passed. The creaking floorboard I trod on cut him off. Silence.

'Nathan, son. Come in here.'

My mum's voice sounded eggshell thin. I pushed the door open to find them both still on their own separate couches in the same spots where I'd left them hours ago. The TV was muted and they hadn't turned any lamps on, as if they hadn't realised it had become dark outside. My mum patted the cushion beside her, beckoning me to sit like I was the cat. I supposed ten o'clock on a Friday night after ignoring it all week was *obviously* the best time to talk about my antics at school. Dad leaned forward, hands clasped, watching my mum, as if she'd missed her lines in their rehearsed conversation.

'Need to talk to you, Nathan.' A flutter behind the eggshell.

I plunged onto the couch, flicking a morsel of sticky popcorn from my cords.

'I'm not going to say anything else to Mr. Young–'

'–It's not about that, pal,' Dad cut in.

The UCAS application then. I sighed, clenching my eyes.

'Well… I just don't think I want to go to Uni. Not yet anyway. I've got other–'

'–It might be just as well you haven't applied, Nathan.' Mum interrupted this time. Something touched my side. I jerked away. Mum pulled her fingers back. The TV's faint glow reflected off her eyes. They were glistening. Too shiny. Frost crept over me, spreading from my ribs where she'd touched me. I turned to Dad. His legs jittered, bouncing his elbows over and over and he stared at the carpet in front of my feet. The shiver snuck up my neck and down inside to my stomach.

'I think you know that we've been struggling with money for a while. Mum's hours have been cut back and the video shop's not exactly raking it in. Mum's been trying with the antiques and that, but–'

'–That's why Aunt Brenda and Uncle Frank were here.' Mum took over again but I kept watching Dad. His eyes were still fixed on the floor. 'They offered to help us out a bit, but that's not going to do much long-term. Jack wasn't meant to say anything to you. Or even know anything. I could've killed Brenda. Bloody typical, I told her not to mention it…'

She wittered on behind me but I couldn't hear anything else. Dad's legs stopped bouncing. He looked at me.

'We've had to make a decision. We've been talking about it for a while now.'

My solar plexus caved in.

'We're selling the house, son. We're going to move… to England.'

Fuzzy ringing whistled through my head. A noise whimpered out of my throat. I don't know who spoke next. Her voice said things. His voice said things. I didn't know which was which. One of them was explaining why it would be easier for us. Someone mentioned a job. Brenda and Frank's names again. Nottingham. Jack. School. Uni. Money. City. Friends. Girls. Boys. Freya was suddenly there, rubbing against my leg, yowling.

'But I was just out with Emily.' My mouth was heavy, my throat pulsing. 'I asked her out.' I sobbed the last part then pulled myself upright, thrusting my hand to shove tears away.

'I'm glad, son. But…' My mum, I think.

'When?' The scream in my head whispered out.

Something about an estate agent. Already been. Photographs. Shrill ringing cut through their words.

The marshmallow floor sank beneath my numb legs as I stood. Stumbling over the cat I forced my way out and staggered upstairs to my room.

My head crashed onto the bed and the moonstone inside the pillowcase jabbed at my temple. I threw the pillow across the room into the bookshelf, the huge amethyst plunging to the floor. Cold wind whimpered through the open window and I remembered granddad's voice months ago. He'd been contacting me back then, warning us about money. And I'd taken too long to understand. Too long to tell even when I did understand.

My fault.

The wind sucked Iris and the circle out into the night. I woke up later in pitch black, the side of my face soaking in a cold damp blotch.

31

This time when I didn't go to school my parents knew about it. They didn't stop me, though. Didn't shout me down from the loft or clamber up the ladders to comfort me or issue warnings about the terrible punishments that awaited. Maybe they thought leaving me alone was best, like I was still a baby and had finally gone to sleep after hours of screaming. Or maybe they'd just figured out that missing a few days wasn't going to make one bit of difference to what it was now clear would be pitiful exam results. They knew from my reports that I'd already thrown the year away. No point in a salvage mission.

My stomach had stopped rumbling by last night. Folded inside the sleeping blanket I didn't feel hunger anymore, just an ache that food wouldn't fix. I'd wobbled down to the kitchen a few times when my parents were out of the house, but only for water and a handful of crackers. I imagined everything else tasting like puke.

That Wednesday night I walked out of the house. They could believe I was going to my book group or not. The For Sale signpost defied my protest, a soldier standing guard, blind to me. I trailed the streets peering around with different eyes. I noticed the colour of each house door, darker than before, and the identical shapes of the roofs. I heard the river ripple louder from under the bridge. I smelled the wet reeks of different plants as I walked past each prissy garden. On Dyrne Street The Book Cover looked smaller. I stopped outside, looking up at the black sign, paint flaking off along the bottom. I'd never spotted that before.

Then it bobbed by me as I kept walking. Its magnetic pull was switched off tonight. It was too early for the circle anyway. Instead, I trudged forward under grey drizzle that spat at me. At the end of Dyrne Street, before the bridge, I swivelled into the path to St. Germaine's, crunching gravel under my feet. A sudden bluster of wind shoved me towards the green doors but they were locked. I thought churches were always supposed to be open for people to come and pray or worship or light candles. Or hide from their parents. Even Germaine's lofty statue looked off in a blank gaze at some spot behind me, her open hands useless, almost shrugging.

When the spit turned to torpedo rain I yanked my mum's umbrella I'd brought from inside my coat and pulled the black sleeve off. Bright pink with white polka dots. Fucking great. I jogged around to the back of the building, out of view of the main road and anyone who might walk by, and slid down the rough stone wall, nestling myself in the pebbles.

I muttered prayers through gritted teeth. Not to 'God' or 'divine spirit' or my peacock or Granddad. Just to whoever, whatever was out there and listening. Prayer could change the future, *had* to change the future. The power of positive thought, like Iris had told me. Send my wishes beaming out into the universe and watch them manifest. It would work with faith. We wouldn't move to England. I wouldn't lose Iris. I'd stay in the circle. Emily would be my girlfriend and they'd all see I was normal.

I let the umbrella fall to the side and wished the rain would cleanse my aura, make me purer so the thoughts would emanate from me. But maybe it would just wash them away, trickling into the river. Maybe the universe had already given me its verdict.

The cold didn't feel cold after a while and I thought about how long I could stay here. Hours? Days? A year? What would the priest say if he found me? 'Come inside,' at least, I hoped.

When the time for the circle to begin had come and gone I unfolded myself. I had to press myself against the wall while everything blacked out in front of my eyes for a minute and my head felt like it had been turned inside out. Once I was steady I closed the umbrella and abandoned my new prayer spot. On Dyrne Street nothing had changed. Puddles rippled and every dripping eave looked as miserable as the next. I shoved my mum's umbrella in a bin.

The door of The Book Cover jingled as I pulled it open.

'Come on, love. Was about to shut you out!' Iris beckoned me in and clinked the lock behind me. The sounds of the others echoed down from upstairs.

'Jesus, you're soaking! Don't you have an umbrella?' I shook my head and she reached behind the curtain to grab a tea towel. 'Here, use this. The towel's just washed, promise!'

'Thanks.' I rubbed it through my hair for a few seconds before limply handing it back.

'Not like you to be the last one here.' Iris held the tea towel and searched my face. Or maybe my aura. 'Nearly thought you weren't comin'… is everythin' OK?'

I could have told her then. But for now I could pretend everything was still the same, could shield myself in these walls. Telling Iris would make it real. I said nothing. Just shook more dripping rain from my fringe and smiled as best I could before scuffing my way up the stairs to the candlelit room and my waiting chair in its usual glowing spot. As I slid my sodden jacket off Marcy gave me a big grin and I forced the smile even harder, focusing on her leaf-patterned skirt and matching green tights. She looked like Peter Pan in drag.

Iris settled beside me, making a joke I didn't hear. The others laughed and I faked a cough. Then the same opening as every week – the call to divine spirit, asking for communication and for us to be protected. Did she even have to think about it or were they just memorised lines by this point?

'We're goin' to start with a meditation tonight. A spirit has been with me all day and I want us to connect with them. I feel they've been waitin' for us all to be here.'

I looked over to Katrina sitting opposite me, expecting a wave or smile after we'd met at the cinema. She just glanced between Iris and her clasped hands.

'Find a comfortable position in your chair with both feet firmly on the ground and your palms facing upward to connect with spirit through the chakra points in your hands. When you're ready close your eyes.'

I bowed my head, sunk into the seat and squinted at the dusty pink carpet. Five rhythms of soft breathing puffed around the circle.

But I didn't want to connect with spirit.

Didn't want to know there was a reason for my parents moving me to another country. Didn't want to know the lesson in it for my soul. Closing my eyes and listening to spirit meant accepting it. I couldn't though. I wanted to feel the anger vibrating in my head and the sadness lolling in my chest and to keep seeing everything through a darker lens. I gripped onto it all and closed my eyes for show while Iris talked about breathing and using our third eye.

Back at home, the pile of newspapers underneath my bed waited for me. I'd folded over the corners of all the pages I'd need: flat rentals, jobs in Perth, even the Citizens Advice Bureau phone number – surely at seventeen my parents couldn't force me to move against my will? And then the non-existent UCAS application floated through my brain, taunting me: if I'd have filled out the bloody thing it could have saved me. Couldn't move to England if I'd been given a place at a Scottish university, could I? Too fucking late.

Straining to peep without making it obvious, I looked towards Iris. Her head was dipped, eyes closed. Safe. She didn't know I was looking. I watched her, slumped in the chair like the others, oblivious. I'd seen pictures like this in a book. Old portrait photographs they used to take of people who had died, dressed in their best clothes, their bodies posed in place.

Was spirit making me think of that? Or just me, on my own?

And why hadn't spirit prepared me for what was happening?

I remembered Iris telling me after Brenda and Frank went home that Mum and Dad had 'something' to tell me. But why hadn't spirit shown her all of it?

Maybe they had. And she'd kept it from me.

In the first reading she'd ever given me – with the cards, before the circle – she'd told me that travel was a big part of my future. I thought she'd meant a holiday somewhere. Or that I'd have some glamorous job when I was older, whizzing around the world. I didn't think it meant this. Maybe she'd misread the cards. That was when The Hermit had jumped out of the pile for me. Maybe that was my omen: that I'd be sequestered forever. An eternal loner, moving from place to place. Mum and Dad should buy me a lantern and a robe.

'Allow your heart chakra to open wider.' Iris was almost slurring, as if she was talking to us in her sleep. 'Envision green energy becoming brighter and beaming from your chest. Send love to the spirit who is with us tonight. Give him thanks for his presence.'

I tilted my head and relaxed my clenched eyes a little more. Sadie smiled on the other end of the circle, leaning back in her chair, drunk on Iris's words. I remembered her trooping along the church aisle, contented, until she saw me, at least. Now, watching her happy face lit by the candles, I realised this was just another kind of church for her, listening to different forms of prayer in a circle instead of a pew, sipping a new wine.

'And when you're ready, slowly open your eyes and return to the room.'

I pretended to yawn, stretching my legs out.

'Well, that was a strong presence tonight, wasn't it? Did you feel that?'

'Mmm.' I felt Marcy nodding beside me and heard the urgent agreements from all the others.

'Yeah,' I murmured at the tail-end of the chorus.

'Anyone feel like this was someone they know who's passed over?' A pause. 'Because I feel that I know.'

'I definitely felt a strong male presence, Iris,' said Marcy.

'Aye, that's what I was getting.' Katrina leaned forward, hand on her chest, nodding.

'Sadie?' Iris asked.

'Yes, yes, absolutely a male figure I tho–*felt*.' I noticed her fidget with a loose thread on her skirt. 'A younger gentleman, maybe…'

'That's right,' Iris urged. 'Not an old man. Nathan, what about you? What were you feelin' from the spirit? Or did you hear anythin'? His voice? A name?'

Fuck.

I thought she'd felt the change in my energy, known I hadn't disconnected from my physical senses tonight. Hadn't she spotted me with my eyes open at the beginning? I inhaled, hoping a sharp breath would bring the right words to say. But Patrick saved me.

'I… I felt something different.'

All heads turned to him. He reminded me of myself: never expected to say much but occasionally speaking up in classes to everyone's surprise.

'I felt… well, I sort of felt it was a female presence. I didn't find it to be that strong to be honest. Felt a bit softer. A kind of… sadness, I thought.'

A pin prick jabbed at my neck.

'Hm, that's interestin', Patrick. You might have been sensin' a different spirit. Someone else here for you. Did you recognise the energy?'

'… Not really, no. Just that it was sort of feminine. And I could see cool colours… like purple and that.'

'Right… right. You know, sometimes we just… feel spirit in different ways, dependin' on who the person is. I might feel a spirit one way because of my aura and my energy, and another medium might feel that spirit differently if their own aura is different to mine. So you and I might interpret the same spirit differently. Do you see what I mean?'

I'd never heard this theory from Iris before, but there were more slow noises of agreement from the women.

'And ladies, what did you feel the young man was here for? Did he know one of us?'

Patrick settled back into his chair.

'I felt like he was very familiar,' Sadie offered. 'Maybe someone I knew.'

'That's funny, I sensed it was somebody *you* knew, Iris. Maybe a nephew or a friend from years ago.' Katrina had her head tilted towards Iris. I thought she was just guessing about the old friend part.

'I felt somet'in' quite different.' Marcy had leaned forward, darting glances between the three other women. 'I was feelin' an angelic presence, or a spirit guide.'

I watched Iris watching her. A smile crept onto her mouth. But it wasn't happy. More like she had figured something out but wanted to keep it secret.

'Maybe it was Dancin' Feather?' Marcy asked.

Iris didn't respond and didn't look to me for my thoughts again.

For the rest of the hour she talked to us about a new set of angelic cards she'd started using in her private readings. She passed them around the circle, everyone sifting through them with care while Iris explained how she used them. Marcy passed the little cardboard box to me. I pulled out the pile of glossy cards and flicked through them. All of the images looked like paintings from churches – saintly beings with long hair and white robes, light beaming from them. Calming words were scrolled across the bottom of each one: Nature, Wisdom, Healing, Patience, Children. Not like the tarot, then. No Hanged Man or Devil or Hermit.

I pushed the cards back in the box and turned it over. On the back was a picture of the woman who'd created them. She'd been photographed leaning against a tree with her head tilted, smiling. Her maroon blouse matched her short, dyed hair.

Even though the hour for the circle was over, Iris didn't close with a prayer. No one stood to grab a coat or rush off with a 'need to get home…' explanation. They'd all pulled their chairs in closer, the circle tightening, swarming around Iris for a reading from the cards. I studied them one by one, staring at each of their faces while they smiled and gasped. I noticed something new about each of them I'd never spotted before: Katrina's eyes weren't blue or green, but somewhere in between; Sadie didn't wear any makeup but her cheeks were always pink; Patrick's right eye twitched most of the time, except when he laughed; and Marcy had one cracked tooth that you could see when she was grinning. I stored them all away like new stones in my pockets that I'd need again one day.

My own secret stone wasn't in my pocket anymore. It was lodged in my throat, pressing my breath and forcing tears that threatened to run. And if I gave in and let the tears dribble and coughed the stone out, the secrets would gush out after it. That we were moving to England. That I would have to leave all this. That I wouldn't see them anymore and wouldn't be part of the circle. That my prayers and my thoughts and my wishes for the universe were nothing.

And the other secret I couldn't even tell myself.

With a mumble I gripped my coat and escaped to the tiny toilet downstairs, squeezing the door closed behind me. The tears came and I rubbed them away with papery toilet roll without looking in the little oval mirror.

Knowing I had to get out, I peeled the door open again and brushed the curtain aside, heading for the door. But warm fingers wrapped around my elbow before I reached it.

'I'll talk to you soon, love.' Iris's eyes glinted and she leaned towards me. 'That spirit was here for you.'

32

I'd started waiting an extra minute outside the front door when I arrived home from school – later than usual after wandering around for as long as possible. Today I examined the patterns in the frosted glass door. It was supposed to look like maple leaves all overlapping one another. I'd never noticed that before. A blurry shadow passed somewhere on the other side. They'd see me standing here. I pushed the handle and opened.

The antiseptic smell was back. The one I'd smelled last year. The one Iris had told me was a sign that spirit was present. Purple flames reignited in my solar plexus. I'd missed their warmth. Granddad again? Had he died in a hospital surrounded by these smells? Was this his way of showing me he was still watching over us? Maybe this was part of the new message Iris had for me. My mum drifted about in the kitchen.

'Mum?'

She appeared in the doorway, pushing her hair back then folding her arms. It was the first word I'd spoken to her since the news. Dad had tried to talk to me again in my room once but I hadn't answered.

'What is it, son?'

Maybe Granddad could keep us here if she knew he was in this house. It was time to open his lost letter.

'Do you smell that?' My voice was thin, almost a whisper. 'The hospital smell?'

She took a step forward and unfolded her arms, lifting her chin.

'Mm.'

'Do you know what that is? … It's from–'

'–the vet. It's Freya.'

She looked back with blank eyes. The ticking from the hall clock chipped into my head.

'What do you mean?'

'I mean it's the smell of the vet like every other time. I took Freya for her vaccinations earlier. She always comes back with that sort of medical smell. It's the flea stuff they put on her neck. You must have noticed it before.'

The purple flame snuffed out. Freya had padded out from somewhere and rubbed against my leg, meowing, a little wet patch of fur on the back of her head.

'I'm making dinner. I think you should sit down here with us tonight. Someone's coming to view the house tomorrow. Need you to help us start tidying.'

The door rattled behind me and its handle jabbed into my back, shoving me forward as I yelped.

'Sorry, pal.' Dad bustled in with carrier bags in each hand, kicking the door closed behind us and looking between us both. 'You finally talking about this?'

I assumed he was asking her but she didn't answer. I shook my head a little.

'Take it she's been to the vet then?' he asked, as Freya followed him into the kitchen.

The pavement scraped and blurred under my feet like a treadmill. I nearly barged into an old lady, only noticing her when she was inches from me. I swerved away onto the empty road, staving my ankle but marching ahead. I didn't know what I'd do when I reached my natural destination. Tell Iris that the medical smell wasn't a spirit and wait for a better explanation that would ease me? Or tell her that her theory was bullshit? Maybe I didn't need her to speak at all; just being in The Book Cover might recharge me. But as I stepped through the door any healing energy the place might have had stopped dead like a power cut.

Crystofer. He stood beside the counter, talking to Iris, with a backpack hung over his bony shoulders and a new, even more ridiculous haircut, all shaved up the sides with a curly mop on top like he was in a music video from the 80s. He saw me before Iris did, smiling as if we knew each other well.

'Hiya, love!' Iris called. 'You never said your pal knew me.'

'My pal?'

'Aye, Crystofer! I gave his mum a readin' a wee while ago. Didn't realise you were at school together.'

'… Well…'

'I obviously already knew you worked here,' Crystofer piped up, 'but then Emily told me about your group with Iris and I knew her name was familiar. I asked my mum about who she'd had her reading with and then, you know, I figured out all the connections.' This was the most Crystofer had ever spoken to me without Gillian or Emily there.

'Spirit!' Iris chimed in, as if that one word was an explanation in itself.

'So… are you wanting to join the circle or something?' I asked.

Crystofer opened his mouth, looking between Iris and me. 'Don't be daft, love. You're gettin' ahead of yourself.

Crystofer's just been askin' about bookin' a readin' himself.'

'You can just phone up and do that.'

We stood in a triangle: Iris leaning on the counter with both hands; Crystofer fidgeting with the straps on his bag; and me blank and limp, still in the doorway.'

'Aye… well… sometimes it's nicer to come in in person. And anyway, he's your pal!'

I clenched my teeth. But Crystofer stared down at his feet, rubbing one heel into the carpet. Some invisible cover over me melted away.

'Yeah, I suppose. So… Emily says you're interested in spirit and readings… and things.'

'Totally. I mean, I already was, but after my mum's reading with Iris, we both just want to know even more.'

We both?

I pictured him, sharing a couch with a woman in rhinestoned jeans and a halter neck top, younger than my mum, legs curled up, pedicured toes touching his, sipping coffee and gossiping. It was a faraway image out of a film or a TV programme. With subtitles.

'Aye, spirit is amazin'. The messages they come through with… Sometimes it's through readin's that we just open up to a whole new level of awareness. Nathan knows all about it.'

'Do you?' Crystofer was staring at me and I noticed how green his eyes were for the first time. Like little emeralds.

'Sort of, yeah.'

'Ach, he's bein' modest. Nathan's clairvoyant, amongst other things.'

'Oh my God. Like he can see ghosts? I didn't think folk our age could do that!'

And I can smell ghosts that aren't ghosts.

'Of course they can. Do *you* ever experience strange things, Crystofer?' Iris asked. 'Hear sounds that don't make sense? Noises in an empty house? Even whispers when no one's around?'

Her voice had softened into breathy hypnosis. I squinted at her through a distorted camera lens. Déjà vu was wrapping around me like someone's familiar, overpowering perfume. Crystofer stood with his veiny hands clasped in front of his chest, one foot crossed over the other, head tilted.

'I'll make some tea,' I said. It would still be a while until either of my parents realised I'd left the house. Mum wouldn't have made dinner just yet. I slipped past Iris and Crystofer.

'One for me please, love.'

Behind the curtain, by the sink, I stared at the kettle gurgling and heard Iris murmuring through the wall – a repeat episode of her sitcom I'd already seen and didn't need to watch again.

'Energies... from spirit... lessons... the cards... passed over...'

The kettle clicked but I didn't move.

I didn't want to hear her.

Didn't want a recap of her explanations of how spirit was always guiding us, sending us messages. And fake smells. I still didn't understand why I hadn't been given messages about my parents' decision to move me to another country. Where had my warnings about *that* been? And why was it even happening in the first place? There must be a lesson in all this, I knew. Maybe starting life over in Drichton hadn't worked and I had to do it all over again, move somewhere else, force myself to make friends and adapt. Maybe this was why I hadn't filled in those UCAS forms for uni. Maybe my soul knew I wouldn't be in Scotland for much longer. Or maybe I'd learned what I needed from Iris and the circle. Was it time to start developing my gifts on my own? Giving readings? Really becoming a medium myself? Iris hadn't been happy when Melissa had left to do the same thing.

I sighed and other sounds filled the air around me again: Crystofer rambling, a car zooming by outside, my own hand tapping a teaspoon on the counter.

'Nathan, are you away to China for that tea?' Normal voice again.

I poured three cups, plonked them on a tray we used after the circle sometimes and grabbed a carton of milk from the fridge. I edged out from behind the curtain and rested the tray on the counter.

'Thanks,' said Crystofer. 'Glad you didn't put milk in mine, I just like black tea.'

'Hm, that's quite unusual. Most young folk don't even drink tea. See, Nathan's intuitive. He senses little things like that from people.'

Crystofer looked to me, his mouth open in a smile of shock. I shrugged back, thinking I was capable of a little more than just sensing how people take their tea. And anyway, my intuition wasn't the reason I hadn't bothered pouring his milk. I just hadn't brought it through yet. As I watched them sip from their cups the aroma of déjà vu stiffened the air again. This is how it had been when Iris first told me about what she did and what the spirit in my room last year was. We'd sat together, drinking from steaming mugs and munching biscuits, Iris reciting her wonders, me gulping them down with the tea.

'In fact, Nathan, that spirit's still lingering here. Do you remember?'

The déjà vu scent vanished and ice-cold wind rushed at me.

'The spirit?'

'Aye. From the circle last week. The one everyone was sensin' in our meditation. I told you it was for you but you were zippin' away that night. I've been feelin' him here ever since. And he pressed on my crown chakra as soon as you walked in. Do you know who it is?'

Granddad again?

Was it ever Granddad at all?

'I... well... I think...'

'Remember – feel it, don't think it.'

All I felt was Crystofer's gaze but somehow I didn't care as much, like he'd floated away as an audience member in a dark theatre and it was only Iris and me on the stage under a bright white spotlight.

'... Is it Granddad? Neil?'

'No. Don't just guess.'

I felt the blush bubbling up through my neck. But looking to her, she didn't seem to care I was getting it wrong. I doubted her grin could widen any further. She knew. She knew I was moving and was more happy she'd sensed it from spirit than she was sad that I'd be leaving.

'You can sense it in other ways. What's your clairsentience tellin' you? What's your third eye seein'?'

I swallowed, tasting sour stickiness. The only things my senses were communicating were nausea and blood pumping too fast and too loudly. Iris urged me on with coaxing eyes.

'It's not a man. Not a grown man, like granddad.'

'Right…'

'It's someone shorter, younger… A teenager?'

She clapped her hands together and leaned forward, a blue, plastic-looking crystal dangling from a silvery pendant. I hadn't seen this one before.

'That's it. There's a boy here, Nathan. He's showing me numbers… seventeen. Same age as you. There's a close connection. This is someone you knew. Is this a cousin, Nathan?'

Nothing about the house. Or England.

'No.'

'Or a friend you had at school?'

'No.'

'Someone you knew who was your age who passed over? Who is this spirit, Nathan?'

No answer. I didn't want to speak anymore.

'Oh my god,' Crystofer whimpered from his distant, dark spot. 'Nathan, isn't it…? Don't you think it must be…?'

Does he know? Don't say anything.

'Nathan's brother.'

Furrowed eyebrows.

'Brother?'

Tilted head. Crystofer filled the static air, a sudden spotlight on him too. Red.

'… Nathan had a twin. He… died. When they were at primary school.'

Iris's eyes gouging me.

Stop.

'And Emily said it's your birthday next month, Nathan. Maybe that's why he's around you.'

'Emily,' I croaked. 'Does Emily know about *this*?'

'I… don't know. No. Don't think so. I've never spoken to her about it anyway.' His voice had shrunken too.

'Oh… Nathan.' Iris sat back, unclasped her hands. 'You've never ever mentioned–'

'–Who told you?'

'It… it was just someone in your year at school. I don't even remember who. Actually, I think a couple of people have mentioned it…'

'A couple of people?' I heard myself taper off to a whisper, a distant recording of someone else speaking. 'Why did they…?'

Their stares burned my skin like the fire in my dream. The distorted camera lens rested in place again and they shrank away from me. Tea spilled from my cup, dribbling onto my shoe. Iris was talking again, fluttering.

'He's here, Nathan. Your brother is here today. He must have been tryin' to communicate with you for so long since passin' over. Aye, I can see him now. Oh my God, an identical twin? No wonder you're so sensitive to spirit. You have such a strong connection on the other side.'

I touched the wall to stop the floor from zooming towards me.

'I want to go now.'

Iris stood from the stool and said something else I didn't hear.

Somehow I had my coat hooked over my arm and was pacing back down Dyrne Street, the whistling laser in my head dissipating with every step away from The Book Cover. I looked down at my hand, counted my fingers, squeezed my eyes shut, opened them, and then looked again. Still five. I wasn't dreaming.

33

In the twilight I swallowed five of my mum's sleeping tablets instead of the one you're supposed to take. Just herbal things that probably didn't even work; not anything as exciting as a real overdose. While the sky darkened, I stared into a quartz orb, waiting for an image to materialise. Scrying, Marcy had called it. I'd thought it sounded painful. Now I knew it was just boring. I abandoned the crystal ball, letting it roll away and clunk into an old framed family photograph.

With the unzipped sleeping bag draped over my shoulders, I pushed down on the cobweb-covered bar of the skylight and shoved it open above me. Cold air blew at my face and I folded my arms on the mossy slate, resting my chin on them. The river rippled and a magpie hopped along the far edge of the roof, pecking and tapping at something I couldn't see.

I looked ahead into the little lit up window in the side of our next-door neighbours' house. An older couple lived there and I saw them climbing the stairs, looking like they were laughing and talking to each other. On the wall beyond them a photograph was hung in a white frame, although it was too far away to make out the details. I guessed it was a picture of them on holiday or of their two children when they were young. The light in their house cut out as I was squinting to see.

Then I watched the river, wondering what direction it was gurgling in. North or South? Which way to the sea? Could I follow the water there? At this time of year it wasn't easy to spot many stars until after eleven, but I craned my neck back trying to see how far into space my eyes could reach. Which way was it to spirit? I thought about climbing out onto the roof and lying on my back to stare at the sky, but maybe the tablets would kick in and I'd fall asleep out there. I'd end up rolling off the edge and plummeting into the garden.

Even with the sleeping bag around me my hands had started shivering so I ducked back inside, yanking the skylight shut behind me. I lay down and pulled the zip all the way up to my neck before cradling my knees into my chest and closing my eyes.

I had only told three people at school about the twin thing.

But why? Mum and Dad had said high school and Ballahan and Drichton were a new start for me. For us. Why couldn't I have just fucking listened? Kept my mouth shut, or just told everyone I was an only child. Maybe if I'd had that fucking secret stone back then…

Was that why Gillian and Stacey and Nick were ever friends with me? Did they feel sorry for me? Invite the new dead twin boy to the cinema, do a good deed. And Emily? The same? But Crystofer said she didn't know. She can't know. Can't be told this.

I thought about him until the room sank under black sand.

I was in St. Germaine's at night. Moonlight glazed the windows coating everything inside with cold, shiny velvet. I kneeled on the padded bench in the back row with my hands clasped and shaking as if they were being crushed together in a vice.

'Please make it go away. Please please please please please…'
My sibilant voice echoed round the empty chamber

amplifying itself and reverberating through my head.

The bench beneath me splintered and my kneecaps cracked into the tiled floor, lightning shattering through my body. And I kept praying and begging. Eventually the moonlight dimmed to nothing and I was blind.

But then yellow light was back, glowing from behind me. My knees pressed into the sleeping bag, my elbows on a pile of books. Hands rested on my shoulders and squeezed me.

'Come on. Back to sleep.'

I made the sign of the cross with a flopping hand. Mum held my shoulders and I crumpled back onto my side.

'Pls mk g-way. Pls ps ps ps s s s.'

She wiped my wet face. The floor creaked under me and my body shifted. Footsteps back down the ladder. Darkness again.

34

They let me sleep up there for another two nights and even when I came back down to my own bed it was because my back ached so much. In the morning, cutlery and crockery clinks filled the quiet over cereal. It was the first breakfast I'd had with them in weeks. First breakfast I'd *eaten* in weeks. But I knew stewing in my room wasn't helping come up with any new ideas about how to change their minds about the move. I'd have to interact with them, hear more about their plan, figure out an angle I could use for as long as I could stand it.

They hadn't asked me about my nightmare or why I'd been sleeping in the loft. I wondered if it was their guilt that was letting me do what I wanted without question. Or maybe they'd let me stay up there because they knew, somehow, that something had happened. That the past had come bubbling up to the surface.

'... Frank's looking into getting your dad a job at his place. Been speaking to his boss...' Was that who Frank was passing Dad's number on to? 'And Brenda's keeping an eye out for me at the shopping centre. She knows most of the other managers...'

'... So you'd be able to get to know Jack better. It won't be like when he visited – you hadn't seen him for about five years. But you'll get to spend a lot more time together...'

'... This way you can think more about university or college... or whatever. Don't need to make a decision right now...'

'… and Mum'll be nearer the rest of her family too. I don't really have anyone left up here…'

I knew I should be listening for clues. Investigating. Find the loose thread I could pull that would unravel everything they'd planned. But I couldn't grab hold of any strand they started. Their words slipped free each time and my mind shifted to some other thought: the soggy flakes swimming in my bowl; the vet smell that wasn't a spirit; what Crystofer had told Iris.

'Nathan? You listening?' asked Dad.

'Mm. Yeah.' I swirled the cereal with my spoon again.

'You know we'd stay here if we could. But it's all just become unmanageable. Hey, don't you want to get out of Drichton anyway? Not much here for you.'

I stopped swirling. Had he been in my room? Found the Observer folded open at the flat rentals page? Even if he had, it felt stupid now. He'd have laughed at how pathetic it was. As if I could afford to move out on my own, or even figure out how. Citizen's Advice would hang up, laughing, before I could even finish explaining.

'What if you don't sell the house? Can't go anywhere until then, can we?'

Dad sighed, clattering his knife and fork onto the plate.

'We live in Drichton, Nathan. Have you seen this place in the summer? It's a highly desirable location.' He was talking like an estate agent. 'Houses always sell quickly here. And we already have this viewing this afternoon.'

'Only a viewing. They might just be curious. Katrina said houses around here *aren't* selling that fast anymore.'

'Who's Katrina?'

'… someone at school.'

'Look, son.' Mum stood. 'It's going to be sooner rather than later. Need to get used to the idea. What did your friends say?'

The black piece of onyx in my pocket throbbed and I pictured Iris's little label for it in the shop reminding me of its properties: 'a steadfast stone that promotes secrecy'.

'Dunno. Just asked why we're moving and when and stuff.'

She watched me for a few seconds then lifted my half-finished bowl and took it to the sink. Dad leaned on the table with his elbows, hands clasped, still chewing toast. He spoke again, more softly, without looking at me.

'Be good for you to find other lads to spend time with. Leave all these girls at school behind, eh?'

His eyes flicked over to my mum in complicity, like they'd discussed this together and drawn straws to decide who should say it to me. I wanted to yank the straws back from both of them.

'Can Emily come over for dinner one night this week?' I stared at the ceramic cat saltshaker. 'She's the girl I'm... I'm going out with.'

Louder clinking at the sink before Mum plopped back down in her seat across from me.

'If you like.'

I heaved out the breath I'd been holding. Dad watched me.

'Don't get too attached,' he said.

At school, I glided from classroom to classroom with my head tucked down, avoiding the eyes of everyone who might be inspecting me, feeling sorry for the boy whose twin had died. If Crystofer had heard about it, the story might have infiltrated every classroom and canteen table by now. At least they still didn't know I was the boy whose parents were moving him to England. I'd tidied myself behind a desk in the reference corner of the library at lunchtime, my back to the door. By the end of the day, I'd managed to avoid talking to anyone except Emily. She spotted me at the end of an afternoon assembly.

'Bookworm!'

I spun around, scanning the area for any signs of Crystofer, or anyone else I knew.

'Still OK for dinner some night?'

'Mm.'

'Figured it makes sense if I just come home with you on the bus. Told my dad he can pick me up from yours after. That OK?'

I nodded quickly.

'Or… we can forget it if you've, you know, changed your mind or whatever.'

'No!' I leapt towards her. 'I still want you to come. Please. Tomorrow.'

'Yeah, alright, steady on!'

'Sorry.'

She watched me lurch around for a moment before smiling, patting me on the arm and walking off.

35

When the young couple came to visit the house that afternoon I hurried to the river, avoiding them like Freya hiding under the bed when the hoover is on. Took my schoolbag with me, of course – my mum didn't want it lying around cluttering up the newly-minimalised décor. My mind stretched and wound with the rushing water into the future, seeing the sign in the front garden for months, day after day, greying in the rain and sun, even tipping over a little, pathetically lopsided. After I'd traipsed back home, I'd found out the visitors had only stayed for five minutes. I'd already heard Mum talking about lowering the price. Dad shouted and slammed doors. Their echo sounded different than usual, aimed at someone else.

I still kept my head lowered as I stepped onto the bus with Emily the next afternoon. I scuttled my way to my usual spot and she followed, sitting beside me on the shredded red tartan seat, probably horrified at the stale bus stench everyone else had grown used to over the past six years. I anticipated hootings and lunatic shouts from Jonnie and his sidekicks at the back, losing their minds over the idea of me taking a girl home. Luckily, Hannah had plopped into the seat in front of us and she and Emily chattered together for the entire journey to Drichton. The boys would assume Emily was going home with Hannah rather than me and I was left to press my forehead against the window under my jacket hood and close my eyes.

After the bus dropped us off, Hannah and Jonnie scattered off in their separate directions. Emily and I plodded along Dyrne Street together and I'd avoided looking towards St. Germaine's.

'You want to nip into the shop and say hi to your boss?' she asked.

'Mm-mm. Not today.' I gripped the straps of my backpack and powered across to the other side of the road, not even peeking towards the shop and the possibility of Iris's face peering out.

When we stepped up onto the other pavement, I bashed my leg against the wing mirror of a parked car and swore. The onyx dug into my thigh and I clutched at it.

'You OK?'

'Mm. Yeah.' I let her walk forward and we turned the corner. 'Emily...'

'Nathan?' she turned around, parroting me.

We were a few steps from my front garden and the For Sale sign. 'Listen... There's something going on that I should have told you. I haven't told anyone at school. I–' my throat tightened again and I pulled at my t-shirt collar. 'We're – my parents, I mean – they're selling our house.' I swallowed more heavy lumps. 'They want to move to England.'

Emily's focused gaze flitted back and forth as if she was reading tiny writing printed on my eyeballs.

'When did you find this out?'

'Just a few days ago,' I lied.

'Oh. Well, that's... shit.'

293

'Yeah.' I chewed my lip. She kept looking at me, swaying a little from side to side.

'I thought you were going to say something else.'

My collar gripped my throat again. 'Like what?'

She kept examining me, opening her mouth and pausing.

'I… told Crystofer about your spiritual group thing. Sorry. Didn't know if it was a secret or not.'

My collar loosened. But my solar plexus was cramping. I couldn't tell if she was lying. Was that really what she wanted to say?

'… It's OK, I know. He came into the shop the other day. You've not spoken to him since then, have you? About… anything?'

'Not really, no. He didn't tell me he'd come to see you at the shop.'

'He hadn't. I mean, I just happened to spot him in there. He was talking to Iris, weirdly.'

Emily had started chuckling to herself. 'Nathan, Nathan, Nathan.' She shook her head, grinning. 'Trust me, Crystofer had come to see you.'

'Eh? How do you know?'

'Oh God, you're so oblivious.' My cheeks began sizzling. 'He's kind of, like, obsessed with you.'

'What!' I choked on the word and Emily smacked me on the back.

'I mean, not *obsessed*. But, you know, well… You know.'

'No, I don't know. Don't think I want to know… How do you know?'

'Ha! Well he did try phoning you on Christmas Day.'

The ringing in my ears didn't even happen right away.

'Christmas Day?' I muttered. 'Are you… How do you…'

'He got your number from Gillian or Stacey, I think. Wanted to wish you Happy Christmas. Kind of sweet. Said he chickened out, though.'

'Mm.' My eyes had blurred over from staring down at the stones of my driveway. Why was she telling me this? Did she think it was funny? Or that Crystofer was my friend?

Or that it might make me happy?

'So… is this your house or are we just standing here for a while?'

'Sorry.' I crunched up the driveway and Emily followed me to the front door. 'Listen, can you just… not mention Crystofer to my parents… or my spiritual group thing.'

'Sure. Although wouldn't your mum be interested? I thought she liked this kind of thing.'

'Huh?'

'You said your mum had a dream dictionary.'

'Oh. I know but…'

I didn't bother finishing. Just unlocked the door and led her inside.

I made her stay downstairs in the living room like she was in a waiting room for a job interview, while I changed from my uniform upstairs and pushed away the memory of the Christmas phone call. And Crystofer on the other end of it.

Not granddad.

I focused on Emily and wondered if she was mulling things over, and if maybe when I went back down, she'd be gone. What was the point in hanging around for a quasi-date with someone who was preparing to leave the country? Or was that even what this was? Was she just another friend? Here to tell me about a boy who was 'obsessed' with me. But as I creaked down the floorboards, I saw her perched on the couch where I'd left her. Even then I didn't invite her upstairs. Instead, I sat on the other couch, mirroring my parents' TV-watching positions. I rubbed the fabric underneath my thighs as Emily chatted and I tried to focus on every question she asked rather than the sweat trickling down my sides.

Car tires on the driveway gravel signalled their arrival. When my mum and dad bustled through the front door, I leapt up, wiping my palms on my jumper and squeezing the carpet between my toes over and over. Looking down at Emily, she rested with her hands clasped around her knees, smiling coolly. I glanced at myself in the mirror above the fireplace and realised everything was the wrong way round; I was preparing to 'meet' my own parents like they were strangers to be impressed.

I didn't move and watched their reflection as they popped their heads into the room.

'Hi, Emily. Nice to meet you. We'll get dinner on soon.'

'Thanks, Mrs. Love.'

Dad hovered behind my mum, peeking his head over her shoulder and offering an uneventful wave before disappearing.

Later, while we waited at the table, Mum peppered Emily with questions as she made dinner, thrilled to have someone new in the house. Where did she live? Who were her parents? What subjects was she studying at school? Who were her friends? Was she ready for her exams? Emily obliged with every query, smiling and talking as if conversation with my mum was ordinary.

While they talked, I imagined Iris had seen me walking past The Book Cover, ignoring her. I pictured her following us here, chasing me down to continue her impromptu dead twin reading. When I heard Freya leap down the stairs I twitched, thinking Iris had come knocking on the door. But she would've left the shop long ago to go home. The seasickness swirling through me subsided to a gentler nausea. I wouldn't be seeing her again for a couple of days, maybe even longer if I could think up an excuse to avoid the circle this week. Enough time for her to hit her head and develop amnesia?

Dad only stood listening to Emily and Mum for a few minutes with his arms folded before drifting off upstairs, but resurfaced when the meal was ready, joining the happy family to eat. During the meal the water in my glass trembled as I held it. I darted glances around the table to see if anyone was watching. But they smiled together, eating and laughing at one another's jokes. They were a happy advert on TV for a new cooking sauce or multivitamin tablet. I was a kid from a different advert. Maybe for lice shampoo or diarrhoea.

'So, are you and Nathan in any of the same classes?'

Emily looked to me as if I might answer, but I swallowed down another forkful of pasta.

'No, we mostly just know each other from, well, the book shop, I suppose. Seems to be our usual meeting place.'

'You like reading too?' Dad asked.

Every question was directed to her, none to me. They were probably worried I'd say something weird to fuck it all up. Must be nice to have Emily in the house – talkative, polite. Normal.

'It's... OK.' She made a screwed-up face and the three of them chuckled together. 'I just go into the shop with my mum or to get books for school. Nathan helped me out with *The Great Gatsby*.'

She obviously thought she was doing me a favour, throwing out fishing hooks to yank me back into the conversation. Suppose she didn't know I just wanted to observe from deep underwater.

'So,' Mum asked, 'do you go along to Nathan's book group then?'

Shit!

'Your book group?' Emily turned to me, surely seeing the red blotches creeping up my neck.

'Yeah, I'll… tell you about it later. Mum, this is really boring, Emily doesn't want to hear this.'

'Nathan,' Dad warned.

I gave up on the pasta, pushing what was left around the plate, trying to compact it together into a neat little mound to make it look like I'd eaten most of it. Dad talked to Emily about the cinema, asking me a question at some point to which I grunted a noise of agreement. He carried on; my response inconsequential.

Throughout everything, pressure gripped my head, squeezing my skull. The kitchen had become an unfamiliar stage set, wobbling around me, its thin, papery walls ready to tip over.

'Nathan, you should have introduced Emily to Jack when he was here.'

All three of them looked to me, pinning me to the chair.

'Oh, I met him one day,' Emily said. 'Briefly. I think it was on Easter Sunday. You'd all been to church.' She sipped from her glass and I felt her foot tap against mine under the table. I jerked my leg away.

'Well,' said Dad, 'probably won't see him again, I'm afraid.'

'Colin,' Mum murmured, gripping her fork. Dad looked to

me, about to speak, then closed his mouth.

'It's fine... I've told Emily we're moving.' I watched my parents after I'd said it, waiting to clock them smiling slyly at one another or maybe even shrugging with a 'Well actually, Nathan...' and revealing their change of heart.

But they both exhaled. The first long silence at the table. They continued chewing, Dad drumming his fingers on the table, my mum analysing her plate for an inordinate amount of time. No denial. No uncertainty. No change of heart. I copied her, staring at a red square on the checked tablecloth, forcing a cough to clear the thick pain from my throat.

'A fresh start for the family.' Mum finally shattered the stiff air. She sniffed and gulped. I didn't even know if she was speaking to Emily anymore, or Dad, or me.

'Yeah... my auntie had a wee girl who died,' Emily said. 'She lives in Australia now.'

Sirens blared in my ears.

Crystofer told her.

'Emily,' I croaked, shoving my chair back. 'Let's go. Upstairs. Or out.'

'Hold your horses, we've not even had pudding yet,' said Dad.

Mum turned back to Emily. 'Oh, that's awfully sad. Losing a child... it's...'

My legs pushed me up and I stood with hands jittering at my side.

Crystofer fucking told her.

'Sorry... I shouldn't have brought that up.' Emily shuffled in the chair, glancing up at me, her cheeks red.

'Och, are you still upset about it?' Mum reached forward to

touch Emily's hand.

'I'll get the plates!' I blurted, lunging forward to clatter everything together in a pile, hoping loud noises would kill their words. But Emily penetrated the din.

'No, no, it was years ago, before I was born. My mum just told me about it.'

I turned to the sink, crashing the dishes in and thrusting the tap on.

'Steady on, Nathan!' Dad shouted. But Mum and Emily were oblivious, intent on resisting every interruption. I watched their reflection in the window, water gushing into the sink below me.

'I see.' Mum tilted her head. 'So what made you bring that up?'

'Well... I just...'

'Emily.' I wanted to yell but it fell out as a murmur.

'... I heard about Nathan's brother,' said Emily.

My hands slid into the food-smeared plates.

'Eh?' Dad's ghost reflection sat up in his chair.

I closed my eyes to the rest and felt static shivering off every object in the room. The lightning was coming. Which one of them would strike?

'Nathan doesn't have a brother.' Mum's voice had changed.

'Sorry, I mean... his brother who... passed away.' Emily sounded muffled, as if she was covering her mouth or had her face tilted into her hands.

'Passed away?' Dad again. His chair screeched on the lino. He must have stood up. 'Nathan!'

My hands trembled. My jaw juddered.

'Is that what he told you?'

'No. I just… heard it… at school.'

Sandpaper breath grated my lungs.

'Emily, Nathan has *never* had a brother.'

Drip. Drip. Drip.

I opened my eyes to the water dribbling over the edge of the overflowing sink, spattering onto my socks. Dad's hand shot forward to turn the tap off. His elbow jabbed me aside.

Another chair squeaked and scraped behind me.

'I think you'd better go, Emily. Nathan's Dad'll give you a lift.'

All three of them clattered off into the hallway and Emily's wittering faded. The last things I heard her say were, 'Crystofer,' and, 'Iris'.

The front door clunked open and then closed.

36

I peered at my tiny upside-down room through the crystal ball. It looked like the kitchenette in The Book Cover: cardboard boxes strewn around, precarious towers of books and little room to navigate through it all. For a while I tried twirling the glass sphere in my hand like David Bowie in *Labyrinth*, but it was much heavier than it looked and I nearly dropped it. A hospital visit and a broken foot would be a nice addition to everything else. At least the explanation would give the doctors a story to laugh about. Eventually I gave up, wrapped the ball in old newspaper and shoved it to the bottom of a box. Most of the big gemstones had been removed to the charity shop donation pile along with my tarot book.

Iris had been amputated from my life after my Mum and Dad quit my job for me. They both visited The Book Cover the day after Emily had been over for dinner. They knew now there had been no book group; Emily had had to tell my mum all about what I really did on Wednesday nights. Suppose she couldn't avoid it. One explanation must have led to another until it all tumbled out like handkerchiefs from a magician's sleeve.

The story about a dead twin was the first I'd told at Ballahan High. With a hundred new kids who'd all gone to different primary schools from me, I was the odd piece in their jigsaw. Might as well fabricate my tragic backstory. I thought it would stop them making up their own *for* me – the new boy with the soft voice who collected pretty crystals. Or at least it would give them something else to focus on; a reason to feel sorry for me. I think it worked for a week or two. Jonnie had decided to sit next to me in most of my classes and Nick invited me to his twelfth birthday party. Had no idea the myth had survived the subsequent six years for Crystofer to remember it and believe it. And pass it on.

I don't know what my parents said to Iris. They could have gone in there screaming at her for allowing their seventeen-year-old son to join a spiritual circle with five adults, the youngest of whom was in their forties. Maybe they'd threatened her with some sort of action. Had she done anything illegal? Or maybe they'd grilled her for information. I pictured them wringing their hands and stamping in front of the counter, begging for answers about how she'd managed to make their odd son even odder. I couldn't read any of this from their auras when they came home that night, though, arm in arm in silence. Couldn't even see auras. Could I ever?

Of course, they accepted the first offer on the house. Desperate to get the fuck out of here. Well done, me.

The last of my *Mysteries Unsolved* books on the shelf was next to be packed. Normally I'd hand them over to Iris for the shop. Couldn't do that anymore. Wouldn't be seeing her or the circle members, or taking books out of boxes, or leafing through old dusty pages, or sitting on the pink-carpeted landing.

'Nathan?'

I scrubbed stinging tears away with the butts of my hands as Mum pushed the door open. Usually I would have told her not to come in, and usually she didn't ask, but there was no point anymore. Half of my things were either in black bags or cardboard boxes or just gone. It wasn't my room anymore. I lifted the row of books and dumped them in a new box together.

'Need any more rubbish bags?' She perched on the edge of my bed and I knew she hadn't come in to ask what I needed.

'Nope.'

I turned and leaned against the bookshelf as she bent over to pick something up from the floor. She held it up between thumb and forefinger, examining it. Moonstone. She glanced to me and I folded my arms.

'I still don't really understand… What did you do at these… meetings?'

'I told you. It was just… about psychic stuff. Just talking about it.'

'Just talking about 'stuff'. For a year?'

'It's not been a year. I didn't join the circle as soon as I got the job in the shop either… It took a while.'

'Nathan, the amount of time's not even the point. What the hell were you doing there every week?' Eyebags cushioned her stare and she was playing with the moonstone. Maybe she needed it.

'We did… meditations. Analysed dreams… Learned about crystals.'

'Hmph.' Almost a laugh. 'Yeah, well, you've always liked them.'

That was when I imagined another scenario in the bookshop. Maybe they hadn't screamed at Iris or threatened her or demanded information. Maybe they were sad. Confused because she'd found a way to connect with me when they never really had.

'… That's moonstone you're holding.'

She looked down at the milky silk stone, as if she'd forgotten she was holding it.

'It's supposed to be soothing and calm. A lady at the circle told me I could put it in my pillow to help me sleep better. Haven't been having those nightmares anymore. Well apart from….'

She looked at me, squeezing her lips together. Neither of us had mentioned her crawling up to me in the loft. I'd even wondered if that had been part of the delirium too. But her glance let me know it had been real.

'Moonstone's connected to female energies and stuff too…' A picture flashed into my mind of me in primary again, dressed up as a girl for the day. 'We learned about auras as well. That kind of thing.'

'Wait a minute… auras? Oh my god, this is why you said those ridiculous things to your English teacher, isn't it?'

I looked to the carpet. No need to nod in agreement.

'And you said something to him about a ghost. His mother who had died, wasn't it? That's not just doing meditations, Nathan!'

I traipsed to my side of the bed and plunged myself down, shoving the bedside drawer closed, concealing my yet-to-be-packed journals.

'And your dad thought it was because of that stupid dream book of mine you found.'

'… Well, why did you have that? Who gave it to you?'

'Och, I don't remember.'

'Did you just buy it for yourself?'

She sighed, shaking her head and suddenly we were in a new

mirrored world.

'Why is it so bad anyway? Why are you and Dad so angry about it?'

'Because,' she turned with a puff, 'it's not exactly what the Church teaches is it? You shouldn't be getting involved with this sort of… weird… stuff.'

'Mum. We don't go to church. I'm not even in a Catholic school.'

'Only because it's too far from here!'

'Yeah and St. Germaine's is just around the corner. The last time we went to Mass was when Brenda and Frank were here and that was just for… never mind.'

'Look, we're angry because you've been lying to us. You told us you were in a book group! And you told your pals that you had a dead…' She pressed rigid fingers to her eyes. 'We thought you had grown out of all this… shit.'

I'd never heard her swear before.

'I *have* grown out of it. I made up that story after we'd just moved here… and besides, you and Dad lie to *me*.'

'Excuse me?'

'It was Jack who told me you had no money, or were in debt, or whatever you are – I still don't even know.'

'Nathan, it's been bloody obvious for a long time that we've been struggling. You know not as many people come into the video shop anymore. Dad's had it. My salary alone wouldn't have been enough to pay the mortgage on this house. And even my job's not guaranteed. Why do you think I've been buying and selling all these antiques? It's not for fun.' She shoved herself up from the bed.

'Did you sell those cards I bought in First Year? The Fortune

Telling Game?'

'Eh?'

'We saw them at an antiques shop but you and Dad wouldn't let me get them. Then I went back later with… with Jonnie and his mum. And I bought them myself. But they disappeared.'

'God, those things.' She held a hand up to her forehead. 'We got rid of those as soon as your dad found them. Didn't think you should have them. I'd forgotten about that…'

'So you *did* sell them? Another lie?'

'No, I did not. And don't you speak to me like that.'

I lay against the headboard, pulling my legs into my chest and resting my chin on my knees.

'I didn't sell them, son.' Her voice softened. 'I think I gave them away to a charity shop or… in fact, I think I handed them into the book shop. To Iris.' We looked at each other. Her mouth curled into an almost-smile at one side, a strange mask on her. 'Didn't realise then that you were going to start going in there to buy books so often. I'm surprised you didn't find them again.'

'I never saw them… Iris probably kept them for herself.'

'Look… keep packing, son. Dad'll take the rubbish to the dump soon.'

As she stood, fire burned through my chest forcing words out.

'Mum,' I said.

'Mm?'

My head pulsed in hot, painful waves. I screwed my eyes closed.

'Iris gave me a message once. For you.'

I opened one eye, peering at her.

'From Granddad.'

Her lips opened.

'It was a while ago. Months. She knew his name. Neil. And she knew he was my granddad.'

She sighed. 'She could have guessed one of your grandparents was dead, Nathan.'

'But Neil? His name?'

'It's... she... you must've mentioned it at some point. She's just picked up on it and remembered it.'

'And she said he was here, protecting us. He's been in the house. I've heard him. And Iris said that a big change was coming for you, me and Dad.'

She shook her head, looking around as if searching the room for the right excuses.

'Of course she'd say he was protecting us. Any psychic could say that about someone who's died. Who wouldn't want to hear that? And 'a big change'? What does that mean? It's vague, Nathan, it could mean anything to anyone.'

'But he knew about the money! That was his message. To tell you to be careful with money. Iris told me this even before Jack was here.'

She squinted. Not at me, though. She was thinking it through, solving the riddle, trying to figure out how Iris could have known. She stepped closer to me.

'And Iris also told you your dead twin brother was there.'

The pulsing heat vanished. Ice instead. Every part of me sank. Mum touched my knee then left, bending to pick up one of her old catalogues from the floor on her way out.

⭐

During the week I was forced to watch TV in the living room for 'family nights', especially on Wednesdays. The books Mum and Dad always encouraged me to read were tainted, laced with 'funny' ideas to be avoided. One couch would be left empty as I was sandwiched between them in some bizarre conversion experiment, bombarded with *Mr and Mrs*, *Changing Rooms* and *The Bill*. Their offering was that we'd eat dinner while watching, sometimes a takeaway Dad would bring home after work. We'd even speak, muttering answers during *Who Wants to be a Millionaire?*.

Some other game show was presented by a man who always wore glittery or flowery suit jackets. One Wednesday he twirled on with a pink-sequined blazer, fluttering his hands around as he spoke with a voice that sounded like mine. He'd been on one night when Frank and Brenda had been here.

'This nancy again?' Frank had said. 'Change the channel, will you, Helen?'

I remember my insides shrivelling and combusting at the same time.

Now Dad laughed and broke my daydream.

'I quite like him,' he said, and squeezed closer to me.

37

I clutched the hem of my too-small blazer like a suit of armour as I wormed through the corridors. The Head Teacher had sent a letter home insisting we still wear our uniforms to the exams, even though we weren't in classes anymore. Focusing on the filthy speckled lino under my worn shoes, I tried to ignore the flashing siren above my head. Emily must have told other people about my twin brother lie. Probably about the circle too. Even if she only told Crystofer or Hannah, I knew the story would spread like a contagion from person to person, infecting the teachers eventually.

The Advanced Higher English exam was in an unused Religious Education classroom with plaster crumbling off the walls in patches and broken blinds barely hanging from the windows. I avoided looking at the other pupils as they came in to take their seats. I was granted a 'Hey' from Stacey when she arrived, though. Untouched by the rumour plague so far.

An extract from a Robert Frost poem, 'Maple', was printed in the exam paper with a series of questions about its meaning. In between reading the blurred stanzas over and over for the next half an hour I glanced up at the others around me, the unanimous racing scrapes of their pens drilling into my eardrums. Eventually I scribbled down some half-formed guesses and margin illustrations of an albino peacock before stopping early to watch the invigilator at the front of the room who glanced at a newspaper behind the teacher's squint desk. I looked for her aura but my third eye had hung up on me.

When the time was over and our papers were collected, I grabbed my near-empty backpack from the front of the room and filtered out behind the others, ignoring their discussions of what 'Maple' was about. Mr. Young was in the corridor, hands splayed, bobbing up and down as if he was waiting to catch a tennis ball. His sleeves were even rolled up showing carved, tanned forearms. My classmates gathered round him in pairs and trios to debrief and perhaps fight over who had the most abstract interpretation of the poem. I shuffled past, head down. But after a few paces he called out to me over his shoulder.

'Mr. Love, how did it go then?'

Walking backwards, I offered him a thumbs up and the most difficult smile I've ever had to force.

'Nathan! You're moving?'

Gillian closed in on me on my way to the school library where I had to hand back a three-year-overdue *Goosebumps* book I'd found during the final clearing out of my wardrobe.

'Yeah. In the summer.'

Behind her, bleached curls bobbed towards us through a crowd. Crystofer glimpsed me through swarms of shoulders and nudged his way towards us, linking arms with Gillian as she noticed him beside her. I could see his pink scalp underneath the new hair. He avoided eye contact for any longer than a second and I pictured him with a telephone clamped to his ear, breathing into the mouthpiece, listening to me.

'You didn't even tell us!' Gillian said.

'… Sorry. Didn't think… How did you find out?'

They glanced at one another and Gillian shifted around on her feet. 'I... someone mentioned it the other week... Can't even remember who.' Crystofer shrugged along as if he had no idea and as if I had no idea. It was almost funny.

'So why is this happening? Your mum or dad have a new job or something?'

'... Yeah. Dad. In England. Near family down there.'

'Doesn't your dad own a video shop?' Crystofer asked, quietly.

'Mhm. He's...'

My brain started its familiar hyper speed assembly line, crafting possible stories.

What's the point?

I stopped the machinery.

'... Actually, he's going to close the shop. We're struggling for money. Fucked.'

Crystofer looked me in the eye.

'Well,' said Gillian, 'we need to have a few last cinema nights before you go! There are loads of films coming out this summer I want to see.'

'Mhm.'

'I'll phone you at home.'

I looked to Crystofer and acknowledgement flickered between us. Maybe he was psychic too. Could be Iris's new protégé.

'We can figure out what day's best,' Gillian went on.

'OK,' I answered, knowing it would never happen.

Then she reached forward and pulled me into a hug. My useless hands patted her backpack and I blew her hair out of my mouth. She let go and turned, waving. Then Crystofer stepped forward. Arms wide, he closed them round me too, pressing against my chest.

'Bye, Nathan.'

My hands touched his sides and I felt bony ribs through his shirt.

I didn't know if it was his heartbeat I could feel or my own. I smelled the skin on his neck, some sort of paint-fresh aftershave. He let go and grazed my hand as he turned away. I think that was the first time I really did feel my aura as it vibrated.

Escaping out the back doors of the school, I squinted in the sun, peering around for a final survey, committing it all to a scrapbook in my brain. I dropped my bag and pulled my blazer off, bundling it into a ball and stuffing it into a nearby bin. I imagined it meeting up with Mum's pink umbrella in a landfill somewhere. Then through heatwaves on the tarmac I saw Emily walking with other girls in my direction. They all wore blazers but her leather jacket hung defiantly from her shoulders. She looked from side to side at the others, never straight ahead, and I knew she had seen me but didn't want to look. I was thankful. Whether she meant to or not, she was sparing me from explaining why I'd ever invited her to the cinema and to dinner with my parents. I hadn't been using her to lie, not deliberately, but I knew I couldn't convince her of that; I was better at persuading people to believe lies more than truth. I'd wanted her to help me be someone else. Someone who didn't need to lie.

Turning, I slipped out of the black gates, free from the contamination zone.

38

Crumpled and bent faces of film stars looked back at me from the skip. Their shining pixel eyes didn't seem to care. Inside, Dad mumbled that he could finish tidying the last few things alone and that I should wander for a while. I imagined him climbing into the skip, marinating in the debris of his failed business.

Shuffling down the high street of Ballahan, a few familiar pupils from school smirked back at me. I didn't know their names – kids from other classes, younger than me. Usually I'd have stared at the pavement and hurried to an imaginary destination, but I glanced back, keeping the same pace. It was like being on holiday abroad and not caring which locals saw you with a peeling sunburnt face and Bermuda shorts; you'd be leaving soon.

Further downhill, I stopped outside a charity shop. A woman was dressing a mannequin in the window display, a pile of board games at her feet. I tilted my head to read what they were and as I squinted in the sunlight I spotted it: nestled behind an old tea set, my Empire State Building model, still unfinished. I'd put it in the rubbish pile at the house. Dad must have brought it here – obviously thought it wasn't too bad. Some other loner teenager with insomnia could finish it off. I wondered if Dad had handed in all the little pots of paint too. Then I searched the rest of the display and found the picture frame behind them. A peacock. My spirit animal. Mum's picture from under the stairs. What had been the point of that? Made me happy for a little while then ended up dumped here. What was it guiding me to this time?

As I thought about going inside to check for more remnants from our life here, something moved beside me and my distorted reflection shifted back into focus. Another, shorter, silhouette beside me looked back.

'Hi, love.'

I turned to see Iris haloed by sunlight. She clasped her hands in front of herself, as if holding them back from hugging me. She'd dyed her hair black.

'Iris! Hi.' I almost squealed, taking a step back to figure out if she was real.

'What you doin' in Ballahan? The schools are all finished for the holidays, aren't they?'

'Was just helping my dad tidy out the video shop, but he's finishing the rest himself. It's pretty much empty now. Someone else'll be leasing it out soon.'

'Aw, love.' She frowned but still didn't move any closer.

'We're moving... I never told you. Going to England.'

'I know.' She nodded. 'Your parents told me.'

All the things we couldn't say clogged up the air between us. She was supposed to be forbidden to me, and I to her. What if Dad stepped out from the shop and looked down the street? Or if Mum appeared in the car to collect us and pulled up beside me? And the imaginary twin brother lay between our feet, neither one of us wanting to tread on him. But Iris smiled and I imagined her white light protecting us like a big quilt. For a few moments we were safe.

'So... how are you?'

315

'Aye, aye, I'm fine, just enjoyin' the weather. Jimmy's around somewhere, away gettin' somethin' for the house.'

I nodded, a pit opening inside me. I wanted to fill it with purple flames again, ask about spirit or what my aura looked like, tell her my last dream, talk about the smoky quartz pendant around her neck. But really I knew it wouldn't work anymore. Those flames had been stamped out forever. All we could manage was Jimmy and Dad's shop and weather.

'Have you heard about Patrick? Away in the hospital for another operation.'

'Patrick? What operation?'

'On his leg.' She said it as if it was obvious. I'd never found out why Patrick always limped. Had never asked.

'Is he OK? Is it serious?'

'Well, it's about his fourth operation now. I don't know if it'll ever get any better.' She waved a flippant hand as she spoke.

'Oh. Hope he's OK… I had no idea.'

'Aye, well that's why he started comin'… to the circle.'

I glanced down, chewing the inside of my cheek. We both knew we'd broken a pact, uttered some treasonous language. She spoke again, softer, almost in her meditation-voice.

'He'd had his other operations and nothin' was really changin'. He'd come to me for a readin' and then we'd started doin' some healin' work. Seemed to make a difference. He just kept comin' and eventually joined. Must've been–'

I didn't hear what else she said. Another sound had taken over, coming downhill behind Iris. Loud, laughing, obnoxious, piercing our quilt. Jonnie and two followers from school strode down the pavement towards us, swaggering with hands in pockets, guffawing like they were the most important people in the street. I think it was my shoes scuffing the pavement as I shrivelled back towards the shop window that made him look at me. Right in my eyes. Just for a second. He even slowed down. Then kept going, laughing even louder as he jaunted off.

'Who was that, Nathan?' Iris's voice had cooled completely, like this was a reading and Jonnie had been the first tarot card. And like she always did, she shone a torch into my head and pulled out words.

'That's Jonnie Knight. Jonathon. You said his name in my very first reading.'

'I've seen him in Drichton walking past the shop,' she said, her gaze following him off behind me.

'He walked in once a few weeks ago. Saw me and then walked back out.'

'Aye, I remember. You know him. Well.'

I looked over my shoulder at Jonnie springing downhill, elbowing one of the other boys. There *were* sparks inside, flickering into little flames. But they were scarlet, not purple.

'I used to. Jonnie was my best friend in First Year. We were the only two boys who lived in Drichton, getting on the bus together every day. Made sense. And my parents were happy. Relieved.'

'You've never mentioned him.'

'No. He doesn't like me anymore. Don't like him much either. I think.' The flames warmed my lungs and smoke climbed my throat. 'We spent every day after school together, though. And weekends. Came round for dinner. I went to his. His mum took us places. I was with him when I bought that old Fortune Telling Game I told you about.'

Iris didn't ask anything else but the fire was crackling and more words billowed out.

'He thought it was a bit weird. But it didn't matter, just didn't say anything else about it. Then when he was staying over one night... our sleeping bags were on the floor together...'

The final ribbons of smoke flew out of my mouth.

'... I tried to hold his hand. He shoved me away. I jumped up to my bed. He left really early the next day. Didn't speak to me after that.'

My eyes had blurred over staring at Iris's skirt.

'Oh, hi.' Her voice was back to normal.

'Hiya, pal.' Jimmy had appeared, hands in jean pockets, giving me a nod.

The charity shop door squeaked and clanged beside me. Cars rumbled past. Shouts and laughs up and down the street funnelled back into my ears.

'Got what you were lookin' for?' Iris asked.

'Aye.' He lifted a carrier bag and something metallic jangled inside. The heat had dissipated and I was on the periphery, watching their conversation. They talked about the tool he'd just bought at the little DIY shop and where else they needed to go to. I knew Iris probably hadn't told him about me leaving my job or my parents visiting her or my lies. Either that or she had and he didn't care.

'Right, Nathan, we'd better go. You get back to your dad.'

'Yeah.' I shoved my hands in the pockets of my hoodie, knowing this was it and swallowing the hard stone back in my throat harder than I'd ever had to before.

'He might be needin' you more than he says,' she added, winking. 'Take care, my love.'

Her voice cracked with the last few words and she turned around with Jimmy then walked away. I wanted to call something else out – something about saying bye to everyone at the circle, or at least telling Patrick I hoped he was OK. But my throat had swollen too much and the white quilt was gone and Iris was just a woman in the street with her husband again, turning a corner and disappearing.

39

The ceiling was too far away when I opened my eyes. I rolled onto my side, feeling the solid floor through the thin sleeping bag and remembering the bed was gone. The bare walls gaped back at me. Little blue tac marks and pin holes dotted them like bullet-fire. Bumps and bangs downstairs told me Mum and Dad were already awake, packing the final boxes into the car. They must have let me sleep in so that I'd stay out of the way.

Or maybe they just wanted to let me savour my last moments. Make it easier for me.

I crawled to the window, leaned on the stained sill, and peered out. Mum was in the garden, cajoling Freya into the cat box with a treat. Freya crept forward, ears peeled back, sniffing but holding her ground and every time Mum lunged forward to grab her she'd spring away. I smiled, picturing the human-sized box they might have built downstairs for me too.

'OK?'

I turned to see Dad in the doorway, hands fidgeting in his pockets.

'Mm.' I pulled the sleeping bag back up over my shoulders.

'Everything's just about ready. It'll be a bit of a squeeze in the back seat for you.'

He walked in and closed the door a little behind him. I turned back to the window and looked out at the river rippling past on the other side of the fence. Then Dad's warm hand gripped my shoulder and he huffed, sitting down beside me. I grabbed my t-shirt from the clothes bundle against the wall and pulled it on.

'Going to miss it,' he said. I couldn't tell if it was a question or not and didn't say anything. He sighed. 'Lot happened here, eh? Time for a new start, though.'

'New start how? Are we suddenly going to be rich in England?'

'Well, we've made a wee bit of money on the house. And we'll save more staying with Brenda and Frank for the next month or two until we find a new place down there – somewhere less expensive. Money's not the *only* reason we're going, anyway.'

I knew.

'Your mum's missing her side of the family down there.'

'What, Brenda and Frank? Jack?'

Freya was perched on the fence now, observing Mum below her.

'And everyone else,' Dad said. 'She has cousins and old friends, too, you know. And you always liked it down there when we used to visit.'

'Did I?'

I waited for him to leave, wondering why he hadn't given up already. He lifted his hand, surely to push himself up and go. But it rested on my knee. He didn't move.

'Nathan… Mum told me what you said about Granddad. About the… psychic message… thing.'

Pins and needles prickled where his hand touched me.

'Mm.'

'Do you think the house is haunted? Maybe we should've

warned the people moving in!'

He shook me, laughing and I shoved his hand away. It reappeared, though, around my other shoulder, pulling me into him, almost tipping me over.

'I'm only kidding, pal. But… what made you think Granddad was here? How did this all start?'

Dad asking about spirit was like hearing Freya bark. I shrank beneath his fingers.

'You wouldn't get it.'

'Come on,' he rubbed my upper arm again, 'I want to know.'

I sighed. 'Well… I heard him. One night last year.'

'What? Heard him talking?'

'No. I heard his voice, but not talking. He was… groaning or something. Like he was in pain. The window was open one night and I thought it was somebody outside at first.'

Dad's hand loosened and slid from me.

'It was almost like crying. And then I saw him when I was in bed. Standing there.' I nodded over my shoulder towards the door. 'I started working at The Book Cover right after that and, well, Iris explained to me what it was – that it was Granddad. She described him and had a message from him.'

'Mm… Mum told me that part.' Dad's voice had deepened. 'When was this, Nathan?'

'Last year, I told you.'

'Yes, but when?' He had started mumbling.

'End of the summer holidays. I think it was the night before I went back to school.'

Outside, Mum finally snapped the door of the cat box closed, Freya tucked inside. Beside me, Dad's silence buzzed in my eardrum. I pushed myself onto my knees, leaning towards the rest of my clothes in the corner. Dad's hand folded around my wrist, though, pulling me back towards him, his thumb grazing the back of my hand. I leaned back down and he didn't let go.

'Nathan, that was me.'

He was staring at the floor.

'What was you?'

'The voice you heard. It *was* outside. I was in the garden. Standing outside the back door. Right under your window.'

'What were you doing? How do you even remember? It was—'

'—And it was me you saw.' He nodded back towards my door. 'I was watching you, just for a minute. Pushed the door too hard and you woke up.'

'Eh? Why were you watching me?'

'I didn't want to tell your mum.' Now he was looking out the window. 'I knew what it meant. What I'd found. Couldn't let her know yet.'

My stomach yanked and pushed. Throat seizing. I pulled my hand back but Dad held on. He breathed heavily through his nose, nostrils flaring. I was little again and he'd caught me lying or saying something weird or hiding a dead cat or dressing up as a girl.

'I'd been looking for the letter about buying new uniforms. Mum kept going on about how your blazer didn't fit. Hadn't been able to afford a new one yet. Thought the letter might be in your room. You were in the bathroom.'

Spiders climbed up my neck.

'Had a look in your bedside drawer.'

The spiders crawled through my hair, sinking fangs into my scalp, drilling poison into my brain.

'I found all the pages you'd torn out. Mum's always looking for those catalogues.'

I wanted to puke out words, stop him talking, but the poison pulled them back down my throat.

'Pictures of men. Underwear. You had dozens of them, Nathan.'

Kaleidoscope eyes spun the room. Chin shaking. Dad's shoulder punched my cheek. Thick gulps and sobs into his t-shirt. His chest shuddered beneath it. Heat from him and arms holding me. My legs curling up and hands clinging. Spiders gone. His hands in my hair, stroking. Rocking.

'I was crying, son. It was me. I stood outside, crying.'

Everything pulsed: Dad's words, my whimpers, my body, my fingers gripping to him. The world shivered.

'That's why I jumped back to my room when you saw me. Didn't want you to catch me so upset, you know. I came back in here the next afternoon. Even left work early. Don't know what I was looking for – a diary or… maybe just to check those pictures were really there. You came home from school, though. I tried to sneak out and managed to whack stuff off your shelf. Think I broke something. You were shouting out to see if I was home but I hid in our room for hours.'

'Dad,' I sobbed, not even knowing how I wanted to finish the sentence. I don't think there was a sentence.

'Shh.' He rubbed my shoulders. 'You know, I thought about talking to you before. It's… not easy for me. Or your mum. Came over to the book shop one day to talk to you without her there. Thought it might make it easier for you. Then I saw you talking to Emily. Thought maybe I was wrong. Maybe you had a girlfriend.'

My wet cheek pressed onto Dad's chest, bleeding into it, and I heard him wipe his face above me. Then he squeezed me tighter, powering on.

'But I knew later I was just convincing myself. I knew, really, son. Just different for me. Not the kind of thing I've ever been used to. Wasn't OK when I was growing up. Even now. But it was always girls you had as friends. The boys never lasted. Jonnie. Nick. Even you and Jack were never pals. I do know that.'

I crumpled and cried again, like my heart was pumping tears instead of blood.

'You don't have to hang around with him all the time if you don't want to.'

'Colin! Nathan! You ready?'

Mum's shout jolted both of us. I was on a backwards-facing train that slammed to a halt. Dad pulled me upright with both hands on my arms. I looked at him through stinging blurriness. His face was pink and he looked right at me with new eyes, blue and glimmering.

'You know we love you, Nathan?'

I didn't know.

I dressed in a daze, bundling up the sleeping bag with numb hands. Dad had distracted Mum when she began climbing the stairs to us, diving out of the room and mumbling in the hall. I had that feeling like when Iris first talked to me about spirit – that feeling that I knew something everyone else didn't; that I could see things they couldn't. Dad had lifted me into a new room in our house I hadn't known was there and everything

325

looked different and brighter from here.

Now the rough edges of a bursting cardboard box scratched my forearms and I was downstairs without remembering how I got there. I hoisted the box out of the front door. I couldn't see my feet over the top of the flaps so trod carefully towards the open boot of the car and dropped the box on the stones of the driveway.

'Need a hand?'

I turned, squinting in the sunlight. An alien silhouette about half a foot taller than me. Then Jonnie's brown eyes.

'Um, no. No thanks.' I waited for some sort of jeer. 'Good riddance,' maybe.

'Here.' He stepped forward and lifted the box, shoving it into the last space in the boot, wedged in between packed plastic bags and a hoover. Then he turned to me, looking like he was trying to smile. He didn't look like a Jim Henson monster anymore. Didn't ever really.

'Cheers,' I said, deepening my voice, hoping he couldn't see how red my eyes still were.

'Heard you were moving. Are you seriously going to England?'

'Yeah.' I cleared my throat. 'Got family down there, so…'

'I remember. Think I met your aunt and uncle when they came to visit. In First Year.'

'Mm. That's right.'

Footsteps crunched behind me.

'Hiya, Jonnie.' Dad chucked another bag in the backseat then patted me on the back. 'All ready, pal?'

I nodded. My throat still burned and I tried to cough the pain away. Dad retreated into the house.

'Just came to say bye, really.' Jonnie coughed too. 'Bit stupid. Know we don't speak or anything.'

'Mm.'

'Saw you were working in the book shop. Came in at one point to say hi, but…'

We both nodded, knowing we'd run out of words. I scuffed some stones with my shoe and looked at his trainers. He swayed from side to side.

'Well… good luck, Nathan.'

His balance changed and I looked up to his awkward hand outstretched towards me. I took it and looked at him again, smiling.

'Thanks.'

His skin wasn't smooth like mine, but it was warm and the heat crackled up my arm. I remembered him in my room. In the sleeping bag. This time *I* let go of *his* hand.

As he turned and walked out of the driveway and along the pavement, I called out to him.

'Hey! You still have my Game Boy!'

We laughed together as he kept walking.

I crammed myself into the back seat with everything else that hadn't made it into the moving van. The new notebook I've been writing in was nestled between my thighs. Nobody gave me this one: I bought it myself. Tucked up in her own soft fur, Freya glowered at me through the plastic gridded door of her box. A folded garden chair dug into my ankle and as the car bumped out of the driveway and off the kerb a frying pan handle bashed against my temple. Dad's wailing voice from last year echoed in my head then vanished out of the window.

'Alright back there, son?' He reached a backwards hand through the furniture and squeezed my knee. In the rear-view mirror his eyes smiled at me.

I didn't see the house as we drove away. Everything piled up in the seat beside me blocked my view on that side of the car. Saying goodbye to a building felt trivial now anyway. That fear had been overlapped this morning.

The sun gleamed off the window of The Book Cover as we glided down the main street. The door was closed, dark inside – usual for a Sunday. I still peered in to catch a glimpse of the counter, though, wondering if Iris might be there. Maybe dishing out new books onto the dusty shelves; maybe setting up the octagonal table upstairs and arranging whatever crystals took her fancy; maybe leaning against the cluttered sink in the back, interviewing someone new to take my place. But the car jerked forward and we powered ahead.

Just before the stone bridge we slowed to a stop at a temporary set of traffic lights. There didn't seem to be anyone doing any work on the road, though, and Mum muttered something and laughed. I squinted out the window at my side. St. Germaine's was at the end of the gravelled path, frozen like a painting. I gripped the knob in the car door and rolled down the window a few inches further. Beneath the rattling of the car engine, I heard voices, all singing together; a hymn rising to a crescendo. The green doors opened and for a second I saw myself in my dream, kneeling on the bench, praying. I blinked it away and instead the priest marched out followed by other people, chatting and smiling like always.

Then Sadie was there. Hands clasped, shuffling out. She

nodded to the priest and shook his hand, mouthing happy words at him. The lace of her little hat covered her eyes like a veil. I think I had more in common with her than I'd ever realised.

I slid my hand into the pocket of my cords and rubbed the onyx between my fingers. I couldn't feel its vibrations or protection anymore. It was just a black pebble after all. As the amber light blinked on in front of us, I reached out of the open window and dropped the secret stone on the road. The traffic lights glowed green. The colour of the heart chakra, Iris would have said. We juddered forward, rising over the hump of the bridge and the circle floated off behind me, letting me go.

'Mum.' I leaned forward, looking at Dad's new eyes in the mirror again. 'I have something to tell you…'

THE END

Acknowledgements

Firstly, thank you to everyone who has just finished reading *The Stone in My Pocket*. There are innumerable books out there that you could have chosen and I really appreciate that you spent your time with Nathan. If you enjoyed it, please leave a review at the outlet you bought it from to help other readers find it.

There are some wonderful writers who helped me along the way in the writing and redrafting process. Thank you so much to S. Mae Tyler, A. Steiger, and Nat Kennedy for all of your time and help. In particular, I want to thank Victoria Pantazis for your ongoing advice and support and for your emails that keep me going! Another specific thank you is to Melissa Wiggins for your kind feedback and positivity. And, of course, a special mention for Pumpkin.